CIN

CINDRA GOLD

Trudi Jordan

VANTAGE PRESS
New York

FIRST EDITION

All rights reserved, including the right of
reproduction in whole or in part in any form.

Copyright © 1994 by Trudi Jordan

Published by Vantage Press, Inc.
516 West 34th Street, New York, New York 10001

Manufactured in the United States of America
ISBN: 0-533-10779-2

Library of Congress Catalog Card No.: 93-93533

0 9 8 7 6 5 4 3 2 1

To those romanticists who love to dream

Contents

Acknowledgments ix

1. A Long Journey — 1
2. Saint Louis at Last — 7
3. Getting Acquainted — 10
4. The Men in Their Lives — 13
5. A Quiet Evening — 14
6. Sunday — 16
7. A Newfound Friend — 23
8. A Decision — 28
9. The Office — 30
10. Telling about It — 38
11. Pleasing and Not So Pleasing Discoveries — 42
12. The Little Child — 48
13. Another Phyllis — 51
14. A Mystery and a Shopping Spree — 55
15. The Mystery Solved — 63
16. Auntie Phyllis — 69
17. A Visitor from Canada — 74
18. A Birthday Party — 79
19. A Guest for the Weekend — 86
20. A Suggested Solution — 91
21. A Lost Child — 97
22. A Nice Diversion — 103
23. An Estrangement — 108
24. A Forced Decision — 112
25. An Unfortunate Incident` — 115
26. Comforting Thoughts — 122
27. Affairs of the Heart — 125
28. A Disappointment — 129
29. A Proposal — 132

30.	A Joyous Occasion	136
31.	The Three Phyllises	141
32.	Pre-Wedding Arrangements	143
33.	The Wedding Day	146
34.	A Problem Solved	150
35.	Paris in the Spring	153
36.	A Choice	155
37.	The Voyage Back	156
38.	A Happy Reunion	157
39.	"The Wishes"	159
40.	The Attention Seeker	161
41.	Cameron Introduces His Wife to High Society	163
42.	Their Social Life	167
43.	A Babe Is Born	170
44.	To Seek and Find	174
45.	A Name for Baby	179
46.	Another Baby	181
47.	Brumby "Goes"	186
48.	A Sad Farewell	190
49.	Tearless Morn	194
50.	Good for Uncle Clive!	199
51.	Cameron's Resolution	209
52.	Life Goes On	214
53.	A Bitter Quarrel	216
54.	Events at the Columns	219
55.	Claudia's Conspiracy	222
56.	Graduation at Last	227
57.	A Mother's Compunction	234
58.	Hurray for the Children	237
59.	A Dream Come True	239
60.	A Joy Repeated	244
61.	The Offspring Mature	247
62.	A Tradition Ends	252
63.	The Greatest Is Love	256

Epilogue   261

Acknowledgments

Saint Louis Public Library, Saint Louis, Missouri

The World Book Encyclopedia

Cherry Diamond, seventy-fifth anniversary issue of Missouri Athletic Club Magazine

Excerpt from writings of Charles Fillmore

Chapter 1
A Long Journey

It was the year of our Lord 1946 and Cindra was at last on the train, leaving her hometown of Belleville, Ontario, Canada, "and headed for God knows where!" her mother remarked. *A typical comment,* thought Cindra of her mother's expostulation; she had always been jealous of Cindra. How deep those feelings of jealousy had been for Mrs. Gold towards her youngest child Cindra.

As the train roared onward, Cindra reminisced about her family. Mr. and Mrs. Jack Gold had struggled, during the Great Depression of the early 1930s, to raise their four healthy, rather demanding (so it seemed to them!) girls.

Jack Gold, who did not bother much with ancestry and the like, a struggling businessman in the lumber trade, had married Bonnie May Fairfield of "United Empire Loyalist stock." Cindra always remembered her mother stating this fact. Four daughters were born to them, each two years apart, except for Cindra, who had come along after double that time.

There was Madge, a comely girl with dark brown hair like their mother's, and Cindra's favourite sister, if she had a favourite, for the girls all got along fairly well, as sisters go. Madge had married her high school sweetheart, Karl Reidit, after she had finished high school. Karl had started out to be a veterinarian, but after two years at college, he was needed back on his father's farm as his dad was ill. Cindra figured that was why Karl never did have to become involved in World War II; and since there was a small house on his parent's property, he had moved into that with his new bride. They now had a little blond-haired fellow, Jody, and Cindra sighed, thinking how she would miss Jody.

Next in line was Marsha, dear dreamer Marsha, the artist of the family, dreaming of living on the proceeds from her paintings for her livelihood but forced to go into commercial art to subsist.

Then there was Barbara May, the nurse. She had gone into nurses' training at Toronto General Hospital and had just graduated in the spring, and how proud her dad would have been, thought the young traveller.

Then came Cindra, baby Cindra. Jack Gold had called her his "Cinder of Gold," the only blonde in the family. She had been a beauty right from the start; and to add to that, she was a gifted child, taking to the piano, as Dad Jack would say, "like a duck takes to water." As a further bonus, she had become his fishing companion. Mom had been too busy for that looking after the needs of the family. And what an excellent job she had done of it, making clothes for her young ones when they were small, preserving and pickling food stuffs galore, and doing the housekeeping in a very competent manner.

The three older girls had not been interested in their father's sporting pursuit; however, he would take his youngest daughter down to the government dock on the Bay of Quinte and there the two "soulmates" (Cindra remembered her dad's endearing term for them) would while away the brief time that Dad Jack had. Their time together was usually either in the early morning before the work day started or in the evening after the day's work was done. Cindra had always felt that this was the real cause of her mother's jealousy, though Cindra's beauty may have come into it too.

Then Dad Jack died suddenly, early that spring, from a massive heart attack. Mom was feeling almost desperate, as she had not been left very well off. The two older girls were out, Madge married and Marsha supporting herself in Toronto as a commercial artist. Barbara, her mother's mainstay, was able to help out with the finances thanks to her job as a nurse at Belleville General Hospital, where she had taken a position on staff right after her graduation.

That left Cindra floundering, or so she felt. She had finished high school, having specialed in a commercial course. During her scholastic years, she had developed her skill at the piano so that she was, as Dad Jack had put it, "a veritable virtuoso."

Dad Jack had also been instrumental in seeing that Cindra, being agreeable, put any extra money she had into a fund; her "piano fund," he called it. He had purchased a rather large bank in the form of an upright piano, and friends and relatives were made aware of this little structure; not that funds were solicited, mind you, but it was considered more of a little token of appreciation when the young pianist played at any of the family gatherings, of which there were a goodly amount, especially on the Fairfield side of the family. Oh, how everyone loved to hear the girl play, her sisters included, though there were understandably twinges of jealousy from all three. But these feelings the girls coped with in a realistic way, so that in later years they were no longer felt, as wisdom had precluded them.

And so, the little fund grew. The young girl had also saved her small allowance, which the girls were all given for helping with the necessary chores that make for the smooth running of the household.

Dad Jack had kept track of the little account, which was first a small bank balance but then became enough to invest in some Canadian bonds, which at that time doubled your money in so many years. Later he invested it in long-term annuities. Her father had hoped that Cindra would become a concert pianist. He was not a type to force this, but just to suggest and encourage. Since Cindra's dreams for the future were in harmony with this, it was clear sailing for both of them.

The young girl's mind brought her back to reality and she again had a twinge of remorse about not helping out at home; however, her mother would not hear of Cindra's giving up her plans, so that was that!

Continuing with her retrospection, she recalled how her dad had gone even further with these plans of his. He had heard of two wonderful artists, both concert pianists, under whom his fair daughter could study. These women, after their performing careers ended, had gone into the fairly lucrative job of teaching. Now both of them lived in the United States, one in Boston, and the other in Saint Louis, Missouri. Dad Jack had been interested in these two centres as he had business contacts in both places. These connections were astute businessmen who were often looking for secretaries of high calibre, and, he reasoned, Canadian girls were so often labelled thus.

Another reason for arriving at these two choices was that Cindra's mother had a relative living in Boston, a distant, but dear cousin, Maude Hailey, by name, who also had a talent for the piano. And in Saint Louis she had a nonrelative but close friend named Phyllis Pindar. They had been school chums. Bonnie May had married before she finished school, and Phyllis had gone off to Saint Louis, as she had met a young man from there, and he had recommended a good job of which he knew. So she had gone down there to apply her commercial course skills and become secretary to a businessman in Saint Louis. This had enabled her to pursue the relationship with her boyfriend, of whom she was very fond.

Bonnie May corresponded quite frequently with this friend of long standing, so ultimately the choice for Cindra had been Saint Louis, despite the fact that it was the farther of the two places.

Now, with her father gone, Cindra felt she should stay in Belleville and assist in supporting the family home; however, though Mrs. Gold had some misgivings, she felt that she should help make possible the dream that both her husband and youngest daughter had held.

As Cindra reminisced on, she thought of how thankful she was that Barbara had a very close relationship with their mother; Barbara felt her father's passing keenly and was willing to help out in every way.

So Mrs. Gold had phoned Phyllis and told her of the plans they were making for the young pianist, and it was arranged for the young lady to stay with her. Phyllis had been delighted. She had met Cindra several times at little gatherings at the Gold home, when she was visiting in Canada, and she was very impressed by the young prodigy. She had always put money in the little bank, hoping to help the girl. She felt very honoured that Cindra was going to be in her charge.

The train shunted and was coming to a stop. The fair-haired girl asked the conductor how much farther the journey was to Saint Louis. Smiling beneficently, he replied, "Quite a little journey yet, Miss."

She felt a curious mixture of depression, excitement, and elation, which was difficult for Cindra to sort out. She was glad she had been brought up in the church. She saw it so clearly now, Tabernacle United Church, where she and her sisters had been CGIT girls. "That stands for Canadian Girls in Training," Dad Jack would explain, proud as could be of his four lovely daughters. And Cindra thought of the church suppers, the pans and pans of good food in which all had been encouraged to indulge to the fullest, and hadn't Dad Jack done just that! Oh, how she missed her dad!

She hadn't planned to throw herself into such serious study so soon, but this move had been precipitated by her father's death. At seventeen she felt very mature, and her dad had been responsible for this. One maiden aunt often said of Cindra, "She's old beyond her age."

The young girl now called to mind the gems of wisdom that her father had taught her as they sat on the dock on good old Bay of Quinte. He would quote from Longfellow, one of his favourite poets, and she recalled one of the lines: "Let us then labour for an inward stillness, an inward stillness and an inward healing." He would quote on, and then they would sit in the silence and put into practise the good poet's advice. Cindra had not realized at that time to what extent these quiet times would later influence her life.

The young girl's reverie was interrupted by the man sitting across from her in the coach; he appeared to be a pensive type, and Cindra again thought of her father. She felt very close to him at this time, very close; she felt him near, in that inner stillness, and she felt beyond any doubt that her father was with God and so a kind of liaison for her with an all-loving God.

Such musings helped to pass the time for the fair one on this lengthy journey. She wiped a tear from her left cheek. It was not that she was crying, but once in a long while her left eye would let fall one tear; her dad would have said that it was her soul getting rid of any sadness that had built up, and he would have gently brushed it away.

Chapter 2
Saint Louis at Last

The train finally pulled in to Saint Louis station; all was alive with the hubbub of the big city. Cindra felt a sudden rush of delight for which she was thankful, as her first feelings had been exactly the opposite, those of sadness bordering on despair.

As our young heroine stepped onto the platform, she recognized a familiar figure, her mother's friend, Phyllis, and how ultra-smart she looked in her navy blue suit, white blouse, and perky little hat to match. Cindra was so glad to see her. They shook hands, and Phyllis came up with a brilliant suggestion, so thought the former, a cup of tea in the flourishing restaurant stuck there for just such a weary traveller! And so, luggage attended to, the two sat at one of the smaller tables. It was all set up as though they were going to indulge in a gourmet meal; however, when Phyllis asked the waiter if it was alright if they just had tea and a bun, he assured her that it was.

There they sat, the older woman and the young one. Phyllis was duly impressed by the composure and calm of her friend's youngest daughter. She expected a flustered young girl, but here, opposite her, sat a beautiful and tranquil young woman.

Cindra, wanting to look older than her age, had styled her long, blond hair in a loose bun at the nape of her neck, a style with which her dad had often disapproved, saying, "Cindy, honey, don't do that to your hair. Enjoy looking young; you'll grow old soon enough."

Also, her wearing apparel added to the deception: she was attired in a severely tailored business suit. It was brown and from Eaton's catalogue and had been a real disappointment to her as it was of a coarser weave than what she gathered as pictured in the catalogue. The dainty cream-coloured blouse relieved the stark look a little, but the overall picture was quite matronly, especially when the description of Cindra's footwear is added to the picture: a solid pair of brown oxfords with silken laces and Cuban heels!

And there they sat, sipping their tea. Phyllis, to her surprise, felt as though she had just met one of her city friends, and they had stopped to chat a while—what a delightful little sojourn it was, the older one telling the younger one a little about the city and their living accommodations, and the younger one giving the older news of her mother and of her home.

Cindra, on the wise advice of her mother, had shipped the bulk of her belongings on ahead in Dad Jack's old steamer trunk, a trunk that he had used on the several trips abroad he had made in connection with his business. And so, since they had only a couple of bags to pick up at the baggage claim and these had been recovered, the two ladies made their way to Market Street, where they hailed a cab, then settled inside for the short drive "home."

The younger woman was impressed by the wide streets of Saint Louis. She had done a little research on that city before leaving her hometown. She had read that "in

1764 Pierre Laclede Liquest selected the site between the Missouri and Mississippi rivers to build his dream town, Saint Louis, named after the French king Louis XIV; it was a trading post, which was a paradox in itself, the 'Paris of America!' "

As they started to head east down Market Street towards the centre of downtown, Phyllis pointed out some of the interesting "show-places" along the route. Cindra had noticed and already had become enamoured with Aloe Plaza, located across from the bustling Terminal Hotel, which served as a haven to weary train travellers. She vowed that she would return to that plaza, read the inscription on the memorial plaque, and study the magnificent fountain.

Phyllis drew attention to the municipal auditorium, known as the Kiel Auditorium, which they were now passing, and Cindra recalled how her dad, on returning from one of his businesstrips to Saint Louis, had mentioned this "opera house", as he had called it. His aim was to encourage his daughter in every way to become a concert artist and play in just such a wonderful opera house. The taxi driver, sensing her interest, proffered the information that the construction of it had begun in August of 1932, and that it had opened in the spring of 1934.

They had gone out of their way somewhat in order to see the aforementioned giant building with the statues of two huge bears guarding its entrance; however, Phyllis, being a creature of habit, asked the cabdriver to turn north along Fourteenth Street, and west along Chestnut Street, to the Plaza Apartments, one of which was home to her, and home it was to become for Cindra.

After the two women alighted from the cab and the older one had paid their fare, they walked into the dwelling. They were happy to set down the bags and catch their breath; though this apartment was on the ground floor, there were a few steps up to the entrance.

Chapter 3
Getting Acquainted

The two women sat down and looked at each other; Phyllis thought, *Oh, this poor kid, so far from home. How strange it must be for her.* Cindra thought, *Golly, the delicious smell from the kitchen.* For her the aroma was like that which emanated from her mother's colourful kitchen, and she could picture her mom in that workplace, with the green ivy wallpaper, possibly at this moment concocting something tasty for Barb's supper when she returned from the hospital. She reminded herself that Ontario's time would be an hour ahead of Missouri's, so Barb and Mom could possibly be ready to sit down to the meal, as Mom liked an early dinner at night. The good woman would say, "So that we can get things cleared away and enjoy a longer evening."

Cindra looked around; what a cosy place it was! She fell in love with it immediately. It was tastefully furnished, but modestly within the limited budget of a middle-class working girl. Then the beautiful girl's eyes focused back to where her benefactress was seated, and she watched the older woman, who was removing her shoes and replacing them with more comfortable soft shoes.

"Now, my dear, I'll show you your bedroom." Phyllis stood up and then led the young girl to what was to be her bedroom. Cindra almost squealed with delight when she saw it, it was so bright and lovely. She had no idea that Phyllis had taken the smaller bedroom in order to accommodate the small, second-hand, upright piano. Phyllis had purchased it from a man who, she was assured by a friend, "knew pianos." Phyllis had been understandably amused by his name, which was Mr. Keyes. As she had browsed in his shop, he'd led her by a host of instruments until he came to one that was excellent. He'd said, "True, the case is a little the worse for wear, Miss Pindar, but I can refinish it and restore it completely." As he spoke, the little stout man performed a few scales and trills, which had impressed the buyer, and she exclaimed, "Oh, the lovely mellow sound!" When the moderate price was quoted, she acquiesced to the purchase of that instrument without any further searching. However, there was almost a heated disagreement when it came to the finish of the piano, but the lady had won out, and Mr. Keyes reluctantly had the piano painted white!

When the young girl's eyes alighted on the little white piano, she indeed squealed audibly, this time with delight, since she had seen no sign of any instrument in the adjoining living room–dining room of the apartment. She had been beginning to wonder if her mother's friend realized the seriousness of her venture; so she silently offered a little prayer of thanksgiving whilst looking at her benefactress who was explaining about the location of the controversial (as far as Mr. Keyes was concerned) instrument. "I have put your piano in your room, my dear. This room borders on the outside, and apparently, above it, is a huge storeroom on the second floor for housekeeping equipment, so you can practise to your heart's content; it's not really going to bother anyone." Phyllis saw a look of relief on the countenance of the young girl, and she knew then that her intuitive need for such organizing was warranted.

"Phyllis, what a pretty room!" Cindra exclaimed as she hugged her mother's friend, who was already endearing herself to the girl. The older woman braced herself a little; she was not a very demonstrative person. One might say she was somewhat aloof as far as any show of affection was concerned; however, she reminded herself of the age of her charge, scarcely out of adolescence. She gave a kindly smile and continued to acquaint Cindra with her new surroundings.

Then off they went to the cheerily painted kitchen. Miss Pindar certainly preferred light colours; the kitchen was appointed in white appliances and cupboards with soft green walls and countertops. There were two little black, wrought-iron chairs, reminding one of an ice-cream parlour. These were cushioned also in soft green, and between them was a black, wrought-iron table, with the top painted a soft green. *What a delight it will be,* thought Cindra, *to eat breakfast with Phyllis in this lovely room!*

However, the aroma of delicious food caught the young beauty's interest, and she found herself assisting the "cook" in dipping out the food. They were having Virginia baked ham for dinner, garnished with pineapple; also peas, scalloped potatoes, and lemon-meringue pie for dessert, which Phyllis announced was an option, she herself having come to the age where she was keeping watch over the calories. The woman was by no means overweight, but she kept guard like a soldier over the midarea of her body. Her efforts had paid off, as she did have a youthful figure, and one that she wasn't about to spoil.

Chapter 4
The Men in Their Lives

The two women sat down to the aforementioned meal in the dining-room. Cindra decided to eat the little salad of lettuce, tomatoes, and cucumbers after she finished the main course; the tomato juice they had both enjoyed drinking in the kitchen before they'd served up the meal. It was Phyllis who broke the silence, asking Cindra if she had still been seeing the young man who had visited her when the former was last in Canada, a year ago. "Oh, poor Lawrence," Cindra said (everyone called him Larry, but Cindra preferred Lawrence), "I guess you knew that he'd finished his premeds at Toronto University before serving in the army, now he's going into his first year of medicine." And she thought of the slender, handsome youth, who had wanted to marry her to keep her from going to Missouri and, he feared, out of his life. What a serious young man he was! But Cindra was just as serious; all she could think about was her career, especially since her dreams were manifesting themselves so beautifully.

The conversation focused on the medical student for a while, then Phyllis updated Cindra on her latest interest, boyfriend-wise. The latter already knew of her benefactress's heartbreak after her immigration to Missouri. The boyfriend who had recommended the job in Saint Louis, which had materialized for her, had been killed in a car accident not long after her arrival; he had been the victim of a drunk driver, and Phyllis, consequently, had an exaggerated antipathy towards the drinking of "spirits." She was adamant in her dislike of that pastime, and made it known to everyone.

She did relate to Cindra, however, a current male interest. He was a divorced businessman, "an excellent escort," she confided, "but I am only one of several ladies in whom he is interested, and," she went on, "ours is more of a platonic relationship; we just enjoy going to concerts together, and other like pursuits, but that's as far as it will go for me. I'm afraid, my dear, I've lived alone too long, and I'm, as one might say, set in my ways."

The meal continued in good-humored fashion, the two people getting to know one another better and finding a mutual feeling of a kind of kinship that was going to prove very precious to both of them in time to come.

After the meal, the two women listened to the news on the radio whilst they cleared up and washed the dishes. This news-listening had become a habit with Phyllis, and thus, in turn, it became one with her new companion. Phyllis would say "I can't take the news in the morning; there's enough of it flying around in the office. But after the day's work, I can settle down to listening to it, and it doesn't seem as soul shattering." It was obvious she was referring to the accidents and various other items that the newscaster relayed to the public.

Chapter 5

A Quiet Evening

Phyllis asked Cindra if she would play the piano for her, the news on the radio having ended. The latter having assented, the two went into the bright-coloured bedroom.

This room had been very thoughtfully appointed: a white wicker screen was standing at one end of the room, obscuring the twin-size bed, which lay behind it. One of the older woman's friends, a traditionalist and an antique dealer of sorts, had scolded her for painting the brass bed white. "That is sacrilege," she had said, "nothing but sacrilege." But there it stood, white, and almost fairy-like, with its gorgeous, flowered taffeta-silk spread, in multicolours of mauve, dark green, white, and turquoise-blue, which blended very nicely with the walls of almost the same blue-green shade. There was a large, oval, braided rug, in matching colour, on the floor. The bulk of the room was fitted out like a sitting room; a pretty wicker love seat, the cushions of which were covered with the same taffeta as was used for the bedspread, stood invitingly in one corner. Even the white wicker dressing table had more of a sitting-room look, with its basket-shaped, white wicker chair and the same taffeta material covering its cushions.

Cindra fell in love with the room! Dear, dear Phyllis had even unpacked the young girl's trunk, which had been sent on ahead; her clothes were hanging up neatly in the roomy closet, actually moderately sized, as closets go, but certainly roomy, she thought, to what she was used to in her fairly large, old brick house in Belleville. Little did she know that her benefactress had spent most of her vacation, which she took in the spring, fixing up this room for her young charge.

It was decided that the traveller would unpack the luggage she had brought with her just before she retired to bed, so, as promised, she sat down at the little, white upright piano with its matching white stool. The stool even had a flouncy cushion in the same matching material as the rest of the furniture.

And the young girl began to play. Phyllis, sitting on the

love seat, watched the beautiful creature, who had released her blond hair from the severe style of a bun and allowed it to fall down over her shoulders. The keys of the little, white upright piano came alive under her limber fingers, and the older woman thought, *How ethereal is this. What a beautiful little treasure is this golden girl.* As the notes came cascading from the musical box, arias from Puccini's *La Bohème*, which Phyllis's trained ear had detected, she vowed, in her musings, to try in every way possible to keep this beauty at her art. She could see in her mind's eye the young swains in the district watching this girl as well, so charming and pleasant to look at was she! Phyllis was now definitely convinced that the hair-bun style was a good idea.

And Cindra, as her fingers flowed over the keys, forming the lovely strains of the lilting melodies, thought, *This is my joy; this is my life. My music is to come first; how fortunate I am!* And her whole being was filled with thankfulness for her father's dream, for her benefactress, and to God. Before she went to unpack her things, she had thought up a name for the little, white upright piano; it would now be called the Dove.

Chapter 6
Sunday

Sunday dawned clear and bright; the weather had warmed and it would be a nice summer day. Cindra decided that a suit would be out of the question for a warm day. She had thought out her wardrobe quite carefully, keeping in mind the image that she wanted to project, that of a mature business woman, intent on doing her very best at the job that had been arranged for her. And so she had selected matronly clothes. Even her mother showed disapproval; she didn't want her daughter to go that far, but the determined one was quite serious about her desire to look older. She sensed what she would face in an office full of prosaic, she imagined, older women, and she couldn't take the chance of appearing her true age.

Well, she would discuss apparel at breakfast with Phyllis, who had popped her head in to greet her with a cheery good morning and an announcement that the coffeepot was brewing.

The two women had breakfast, relaxing in their dressing gowns. Cindra's gown was a little the worse for wear; however, it was a marvellous magenta colour, a redeeming feature, and it was a fine chenille; and with the one small hole (Jody's dog managed that) having been darned, it really did not look too bad!

Cindra announced that she was going to church; this was a habit her family had had from the start. She could not remember a Sunday that the Gold family did not go to church, sometimes three times—in the morning, then home for lunch, then in the afternoon for Sunday school. Dad Jack played the piano for the adult Bible class at that time (yes, Dad Jack was musical too, though he would have been the first to admit that he did not have the talent that his youngest daughter had), then again in the evening. Most of the family attended that service too. Mother in later years stayed home. She sung in the choir, so the ladies processing in for the service would file along and move down, closing in the empty space where Mother would have sat in the choir loft; Mother would have been found at home with her ear glued to the radio, enjoying the comical antics of "Amos and Andy."

The young girl, after reminding her listener of her family's Sabbatarian habit, related to her the story of her would-be lapse from this practice one Sunday evening. It concerned the death of her dear pet cat. However, at this point Phyllis interrupted abruptly, though apologetically, querying, "Did your dad not go to the synagogue?" She was aware that Mr. Gold had been orphaned as an infant and was brought up by a very concerned Jewish family; so the fair-haired girl told her that her father's adoptive family had not been Orthodox, nor did they proselytise, so the young man, using this freedom of choice, decided to embrace the Christian faith of his natural parents. She said he had indeed met his wife in the Methodist church before that church joined with the Presbyterian church to form the United Church of Canada in 1925. She explained that she found it easy to remember the year as it was a year after her sister Barbara was born, and Dad Jack used to say that this daughter was a year older than the United Church of Canada!

There was a pause; Cindra's mind wandered back to home and her family. The older woman saw the expression of anguish on the young girl's face and, looking at her compassionately, said, "Sorry for breaking in upon your story; please tell me about your cat." The storyteller's face brightened, and she continued with the tale of Fluffy Ruffles Gold, the white-and-gray pet she had adored. She related how, arriving at a very old age (she made it clear that this was some years ago), he had come down with pneumonia, and that was the finish of him. What had upset her more was the fact that relatives and friends were quite ruthless, so she thought, in declaring, on her querying, that "no, cats did not go to Heaven," and she, in her grief, had been most dejected. As she continued with the story, a smile appeared on her pretty face, and both women laughed good humoredly. She went on, still smiling, "Well, my dad looked for me to go to church one Sunday evening, but I was determined that no way was I going to a church that wouldn't admit animals to Heaven, but poor Dad, he found me hiding behind the barn (there used to be one of those years ago at the end of our backyard), and he dictated that I was going to church. Well, to church I went, but I felt I had the last word, as true to what I'd said, I didn't wear a hat. It was the accepted thing then that women wore hats to church. Dad Jack, in his wisdom, let me get away with that; you see, he rather thought I might feel uncomfortable. Dad really did win in that one, as I did feel very conspicuous!"

The last part of this anecdote brought more laughter. The young girl was beginning to feel more at home; the feeling of strangeness and aloneness was easing off, and she was so very thankful for that.

The two women finished breakfast, Cindra offering to clean up. Phyllis, however, noting the hour (it was after ten), advised the church-goer to get dressed and then help by drying the dishes if there was time. The younger woman took the advice and a little later emerged from the bedroom wearing a very simple dress. It was a pale yellow, flowered voile, one that her mother had made. Mother had won out in that one and had patterned it in a younger style than what her daughter preferred; however, the latter thought that since it was for leisure wear, she could relax a bit concerning the matronly image she was aiming to achieve.

Having dried the dishes for her friend, the yellow-clad girl left the apartment, after slipping on her white shoes, silk gloves, and matching hat Mother had made from the same material as the dress. Her mother had hoped to achieve the look of an expensive, store-bought hat; she had used starch to stiffen the brim. It didn't have quite the stiffness the young girl preferred, but she would have looked lovely in any hat, and she was not too disappointed in the effect it gave.

On the train Cindra had decided she would go to any church that was handy, irrespective of denomination or creed. Her dad had taught her that the outdoors was God's great cathedral and it was his influence that caused her to believe that it really did not matter where one worshipped. What did matter, in his opinion, was the fact that one worshipped somewhere; as he said, it was a "much-needed rudder" in one's life. She was glad that her dad had been broad minded, especially in regards to religion, as she had seen so many relationships hurt by the religious factor alone, both among her relatives on her mother's side and in the families of some school chums.

She had a warm, glowing awareness as she left the apartment. She was so thankful that the sad homesick feeling that had come over her through the night had disappeared. She thought, *Who could be sad on a gorgeous sunny day like this?* Then she rationalized, as she often did that Dad Jack was just as near to her wherever she was now as he would be at home, since he had gone to his eternal rest. "Eternal rest" was the term her dad used when referring to persons who had passed from this earthly life.

She looked at her watch and could not help being amazed at how fast the time had gone, as she had allowed herself time to spare when setting her alarm clock the night before. Oh well, she would attend Saint John's Roman Catholic Church, located in the square, facing Phyllis's apartment. So a short walk brought her into the little church, where a sidesman smiled a friendly greeting, then ushered her towards one of the pews. She genuflected before entering the pew, which was not the custom in the church she attended at home; however, she had attended Saint Michael's Cathedral in Belleville many times with friends, and so this ritual was well-known to her, and she liked it. After setting down on the seat her purse and the order of service sheet that had been handed to her by the sidesman, she knelt on the prayer cushion in front of her to pour out her thanksgiving to God for giving her this opportunity to develop her musical talent. Her dad had taught her to do this on many occasions when they sat fishing on the Bay of Quinte. Even if things were not going so well, either at home or at his job, he would always find something to be thankful for, and he'd made this known to his fair-haired child as they fished and communed with nature.

She did not feel all that strange in this Roman Catholic church, even though her family's place of worship was quite Protestant. Though her closest friend, Jean, belonged to a Baptist congregation, of her two other close friends, June was Anglican and Helen was a good practising member of the aforementioned Saint Michael's Church in Belleville. Cindra had been in the latter church with her friend on a number of occasions.

The priest was an erudite man, so Cindra thought; his sermon was a beautiful discourse on love, and he alluded many times to Jesus' disciple John. After the service the young girl left the church with love overflowing in her heart; she was feeling somewhat elated by the silver-tongued priest's message. And the strains of one of the hymns they sang kept replaying in her mind. She remembered only a few of the words, "Jesus and the lambs," which struck a deep chord in her soul.

The golden-haired girl had a short walk back to her new home. Her bright blue eyes drank in the luminous crimson red of the geraniums planted nearby, which stood out gloriously in contrast to the lacy-edged, white double petunias. She was greeted by a cheery-eyed Phyllis, who explained to her that she had just come out to see the bright-coloured flowers and enjoy their subtle fragrance. The two women exchanged loving smiles; Cindra would have liked to have hugged her mother's friend, but she was a little shy and sensed intuitively that her benefactress was not a demonstrative person.

Whilst going up the steps and into the apartment, the older woman explained that they were going out for lunch, as she had a club meeting with the women with whom she worked, and doing things this way would allow them more time. She also hastily added that Cindra was quite welcome to come along to their meeting, explaining that since she was going to be doing secretarial work, the subject matter would not be foreign to her and, indeed, might be helpful. Cindra thanked her friend for her kind consideration but asked if she would be offended if she did not go to the meeting. She exclaimed, "Oh, Phyllis, I've just got to go to Aloe Plaza to see the fountain and to read the inscriptions, and I must stand outside that opera house." Phyllis was intuitive enough to surmise that this budding prodigy would stand looking at the opera house and indeed dream of one day being a concert pianist there. And the older lady knew she must encourage the fair one as regards her ambition; however, she, being a sensible, down-to-earth person, was reluctant to have her young charge wandering around the streets of Saint Louis alone, so she suggested an escort for her. She explained that the one she had in mind was an elderly gentleman and a person who needed companionship; she explained further that he was a dear soul with a poetic nature and would, she thought, be the perfect one to accompany the young girl. Cindra was a little piqued at this. She considered herself a free soul, quite independent and confident; she would go anywhere alone in her hometown and was what one might describe as fearless. However, she was mature enough and had insight enough to realize that it would be best to concede to the suggestions of her new living companion. After all, Phyllis had been dwelling in this big city for years, so she knew she must respect her wishes, despite Cindra's ingrained feelings that she was divinely protected. Dad Jack and her mom had fostered such feelings in all of their progeny.

Chapter 7
A Newfound Friend

That is how Miss Gold met John Serenity. Before the two women left for the restaurant where they would have their noon meal, Phyllis phoned Mr. Serenity, who lived in the same apartment building, to see if he would be free after lunch, and if he would like to meet the young lady and escort her on a walk along Market Street. She had previously told the gentleman about her old friend's daughter coming to live with her and to study music, so she asked her favour without much palaver. John had replied that he was free and amicably agreed to chaperoning Phyllis's young charge. "And how about joining us for lunch, John, then you can become acquainted with the girl I've spoken so much about." Both women heard the delighted "Okay" that resounded over the phone, and it was not long before the three were on their way to the restaurant.

Cindra did not take in much about the restaurant, noting only that the food was excellent, she was so enchanted with Mr. John Serenity. If there ever could be a replacement for her dad, he was the one; even his first name was the same, though this man had kept the original John, whereas her dad got the nickname of Jack, as so often happens with that name. The girl even felt the same kind of "vibes" as she had felt with her father, and she was so very thankful that they were kindred spirits.

Having finished lunch the gray-haired old man and the golden-haired beauty parted company with Phyllis, she going off to her meeting, and Mr. Serenity and Cindra walking along Market Street together. The latter discovered that even though John Serenity was old, he was a good walker, just like her dad. What a glorious afternoon they had, strolling in the pure sunlight, not a cloud overhead and the sky as blue as the young girl's eyes.

The girl was telling him of her dreams as they walked in a westerly direction along Market Street. He was a good listener and was quite enjoying the company and the enthusiasm of his young companion.

"I seem to be doing all the talking, Mr. Serenity, do please tell me about yourself," Cindra said as she looked entreatingly at him.

"Well, I'm glad to be enjoying good health at my advanced age, so many of my friends are incapacitated in one way or another." Then John proceeded to tell her about his life situation. He explained that he lived a rather lonely life; his wife had died and his three sons had married and moved away. Though he had seen his grandchildren, there were six of them, from time to time, they had not become very close because of the brevity of the visits. He said that some of his grandchildren were now married, and he had lost track of most of them. He told her he had to be content with the way things had turned out, and content he was, not regretting anything, which some elderly people seem to do. He said he seldom felt really lonely, there was so much he had to do, and Phyllis would sometimes tease him about an elderly widow on the floor above. She would occasionally see the two of them going out for a stroll.

Next John related to her that he had a bird-watching group he had formed, and he also mentioned that he had started a small historical society group, just for his and their own gratification. These few old cronies would meet together on a regular basis and peruse library books or tourist guide pamphlets and study historical facts and dates. The old man said enthusiastically, "The other members and I enjoy this pastime very much. We go to the different museums and landmarks to view the places and to get first-hand information." Then he added mischievously, "It keeps me out of mischief, you know."

"I think that's just great," Cindra announced, looking at him solemnly. She was overjoyed to hear that he had information about so many of the points of interest in the city, but on the other hand she could not help feeling sad that his relatives did not involve him more in their lives. How she had wished for living grandparents when she was growing up, both sets in her family having passed away before she was born.

The two, the elderly man and the young girl, now stood on the street in the brilliant sunlight, directly across from the Terminal Hotel, the fair one having explained to John that the Aloe Plaza was the first spot she wanted to visit, and here they were. They studied the interesting fountain with its water spewing out at various points. Mr. Serenity, in his soft voice, began explaining the magnificent sculpture. He said, "This fountain was designed by Carl Milles, and he symbolizes the union of the Mississippi and

Missouri rivers by those two large figures, male and female, facing each other. The lesser water creatures, the dolphins, and the smaller figures suggest the many tributaries and streams."

Cindra was enraptured by the whole scene, the cascading water sparkling in the sunlight, the playful attitude of the sea creatures, and this dear old man standing beside her, who, she was discovering, had a wealth of knowledge he was eager to share.

Mr. Serenity continued to give more information about it saying, "Milles conceived the sculptures as an embodiment of the freedom and primeval force of the waterways of the great Mississippi Valley, and he thought of the grouping as a marriage or festival celebrating the coming together of these great waters."

The girl marvelled at the memory of the person standing next to her, and she looked at him as he stood there quietly, almost in an attitude of worship, she thought, in respect and appreciation for the God-given talent of a fellowman. She concluded right then and there that this dear person must have a photographic memory, and in her musings the young girl offered a little inaudible "Thank you" to her Creator for this newfound friend with his willingness to share his learning.

Since she seemed eager for more information about the work of art and asked her mentor about the sculptor himself, John proceeded to tell her a bit about Carl Milles, saying that he was Swedish-born and a pupil of Rodin's. He explained that Milles, when sculpturing the fountain, was conscious that it and the entire plaza was a memorial to Louis P. Aloe (1869–1929), who had been a civic figure and long-time president of the Board of Aldermen of Saint Louis.

Then John directed his astute listener over to a plaque

and she read for herself, THE PLAZA AND FOUNTAIN WERE DEDICATED BY BERNARD F. DICKMANN, MAYOR OF THE CITY OF SAINT LOUIS, MAY 11, 1940, and she thought to herself, *Golly that was only six years ago!*

The young lady, having feasted her eyes well on the joyous fountain, next directed her gaze across the street to the Terminal Hotel, with its tower clock and its Juliet balconies. As her eyes drank in all of this, she realized that she had quite fallen in love with this city and she had no trouble in accepting it as her new home.

"We'll go back now and have a cup of tea, Little Miss," suggested the elderly man, looking benevolently at the fair-haired girl beside him.

Cindra looked at her watch. "My goodness, it's four o'clock; how fast the time has gone!" She was amazed at this. She felt very comfortable with John Serenity; even his name put her at ease.

So back they went, sauntering along Market Street. The Kiel Auditorium was clearly visible, just a few blocks away. John was sure that his pianist friend would want to make a visit to this auditorium or "opera house," which he knew was her term of reference, and he suggested this to her. "We'll make it soon," he added.

An expression of gratitude lit up the young girl's face. "Oh, Mr. Serenity, you've read my thoughts. I'm so grateful for your interest; you are so very kind."

Back the short distance strolled the two noble ones, she noble by way of her sincerity and appreciation, he by way of his sharing and consideration for a young girl away from loved ones. "Little Miss" was how he addressed her, which term of reference he would continue to use when talking to or of Cindra. The old man had deep feelings of empathy for Little Miss because of her age and her separation from her folks and home. He realized that this was quite an adjustment for her. Phyllis and he had had chats about it when the former was preparing for the young girl's arrival.

The two sightseers, the older one a little weary, the younger one eager for more information, climbed the few outside steps and made their way to the Pindar apartment. Cindra took out of her purse the key Phyllis had given to her, unlocked the door, and called out for her friend. The said lady was not at home, so John Serenity invited Little Miss to go with him to his apartment one floor up. When he opened the door and Cindra saw the book-lined walls, she could not help but gasp; she discovered that her new friend truly was a lover of knowledge. John proceeded to ferret out books and tourist pamphlets on the city of Saint Louis. The young girl was ecstatic. She read several of the pamphlets and leafed through some of the books, most with coloured pictures for one's enjoyment. What a delightful time she had! Her new friend eventually disappeared into the kitchen to make the tea.

Chapter 8
A Decision

The telephone gave a shrill ring. It was Phyllis on the line asking that Cindra come down for her supper. There was a tone of disappointment in John's voice after he hung up the receiver and spoke to Little Miss.

"Phyllis wants you there right away. She says you don't have time for a cup of tea, that your meal's ready and she's waiting for you." The man looked as disappointed as he sounded. "I did want her to come up and have a cup of tea with us. Oh well, my dear, we'll arrange it some other time."

"Oh, Mr. Serenity, it would have been so nice!" The girl's mood matched John's; however, after thanking her new friend for chaperoning her, she dutifully went downstairs.

"Now, Cindra, I hope you're not too disappointed with not having tea with Mr. S., but I've told you I'm a creature of habit and that's the way it is. It's going to work out well for you with the career you've chosen." There was determination in the older woman's voice, despite the apologetic tone.

The young girl grimaced a little as she washed her hands in the bathroom sink; she would so like to have had that cup of tea with Mr. S. (in her thoughts she used the same nickname as her benefactress's for Mr. Serenity). She wondered why they could not have deviated a little from staid routine, especially since it was Sunday.

The two women sat down to the meal that Phyllis had prepared that morning; it was a simple repast of cold cuts, scalloped potatoes, vegetable salad, and fresh fruit cocktail for dessert. The young girl was hungry, and this was the kind of menu she liked. She looked at her friend sitting across from her and softened. She asked Phyllis how the meeting went.

Phyllis had sensed that the girl was a little piqued and was glad of the opportunity to get away from the unsettling thoughts of the preceding moments.

"We had a great time; all the club members turned out. Mavis, the oldest member of the group, after the official part was over, gave us news of her first little grandchild. That baby's going to be spoilt!"

Then Phyllis, suddenly remembering the phone call, interjected, "Your piano teacher, Miss Grace, phoned. She says you can start your lessons on Tuesday night, if that's agreeable to you; if not, you're to give her a call."

This news startled the young girl somewhat. "I was hoping I'd have at least a week to get settled. There's my new job, Phyllis; I start it tomorrow."

Phyllis used a sympathetic tone but made several points clear. "Dear, this is a career of commitment you're going into, and there's no use putting it off. I plan to cooperate in any way I can. Instead of helping with the dishes, meal preparation, or housework, you can forget these and just concentrate on your music."

The fair-haired Cindra looked at Phyllis with tears in her eyes, tears of gratitude for the caring person sitting across from her who was willing to do this for her!

The musician had ambivalent feelings when she went into her room to practise. She so wanted to read some of the material that Mr. S. had loaned her about the city, but she could not go against the wishes of her mother's friend. Besides, she knew that Phyllis was right; her music must come first. Thus, there flowed from the piano such scales and arpeggios as Miss Pindar had never heard before, and the musician even surprised herself, vowing then and there to keep more control of her feelings and to make a name for herself in the music world.

Chapter 9
The Office

The two business ladies were up early. Cindra wanted to have time to concentrate on her "schoolmarm" image, and conversely, Phyllis tried to make herself look as youthful as possible. The details of both of their toilettes having been completed, they walked out of the apartment, each with a purse suspended from one arm and a lunch bag from the other.

"I'll walk with you to your office building, Cindra. Mine is just a few blocks farther on Locust Street." The older woman had spoken decisively.

Their route took them down Pine Street, north on Thirteenth Street, and east a short distance on Olive Street. The young girl's heart beat faster when they stopped in front of a huge building on the plate glass door of which was printed in large, gold letters, JOHN C. BRENT & SONS, PRINTING & BUSINESS SUPPLIES. Except for its mammoth size and the fancy door, it was not a very impressive-looking establishment; its facade was flush with the sidewalk, though the door was recessed a little and there were a few broad steps leading up to it.

"Well, here goes." The young girl gave her companion a wan smile and hurriedly disappeared into the building, afraid that her courage might wane if she did not part abruptly from her friend.

After ascending the interior marble steps, she paused to stare at her surroundings. The inside of the building was certainly more pleasing to look at than the exterior. There were brass railings here and there, and an air of opulence pervading all. Cindra approached a desk, which she suspected was a reception desk. A very smart-looking, well-dressed, middle-aged woman stood up to greet her.

"You must be the new secretary. Are you Miss Gold?"

Reassured by this, the newcomer replied that she was. Several other employees looked up from their desks, obviously curious about the lady who had just walked in.

Cindra was escorted by the woman up the elevator to the second floor, the woman telling her as they went that

Mr. Brent, Sr., was expecting her. Her escort introduced herself as Miss Frost and said in a kindly tone, "The Brent Company is a fine firm to work for. You'll like it here."

The young girl was further heartened by this as she had found the stares of the other office workers a little unsettling.

She confided to Miss Frost, "I do feel nervous. I hope I'll work out alright." The older woman inspired confidence in her, and she had blurted out her feelings without any reticence.

Mr. John Brent's office door was open and he was sitting at his desk waiting expectantly for the arrival of the new secretary, as Miss Frost had sent the errand boy ahead to let him know that she was coming. The theme of opulence was certainly carried out further on this floor. Mr. Brent got up from his black leather chair behind the huge mahogany desk and came forward with hand outstretched to greet the new worker. They shook hands, and Miss Frost left them to get acquainted with one another.

"Miss Gold, you are a replacement for one of the girls who left to get married." Mr. Brent had a smooth deep voice. "You will be my son Robert's secretary." With that he buzzed another office and a very good-looking, dark-haired young man appeared.

"Robert, this is Miss Gold; she will be your new secretary."

The young man looked at the blond-haired girl with the drab, spinsterlike appearance. Cindra detected an attitude of displeasure in him. He asked to speak with his father alone, so the girl was escorted to the outer office by Mr. Brent, Sr., who asked her to wait on a chair behind one of the desks whilst he had a little discussion with his sons. Then another handsome, dark-haired man, shorter and somewhat older-looking, came out of another office and went into the room Cindra had just left.

Cindra sat there. She could hear the muffled sounds of a lively discussion taking place in the older man's office. She felt uneasy. There were several desks in this outer office, each with a young woman busily at work, one typing, another filing some papers into a large filing cabinet close to her desk, and one affixing stamps to a pile of addressed envelopes. Another of the girls got up and, after having a drink at the watercooler, she came over to the desk where the "new girl" was sitting and started talking to her.

"I'm Catharine," she introduced herself, and seeing the girl was somewhat upset by the previous proceedings, explained, "It's that Robert. He can be such a pain. Don't let it bother you. He wants things the way he wants them and that's that." She took a breath and continued, "Come meet the other girls."

After meeting the rest of the staff in the area, Cindra went back to the empty chair and sat waiting to see what the outcome would be of this odd state of affairs. Her nervousness left her as she rethought the situation, and indignation took over her thoughts. "To heck with this; she would leave. She could look in the paper for another job... Oh, but she hadn't time for that. She had to start paying her board, and there were her piano lessons... She had so wanted to phone home on the weekend, but she didn't want to run up a phone bill. She and her mom, before she left Belleville, had it understood that letters would suffice, and she had written to her mom shortly after she arrived in Saint Louis.... She just had to see this through; she just couldn't delve into her savings." Thus her indignation gave way to common sense, and her thought pattern changed again. "She would stay... she would show them!" Cindra was very confident of her ability concerning her secretarial skills, and her assurance and poise returned.

Finally, the three men came out and approached her apologetically. Mr. Brent, Sr., spoke first,

"I am very sorry for the confusion, Miss Gold. My sons have come to an agreement: Cameron's secretary, Miss Janes, will be assigned to Robert, and you to my oldest son, Cameron."

At that moment a gorgeous, red-haired girl came into view and beckoned to the youngest man, who excused himself and went over to her. Apparently she wanted some papers signed. Cindra learned later that the two men were sharing the same secretary until the new one should arrive. Robert Brent's remark to Jane Janes was, "What a 'Miss Prim' that is!"

After the slight interruption, Mr. Brent, Sr., introduced the young lady to Mr. Cameron Brent, who then took charge of the situation, and in a kindly voice he apologized to her again, saying that he was very glad she was here and he would orientate her to the work as soon as she was ready, adding that if she wanted to have a little break first, it would be fine with him. However, she assured him she was anxious to get started, so the two disappeared into Cameron Brent's office.

It was a nice bright room, and her new employer, she was discovering, was a pleasant man. He was very concise in his instructions, and it was not long before he was dictating a letter. She could see by his delighted expression that he was pleased with her work. She herself had been proud of her rapid shorthand when she was at school and could see it was paying off now.

There came the sound of a soft bell ringing a couple of times, and a scurrying could be heard in the outer office.

"Time for coffee break, Miss Gold. I will get Miss Janes to take you to the staff lounge." With that Cameron Brent pressed on a buzzer. There was no answer.

"Never mind, Mr. Brent. I noticed the lounge as I was coming up here; I'll find it myself." The new secretary felt very assured; she was pleased with her performance and more than pleased with the type of work she would be doing.

The redhead was the first to approach her in the lounge. "Isn't that Robert a character, but he's really a pet, sure has eyes for the women! You just have to take him as he is, and he's not hard to take. Isn't he handsome!"

The new girl looked squarely at her boss's former secretary—what a beauty! She could see why Robert wanted her as his stenographer. She was glad too, as she did not feel like coping with his charm in such close quarters as a private office. She agreed with the red-haired beauty that Robert was indeed very handsome.

Before the blond had time to say anything, the redhead spoke again. "I'm Jane Janes. Come on, let's get our coffee."

As they walked over to the coffee pots, Cindra was about to introduce herself when Miss Frost came in, walked over to her and announced, "Everybody, this is Cindra Gold, Robert Brent's new secretary."

"Just a minute, Lee, there's been a change. She's Cameron's new secretary; Robert's keeping me." Jane informed them all of the switch.

Everyone laughed, they knew Robert Brent; no one was surprised, and the new girl laughed with them. She was pleased that the image she wished to portray had been successful, and also that she did not have to put up with such a male distraction from her work! She, having recovered from the shock of rejection, had to admit she was fascinated by the man!

It was a congenial group. Cindra enjoyed the coffee, which she had been told was provided by their employers. *What a nice gesture,* thought the young girl.

There was not much time to get acquainted with the rest before another soft bell rang, notifying all that their break was now over. There was an unhurried, orderly evacuation from the lounge.

The new girl was happy to be back at her work. With the help and instruction of Jane Janes the pile of correspondence that needed attention was soon cleared away.

Cindra found out that she had access to two desks: the empty one where she had formerly sat whilst awaiting her "verdict," and a small one in her employer's office where she could attend to any correspondence and similar matters that involved the two of them. She liked this arrangement, it would give a little variety she thought.

The time passed rapidly; the sound of a soft bell ringing again alerted all that it was lunch break. This time Jane Janes came for Cindra. They walked together to the lounge. The new girl took her lunch bag from the fridge and sat down at a small table, one of several in the larger lounge area, following the same procedure as Miss Janes. There were only a few employees sitting at some of the other tables, and the red-head explained, "Usually a bunch of us go to 'Miss Hulling's' for lunch. They were going to ask you but I said you might want to talk over the work with me and discuss any problems."

"That's very nice of you, Jane." The new girl tried to think of something to ask her. Everything was coming so easy to Cindra so she replied, "There's quite a lot to it, and you've been very helpful already; I'm just going to take it one step at a time. Oh, now tell me about Miss Hulling's." Cindra did not know if it was a club, a restaurant, or just what it was.

Jane smiled. "It's a cafeteria, at Eleventh and Locust. It's not very far; we all love it there, the food's so good, even the Brent men go there sometimes, and they're used to elegant dining." She lowered her voice to almost a whisper and confided, "I've been hoping Robert would take me out to lunch at the Missouri Athletic Club. It's really exclusive, so I've heard, but these men don't socialize much with their office staff!"

The two women chatted quite amicably, and the hour-and-a-half lunch break sped by rapidly. It was not long before the others returned, some to their lockers to store any little purchase that they had made. The soft bell sounded and all returned to their various working areas.

Mr. Cameron Brent had not returned from lunch yet, so the new stenographer busied herself at her outer office desk, putting things in order and rearranging her supplies to her liking. She was determined to be as efficient as possible. That done, she went to her desk in her employer's office and acquainted herself with the supplies that were there. She glanced at her boss's desk, noting how orderly it was; she could not help noticing a tiny picture in a brass frame. It was that of a little girl. The photo itself seemed shadowy, making the face of the child appear very dark. The little one had beautiful eyes and the sweetest smile. Cindra expressed audibly, "What a charmer!"

She made note of the several phone calls that had come through to the office for Mr. Cameron Brent. Then it was not long before the man himself phoned, stating that he was at his home and would not be back until the morning. In the background she heard the voice of a little child. Mr. Brent asked how she was getting along. She said she was doing fine, and she informed him of the messages that had come for him. He gave her instructions on processing the matters, and when the conversation concluded she busied herself, expediently taking care of the business at hand.

The soft bell rang at 4:00 P.M., announcing the end of the working day. Cindra had not been informed of this closing time and had it in her mind that it would be 5:00 or 6:00 P.M. As her work was finished, she was quite happy to make sure all was secure and gather her things for the trip home. The rest of the staff were scurrying out, friendly good-byes were said, and the new girl was soon out on the street heading for the Pindar apartment. Many of the staff drove off in cars. Miss Frost, as she directed her car out of the driveway, from the parking lot behind the building, honked the horn to draw Cindra's attention and asked her if she could drive her home. The young girl was touched. She thanked the thoughtful lady but declined the offer of a ride, explaining that she lived just a short distance away and really needed the exercise in the sunshine. Miss Frost smiled and drove away.

Chapter 10
Telling about It

Cindra arrived home first. She checked the mailbox; there were several letters for her benefactress but none for her as yet, so she entered her new home. Phyllis arrived some time after, explaining that she was a little later than usual as she had gone to Miss Hulling's to pick up a couple of pieces of chocolate cake.

"I'm usually here before this, Cindra. My boss lets me go at four-thirty, unless something comes up, so I'm hoping to have supper ready by the time you get home. You're a little early tonight; did they let you leave before quitting time?"

"No, Phyllis, guess you thought I'd be getting out at 5:00. Well, closing time at the office is 4:00 P.M."

"That's just great, it gives us a nice long evening. We can catch up on one another's news, hear the radio news, and you'll still have plenty of time to practise." The older woman was not going to let her charge forget the reason for her venture.

Phyllis had prepared Monday's supper the night before. What a pleasant repast it was; the two women laughed good-heartedly as the "Robert Brent episode" was related. From Cindra's description of the man, Phyllis could see that she had some interest in him. Well, she would keep Cindra at her practice!

The older woman carefully removed the two pieces of chocolate cake from the box and, passing a piece to Cindra, she explained, "I told you before how I kind of watch what I eat. That's why I don't get the whole cake. We'll see how it works out; you may prefer a few more confectionaries."

The girl assured her that her food regime was fine. She knew she was more of a sedentary person; her job and practice required it, and she never did care much for sports. She knew she could put on weight very easily, so she was very pleased with her benefactress's attitude towards caloric intake.

"Phyllis, tell me about Miss Hulling's. Usually the girls at the office go there for lunch." Cindra was curious about that establishment and made the fact known.

"The women in our office frequent the place too. She has a large clientele, the food is so good! Her cafeteria's been going since 1928 and her ads say that her food has a better-than-home-cooked flavour. I think her background is Pennsylvania Dutch. I'm sure Mr. S. could tell you about her."

Then Cindra said, "Oh, I'll not need a lunch tomorrow.

Jane Janes, Robert Brent's secretary..." laughter from both broke into the middle of the girl's sentence as they thought of the event again. After this interruption she continued, "Jane has invited me to Miss Hulling's cafeteria. She says I'll probably be finding it hard until I start on the payroll next week. Wasn't it kind of her? They're really nice people down there, everyone's so friendly."

"Now Cindra, you can buy your own lunch; I'll lend you the money. She's a working gal too. Just tell her you prefer it that way."

The young girl decided to accept her friend's advice, and the finances were arranged. She still had some money left after her trip, but she felt she could not allow herself the luxury of eating out. She had helped her mother by giving her a generous amount of her savings, and the rest her mother had arranged to be sent to the bank where Phyllis dealt in Saint Louis. Her mother had cautioned her that it must be kept for emergencies.

After the sharing of their own news and the radio news hour, the two ladies dispersed, the older one to busy herself with the household chores, the younger one to her piano practice. Cindra thought of her music lesson coming up the next evening. Phyllis was insisting on paying for a taxi for her, saying adamantly that she did not want her walking out in this city after supper. The girl had to comply: She just wished she had not said anything about going out for lunch the next day; she did not want to be a burden on her benefactress. She was unaware of the loneliness that her new friend had been experiencing lately and of how much Phyllis was enjoying her company.

The budding pianist's fingers were soon flying over the piano keys. Halfway through she was interrupted by the spontaneous tear that trickled down from her left eye. As she brushed it away she thought of her dear dad. How pleased he would be that his plans for her were already implemented; she felt very close to him at that moment.

She had just finished her practise when Phyllis opened the door and asked her if she wanted a bedtime snack. Cindra declined, saying that she wanted to get to bed early, as next evening would be a late one for her.

"During your practise Mr. S. phoned asking how you made out today at your new job. He said to tell you he was thinking of you; he thinks you're quite a lady!" The woman spoke emphatically.

"That was nice of him, Phyllis." And they both agreed that he was very thoughtful.

"Well, my dear, I'll say good night. Sweet dreams." With that remark Phyllis closed the door gently and was gone, leaving the young girl alone with her thoughts.

Following the example of her dad, Cindra had developed the habit of "meditating" a brief time in the morning and at night when she would become still "to think of 'higher things,' " as her dad would say. This they would do often, out in the boat, when they were fishing. Her father kept a large black memo book of meaningful quotes, and this keepsake she had inherited. She took that notebook from the night-table beside her bed, and as she opened it her eyes were drawn to a quotation her father had copied from the writings of the philosopher Bertrand Russell: "The happy life must to a great extent be a quiet life for it is only in an atmosphere of quiet that true joy can live." She read the passage several times, then thought of what a happy man her father had been, even though his wife had suffered several physical illnesses and was in and out of the hospital for long periods of time, which accounted for the fact that he could never seem to get ahead financially because of the hospital and doctor bills. She also thought of how his cheerfulness had helped his daughters cope with the sadness that a war can bring, when her sisters would come home from school and relate how another former schoolmate had been killed in action overseas. Her dad seemed to know just the right thing to say, and she remembered that he was so glad when V-E (Victory in Europe) Day was celebrated on May 8th. He had been praying for that; he would never forget that date, he had said, as it was his wife's birthday. The time had gone by so fast, she could hardly believe it was over a year ago!

She brought her thoughts back to more tranquil leanings, and at the close of her reverie she gave thanks for the reflective influence of her father and his invaluable bequest, for her new home, for her new job, for dear Phyllis, and for "The Dove."

Chapter 11
Pleasing and Not So Pleasing Discoveries

The next day dawned bright and beautiful. Phyllis again walked with Cindra to her workplace, pointing out again that it was not that far out of her way and she needed the exercise. On their arrival at the Brent Co. building Cindra was a much cheerier young girl than she had been the day before, and Phyllis was glad about that. She so wanted her young charge to be happy.

Cindra was at her desk in the outer office and busy working when her boss came in. The others too were either settled or settling for the morning's work. As Mr. Cameron Brent passed her desk he nodded and beckoned to her to come into his office; there was no palaver with him. She followed promptly, looking very prim in her matronly attire. She closed the door as he had indicated.

"Miss Gold, I must apologize again for yesterday's mix-up. It must have been upsetting for you, but I must confide in you that I am pleased with the outcome." He spoke in a kindly tone.

Cindra smiled and blushed a little as a feeling of pride swept over her.

Her boss continued, "I'm sorry I was not here in the afternoon. My little girl was upset, so I stayed home to read to her." He spoke matter-of-factly, making it clear that his child was a part of his life too. He went on, "You see her mother died when she was born and it has not been easy for her. You managed very well here and I want to thank you."

The young woman would like to have heard more about the little child but Mr. Brent resumed his businesslike manner, and the secretary's second day of work progressed. The man dictated some letters, gave concise instructions, and then told her she could do the typing at her desk in the outer office, as he had some telephone contacts to make.

Coffee break soon came and went. The rest of the staff were all friendly, accepting Cindra as one of them, which helped to dispel any thoughts of strangeness that she was feeling. She had seen Jane Janes only briefly during the morning, but at break time Jane had reminded her of their luncheon date. So after the lunch bell rang, the two of them proceeded on their way to Miss Hulling's Cafeteria, and Jane was full of chatter about Robert Brent, how he related to her his doings of the night before, and how she wished he would ask her out. The new girl would have had to admit that she was listening with only half an ear, she was so busy noting the buildings as they walked east on Locust Street. They passed by a huge building with the name inscribed above the doorway, ST. LOUIS PUBLIC LIBRARY 1893, then, crossing Thirteenth Street, they passed in front of Christ Church Cathedral and Cindra thought how handy it would be. She envisioned her future lunch hours; she could not resist a library and because of her upbringing, the church was the mainstay in her life.

Finally their destination was in view; just a few more steps and they walked into an atmosphere that enchanted the girl, whose curiosity had been overpowering. She was not disappointed. The rooms were appointed in pale colours of pink and green and there was white lattice-work here and there. The place was abuzz with customers. What a delightful lunch they had! Both of the women chose a cold plate with a tuna salad sandwich, and snuggled in a lettuce bed was a quartered tomato with a delectable dressing garnish, a "Miss Hulling specialty," so said Jane. The latter also encouraged her companion to have one of the little custard tarts, another specialty she said. Cindra understood why—she had not tasted anything as delicious before! After they finished their beverage, the two left the eating place. Jane told her friend that she had really wanted to pay for her lunch, but Cindra explained to her the attitude of her benefactress, Miss Pindar, and Jane was satisfied with her explanation.

There was time for the two women to climb the steps up to the huge library and have a look in. Then they proceeded back to their workplace, feeling revitalized by the walk in the brilliant sunshine and by the meal.

The afternoon went by as quickly as the day before—there was a little more dictation by Mr. Cameron Brent, then the typing of that correspondence, then some filing that the typist had been instructed to do, and by the time that had been accomplished the work day was over. The prim secretary soon found herself back at the apartment she now called home, arriving there at the same time as Phyllis. Their greeting was warm and cheery. Cindra followed the older woman's suggestion and had her bath before supper. "In that way you'll be ready for bed on your return from your lesson," Phyllis said whilst getting supper ready.

Before long the budding pianist appeared at the table in her "mid-matronly" outfit. It was a black-and-white fine-checked dress with matching belt and a little red bow at the collar.

Phyllis could not wait to hear and asked, "What do you think of Miss Hulling's?"

"Oh, Phyllis, what a delightful place to eat, and such tasty food!" The young girl, after responding to her query, went on to tell her benefactress about her other surprise discoveries, the library and the church. "And they're within walking distance, Phyllis." The expression on the young girl's face matched the enthusiasm in her voice. "Oh, isn't everything just working out perfectly!"

The older woman was glad her young charge felt that way, and she responded, "Let's hope your music teacher and tonight's lesson turn out as favourably."

The student pianist was soon on her way in a taxi to her music lesson. She tried to pay attention to the streets they took, as she thought that once she was familiar with the route she could at least walk to her lessons, if not back home; she did not think Phyllis would agree to that. It seemed she was there in no time and after paying the cab driver, she walked up the many steps to an imposing front door with a big brass knocker. It was a large house, standing taller than the other houses around; compared to these, it looked like a mansion. A plumpish, stately woman answered her knock. She was elegantly dressed. After introductions, which Cindra thought were very formal, she was led into a huge room that could not be mistaken for anything else but a music room. There was a large grand piano positioned near one of the bay windows and in the opposite corner stood a solid-looking upright piano. The walls of the entire room, with the exception of the two bay windows, were lined with bookshelves laden with books and music.

Miss Grace invited Cindra to sit down on the piano stool in front of the upright piano. She drew up a chair alongside the stool and began speaking in a very grave tone. "Now, Miss Gold, Miss Pindar has confirmed the story that your mother wrote and told me of your desire to become a concert pianist. I am aware that you must work at a full-time job; however, for the students I have, who are in the same circumstances, I require a commitment of at least eight hours of practise before the next lesson besides the written work. Otherwise, you will be wasting both my time and yours, and goodness knows, that is little enough." Miss Grace's voice was crisp and decisive; she added, "Is that clear?"

The young girl was somewhat surprised and felt a little nervous, but her feelings of determination rose to the fore. She could hardly believe it was herself responding in a very confident manner, "Yes Miss Grace, I understand perfectly, I came down here to study music seriously, and that's what I'm going to do."

Without another word the music lesson followed. Miss Grace was very businesslike. Cindra did not know, nor did the piano teacher say, what she thought of her ability; one thing she did know, her music dictation book was full of exercises and homework for her to do, and she left the environs of the music room with a sinking feeling in the pit of her stomach. From the hall phone she called for a taxi whilst the teacher answered the door and ushered in another pupil. They both disappeared into the music room; Cindra was left in the hall to wait for her ride.

The girl did not confide to her benefactress the overwhelming feelings she was experiencing. The hot chocolate and cookies Phyllis had ready for her on her return helped to bolster her spirits, and the chatter of her apartment mate cheered her up, so that she was in an improved state of mind when she finished the snack. She was glad that Phyllis had not asked much about the music lesson.

When she entered her room to prepare for bed, she purposely avoided looking in the direction of "the Dove." Before she settled to sleep, she took her father's black book out of the night table, which stood beside her bed, and by a strange coincidence, as the book fell open in her hands, she read a Bible quote that appeared there in her father's bold hand-writing: "Casting all your care upon Him for He careth for you." Her dad had printed the book, chapter and verse, after the entry. Cindra did not realize her father had such deep religious convictions that he would write down a quote from the Holy Bible. And in the margin, opposite this erstwhile quote, was noted in brackets: "Tell little Cindra next time we are out in the boat fishing." The girl's thoughts flew back to the Bay of Quinte; she was in the boat with her father, and as she read the quote again, it was as though her dad was talking and sharing with her the words of wisdom that obviously had been helping him in his life's struggle. Her composure and hopes were restored, and she exclaimed to herself, addressing her piano, "Little White Dove, I'll work very hard and I will make you sing with joy and happiness!"

She slept well and felt fully rested when the new day dawned.

Chapter 12
The Little Child

The rest of that week sped by so fast. One lunch break the prim young Cindra ate her lunch hastily and then walked to the library, where she arranged for a library card. She also inquired at the information desk and was given a printed plan of the layout of this large place of learning. She even had time to go to the industry section and familiarize herself as to where she would find information on the lumber industry, the pulp and paper industry, and printing businesses. After selecting, with the help of a librarian, some reading material, she returned to work.

And she would never forget a particular day that week when she met Shirlianne. It was a rainy day and Cindra decided that at lunch-time she would stay in the office, eat her lunch, and read the library book about the paper business. However, before lunch a little girl came running into the office area; she was dressed in a red plaid raincoat with matching hat, and on her feet were black rubber boots. Though she had very fine features, her skin was dark. Probably because her boots were still a little wet and she was in such haste, she tripped and fell. This happened right beside Cindra's desk, so the secretary stooped down to help the little one and felt two little arms hug her and a little dark face smile up at her. Following the child was a tall man dressed in a chauffeur's uniform. He was all apologies, saying that he should have carried in the child.

Mr. Cameron Brent, hearing the commotion, opened the door to his office, and with that the little girl ran forward, yelling, "Daddy!" and she was swept up into her father's arms. The businessman gave instructions to the chauffeur to leave and to come back and pick up the little one at 2:00 P.M. Then he asked the secretary to come into his office.

"This is my daughter, Shirlianne. Sweetheart, this is my new secretary, Miss Gold." Mr. Brent's voice was full of love.

Cindra's curiosity was piqued; so it was not shadows that made the little girl's face look dark in the photograph on the desk, and she supposed that the child's mother had been a coloured lady.

The man noticed the somewhat startled look on the young woman's face as she walked forward to meet the child, and he added, "Shirlianne is my pride and joy!"

The little girl, set down by her father, ran forward, took Cindra's hand in both of hers, and exclaimed, "How do you do, Miss Gold. Are you coming to lunch with us?" The child spoke in a manner seemingly old for her age.

"Miss Gold, would you like to come to lunch with us? You seem to have my daughter's approval." Mr. Brent was smiling.

The prim woman thought of the lunch that Phyllis had prepared for her, but rationalized that it was in the fridge and would do for the next day, which she then remembered was Saturday. But she could eat it at home, she further rationalized. So Cindra went to get her purse and raincoat, leaving the excited little girl dancing around the room.

The three went out together. Since it was still raining Mr. Cameron Brent instructed the woman and his child to wait for him in the doorway whilst he went around to the back parking-lot to get his car.

The little girl was all achatter with her newfound friend, "I had two dolls and my daddy got me a new doll who's Raggedy Anne and her eyes don't go to sleep, but my other two dolls' eyes go to sleep."

Cindra thought how articulate she was for a child her age, though her voice still had a babylike quality to it. She asked, "And what are your other dollies' names?"

"There's Sadie, and Pansy. Daddy helped me to get the names."

What a darling little girl, thought Cindra as a large black Cadillac drove up to the door and the child's father came around to the passenger's side to open the car door for his luncheon companions.

They went to a "secluded" restaurant. Cindra found out sometime later why. The waitress brought a thick cushion to raise up the little girl in a regular chair, as she did not want to sit in a high-chair.

The small one proved to be a good little conversationalist and all three felt quite at ease. At one juncture during the conversation Shirlianne asked, "Miss Gold, do you live with your daddy?" After Cindra told her that her father was dead, the little girl leaned toward her father and said sorrowfully, "You'll never leave me, will you, Daddy?" The little one knew what "dead" meant; her daddy was both mother and father to her.

The secretary detected a pained look in her boss's eyes as he answered, "No, dear, I won't leave you."

Lunchtime went by very fast; they were soon back at the office and the chauffeur, whose name was Raoul, was back on time to pick up the child.

Before she left and after her father kissed her goodbye, Shirlianne ran to Cindra's desk and said hurriedly, "I'll come back and see you." Then, "Okay, Role, I'm comin'," and, putting her tiny hand in Raoul's, they walked out together.

The father smiled as he watched from his office door and so did the secretary; they were both amused at the little one who was not quite able yet to enunciate Raoul's name.

Cindra arrived home earlier than her benefactress, and when Phyllis came into the apartment she heard the sounds of piano music coming from the young lady's room. The former had been pleased at the way the musician was applying herself to her art. She knew that tonight there was another lesson for the girl, so she busied herself getting supper, feeling very thankful that there was someone with whom to share it.

The pianist had to be interrupted. Her benefactress did not want her going to her lesson without a bite to eat. As they ate Cindra related the incident of her lunch with Shirlianne.

"I wondered why your lunch bag was back in the fridge." Phyllis wore the expression of one who had just solved a puzzle.

"Phyllis, you've just got to meet Shirlianne; she's the dearest little girl and so mature for her age." Cindra lauded the child; she had been so impressed by her she had forgotten she was dark-skinned and consequently did not tell Phyllis about that detail.

Chapter 13
Another Phyllis

Cindra felt her second piano lesson went better than the first. Upon reflecting on it afterwards, she reasoned that it was her preconceived idea of what she thought Miss Grace would be like that caused the problem. The meaning of her name had conjured up in the young girl's mind a presentation of graciousness and kindliness, but she concluded that the woman had been a successful concert pianist who was devoted to the rigours of her art and therefore would be the ideal teacher. Cindra developed a great fondness for the woman. The teacher still piled on the homework, both written and instrumental; she said little about her new pupil's work, but Cindra had the feeling that she was not displeased.

The weekend went by fast. Phyllis did the household chores on Saturday, Cindra only having to launder her underclothes. The benefactress was content with the arrangement, as long as her musician companion worked at her art. The two women had been invited up to Mr. Serenity's apartment for afternoon tea. Phyllis decided that they had better accept, as she still felt a little uneasy about refusing the last time and had even whisked Cindra away. So the two women enjoyed a tea-break with the old gentleman, though there was no time for the younger one to find out more about the historical sights of Saint Louis. There was time only to get caught up on each other's news.

Mr. Serenity was most interested in hearing how the music lessons were going. Cindra had been amused at his remark, "You know, those professional teachers can be dang uppity." This utterance made her aware of how sensitive and how knowledgeable he was.

The break from routine did not last long that afternoon. The musician was soon back at her practise and in the atmosphere she had chosen to be her life.

On the Sunday the young lady had gone to church. With the benefits of exercise in mind she had chosen to walk to the Episcopal cathedral on Locust Street. She had been impressed by the priest and had felt at home in the beautiful old place of worship. She read in the welcoming brochure that was on the table in the narthex: "Founded in

1819 on All Saints' Day"—she had smiled when she thought that that had been the day after Hallowe'en—"Christ Church Cathedral is the oldest Episcopal parish west of the Mississippi River."

Musing in bed that night after she had finished her nightly ritual involving her father's black notebook, she thought how easy it had been to get the required hours of practice in on the weekend, including the written work. But she knew between Tuesday and Friday it would be a different story. Consoling herself with the thought "Where there's a will, there's a way," she drifted off to sleep.

The young secretary's work at the office continued to be challenging and very interesting, she making it so by her trips to the library to find information about the business in which her employers were involved, by reading the books that the librarian had recommended, and by perusing the pamphlets and tomes that were in her boss's bookcase.

Jane Janes had come in all aglow on Monday morning confiding to her that she had been out with Robert Brent on Friday night. They had gone to a dance, and he had gotten "plastered" (that was the term she used for him getting drunk). Jane did not seem perturbed by this fact, she even made it clear she had been honoured by the date. And Cindra recalled Phyllis's remark that most of those business executives drink spirits and she did not approve of any socialization with those men.

Friday dawned again and the student pianist thought, *Another lesson night!* She had accomplished a large amount of work that morning and was settled back at her desk in the outer office after lunch. Her boss buzzed to her desk indicating he wanted her to come into his office for dictation, so dutifully she went in and positioned herself at her desk in there. As the dictation session proceeded, there was a soft knock at the door. In response to Mr. Brent's "Come in," the door opened and in walked a beautiful blond woman, so fashionably attired that the prim secretary could not help staring at her. The perfume she was wearing permeated the room with its heavenly fragrance.

Mr. Brent came forward, put his arm around the lovely lady affectionately, and, gently drawing her towards the prim typist, he made the introductions. "Phyllis, this is my new secretary, Miss Gold. . . . Miss Gold, this is my fiancée, Phyllis Farrell."

The two women looked at one another. Miss Farrell's steely gray eyes seemed to be expressing approval of the very prim-looking typist; Miss Gold's eyes were expressing the same sentiment towards the aristocratic-looking fiancée, noting well that she was a fair-skinned beauty.

Cindra's boss gave instructions to her to finalize the day, wished her a good weekend, and, taking his briefcase from the desk, walked out of the office with his fiancée holding on to his arm possessively.

It was not long before the prim Miss Gold was heading home too. As she stepped out of the building, the clouds that had been threatening all day caught up with their forebodings and there was such a downpour that she stepped back under the shelter of the doorway, but not before Robert Brent, who was coming out of the driveway, had spotted her. Honking the horn, he indicated that he would give her a ride home. The young lady, who had decided not to take her umbrella that morning, accepted the offer, and they rode off together up Locust Street.

"What a night for the office dance. Are you going, Miss Gold?" the handsome man asked, breaking the silence.

"I didn't know there was one," she responded, wishing afterwards she had not said that; she did not want him to think she might like to have gone. She did not want to betray her image, yet there were certain feelings there, in her heart of hearts!

"You should loosen up a bit and enjoy life," he said. He had noticed her interest in her work and her extreme efficiency.

"Mr. Brent, you know I am studying music seriously." Cindra felt she had to make the "Miss Prim" image clear to him.

"Well, I must say I admire you folks who know just what they want." Robert grinned at her playfully in his carefree attitude, and Cindra noted again how handsome he was.

As the car drew up to her apartment, the young lady thanked him and voiced her appreciation of the ride. He sped off self-assuredly whilst she walked up the apartment steps thinking of her lesson that night, but rather wishing...

Chapter 14
A Mystery and a Shopping Spree

The days were speeding by so fast. Miss Pindar had been enjoying the occasional outing with her divorced gentleman friend. Cindra's lessons were progressing favourably. The portions of philosophy, scripture, and good common sense recorded in her father's big memo book were helping her to cope with her ambivalent feelings. She so wanted to break out of her "Miss Prim" image, reveal her womanly beauty and attractiveness, and, as Mr. Robert Brent had recommended, "enjoy life." But on the other hand she felt a great compulsion to be true to her aspirations of becoming a concert pianist. In these matters, by way of the legacy he had left her, her father was like her mentor, and she was able to deal with her mixed emotions effectively.

Besides, she had been having satisfying feelings of accomplishment at her job. Years before, she had become familiar with the lumber business because of her father's involvement in the industry, which certainly stood her in good stead. And her thrust recently to read about and gather information concerning the business in which she was employed was proving invaluable.

As Cameron Brent's secretary she was expected to take the minutes at any of the board meetings of the company, whose paper and printing business included the lumber business, Mr. Brent, Sr., being a lumber magnate also. And because of her knowledge, comprehension, and proficiency, the prim employee was able to contribute valuably to these important sessions.

And there was Shirlianne. That little girl had come along and filled the void that was left when she moved so far away from Jody, her cherished nephew, who now had a little sister. Her mother had informed her of the birth of her sister's baby in the letter Cindra had received a few days ago. "She's a bonnie wee thing weighing six pounds," her mother had written, "and they're going to call her Patricia."

When Cindra had received the news, how she yearned to hold the little one in her arms as she had Jody when he was born.

Her boss's little girl had come into the office several times on different occasions to visit her father, and Cindra had been going out for lunch with them. She was brought there by Raoul and each time she would run first to Cindra's desk and give her a hug as big as her little arms could reach. The secretary felt satisfied to some extent with this replacement for Jody.

This day Miss Gold was sitting at her desk, awaiting the arrival of the pretty little girl. Her boss had informed her that he had bought some clothes for the fall season for his daughter, but they were not the right size and would have to be exchanged. Mr. Brent requested she take his child to lunch, then spend the afternoon shopping. He was going to lunch with his fiancée.

The other employees had already left, having responded to the cue of the soft lunch bell. The prim secretary had just stepped over to the watercooler when she heard a child's voice exclaim excitedly, "Role, where is she?" The child looked around and saw her friend coming from the watercooler. She ran to the young woman, who had stooped down, and quick as a flash she was in Miss Gold's arms and hugging her tightly.

The little girl was bursting with happiness, "Oh, Miss Gold, we're going shopping, and have lunch and get me some clothes, and Daddy says I can have a ice cream soda."

At that point Cameron Brent opened his office door and walked towards the cheery pair. The little girl, noticing her father, ran to him and was soon in his arms, exclaiming, "Daddy, thanks for the nice clothes."

"Well, Darling, your daddy certainly goofed, none of the things fit you, did they?"

The little girl looked at him. She patted his head and, in a soothing tone, remarked, "Oh, Daddy, you're a good daddy; you always get me nice clothes. I love you, Daddy." The child seemed unconcerned about the garments not fitting her. She knew her father always had a way of making things right.

Mr. Brent gave further details to his secretary about the shopping and instructed her to charge the items to his account at the designated department store if there was a difference in the price of the exchanged clothes. Raoul followed the child and "Miss Prim" down to the first floor, where the latter picked up her things from the staff lounge. The chauffeur soon had them seated in the luxury limousine. Then, settling himself in the driver's seat, he drove away.

"Raoul, we're going the wrong way!" Cindra slid the glass panel that partitioned the driver's seat from the passenger's seat and voiced her concern to the man, as she noticed that they were headed west, away from the downtown area.

"Don't you worry, Ma'am, we're just going back for the little one's clothes. They have to go back to the store and I forgot to pick up the boxes when I left this morning. It won't take long, Ma'am." The uniformed man spoke in a reassuring tone.

The young woman thought to herself that Raoul could have gone back for the clothes when she and Shirlianne were at lunch; however, she said nothing.

The journey seemed long, but eventually they passed a sign on the road identifying the area as the city of Ladue, and soon they were heading up a rounded driveway to the most beautiful house that Cindra had ever seen. Stately Ionic columns stood like giant sentinels guarding the mansion and functionally upheld the high portico, which sheltered the massive front door, with its polished brass fittings. Miss Gold could not help musing to herself about a name for the house: It should be "The Columns." She must discuss it with Shirlianne later on.

The little one insisted that her companion come into the house and see her dolls; within moments the visitor entered a building that seemed to her like a palace. The entrance hall was enormous. There was an elegant central staircase leading down from the upper floors, which stairs the child ascended gingerly to get to her room and procure her dolls. Meanwhile the chauffeur proceeded to put the forgotten boxes into the car.

Cindra, having declined the invitation of the child to accompany her upstairs, stood there in the middle of the hall surveying her sumptuous surroundings. She was impressed by the floor, which was of black-and-white marble tile in a large checkered pattern and polished so highly that it shone like a mirror. But what caught her eye particularly was a huge oil painting of a beautiful young woman. She had fair skin and jet black hair that framed her lovely face. She was dressed in a soft white gown in a style that dated it in the present era. The beholder was consternated by this; was it a portrait of Mr. Brent's deceased wife? It could not have been of his mother, as the whole painting bespoke the present decade. She wondered if Jane Janes could tell her, or Miss Frost might know, as she had been told that Miss Frost was a distant relative of John Brent's wife.

Her musings were interrupted by the appearance of a housemaid, who was attired in a black dress with little white collar and cuffs, and a small white voile apron. Completing the uniform was a white voile frill that stood up above her forehead and was tied around her head with a black ribbon.

The little child bounded down the stairs at that juncture and exclaimed, "Oh, Clarisse, this is my new friend, Miss Gold. She's Daddy's secretary and she wants to see my dolls." The little one then began to introduce Cindra to her dolls in her "trying to be grown-up" little-girl manner. She proudly displayed how the eyes of Sadie and Pansy "went to sleep," and her handling of them was as loving and careful as a real mother's. She then asked her friend if she would tie up the bows on Raggedy Anne's pigtails.

Whilst Cindra was doing this, Raoul bustled in through the front door, remarking that they had better be on their way. He kissed the house maid familiarly, then held open the door for his two passengers.

"Clarisse, please put my dollies back in my room. They're tired right out an will have to sleep. You know, Miss Gold, they're not used to visitors." Shirlianne gave the well-thought-out instructions to the housemaid.

The young woman and the maid smiled at one another, both of them delighting in the playworld of the little child. Then the two shoppers disappeared out the door followed by the chauffeur.

"Miss Prim" and the little girl were soon seated at their accustomed table in the secluded restaurant where they frequently had been having lunch. It was Shirlianne who spoke first, "Golly, did Role ever drive fast, Miss Gold! Wasn't it fun? That's the fastest ride I ever had." The child's eyes opened wide as she talked.

Cindra looked at the child and explained the situation: "Well, Raoul realized he had made us late for lunch by having to go back for those clothes, so he was trying to make up for it."

By this time the chauffeur had parked the car and joined his passengers for lunch. Mr. Brent had insisted that they have an escort at the restaurant. So the three of them had a nourishing repast of soup and a sandwich.

The young woman found the conversation of the child delightful. The little girl was saying, "Daddy tells me I must drink milk and when I told him Raggedy Anne don't like milk he said that's why she's so floppy, cause she's got no bones and milk makes bones. Isn't my daddy funny? And when he saw a place where Raggedy Anne wasn't sewed up he got a needle and thread and sewded her up, he sure is a good daddy." By the way the little one lauded her father, Cindra could see that he was a very thoughtful man who adored his child.

Raoul had a beer with his lunch, whilst the two friends added milk to theirs. Miss Gold thought she had better, after the little one's pep talk on milk. The child had quite forgotten about the ice-cream soda her father had said she could have.

The price of the meal was charged to Mr. Brent's account. This had been previously arranged. Cindra knew of his account there, as she had sent out a cheque from the office for the last month's bill. She thought how nice it was to just say "Charge it!"

Wanting the exercise, Cindra told Raoul that she and Shirlianne would walk to the store, whilst he got the car and took the clothes back for exchange. Afterwards, however, she thought that it was not the wisest thing to do. The walk to the department store was quite a distance. The child walked close to her friend as she felt the stares of passersby. The fair-skinned woman held the little girl's hand tightly, sensing the child's fear. She wanted to shout out and tell them what an intelligent, bright little bairn this was, that the colour of one's skin did not matter, but she remained quiet, and they were soon at their destination and concentrating on purchasing the next season's clothes for the young one.

The shopping spree lasted two hours and Raoul was waiting for them at the prearranged meeting place at one of the entrances to the building. Her boss had told Cindra his chauffeur could drop her off at her house when they were finished with the shopping, and, as they settled into the limousine, the young woman thought what a nice break from routine it had been.

As they passed Christ Church Cathedral Cindra pointed out the large edifice to the child, saying, "That's where I go to church, Shirlianne, on Sunday mornings."

"Clarisse and Role go to church, she says that's where they learn about Jesus, and she says that Jesus is God's son, she says the preacher put her right under the water for her bap-baptims's, and when I told her her clothes are always clean, she laughed and said some day I'd unerstand," the child rambled on, finding the pronunciation of certain words difficult. "An she says that Jesus is the saver of the world an Miss Farrell knows God cause one night when she was there for dinner my daddy was putting me to bed an she said, 'For God's sake, Cameron, hurry up. We'll be late for the show.' She said that to my daddy. What is church, Miss Gold?"

"Would you like to go with me to church one Sunday and see for yourself?" Cindra could see the child's curiosity was aroused and she felt it should be assuaged. She continued, after the little one answered that she would like to go, "Well, I'll ask your daddy if you can go to church with me on Sunday."

With that the little girl clapped her hands joyously, and her remark, "Oh, goody," was an expression of sheer delight. She snuggled closer to Miss Gold, put her little arms around her, and said in a serious tone, "I love you, Miss Gold."

Cindra held the little child tightly to her, then, leaning forward, she tapped on the glass partition to get the chauffeur's attention and motioned for him to stop at the next corner, her home stop.

As the car drove away, the little girl kept waving to her until they were out of sight.

Chapter 15
The Mystery Solved

It so happened that Leah Frost was having lunch one day in the staff lounge. The prim secretary had planned to do a bit of reading of a library book on the printing business, but when she entered the room to have her lunch and read, she encountered the older woman in the process of making a pot of tea. There was something about Miss Frost that Cindra had sensed, even from their first meeting, sort of an aura of friendliness, which made Cindra feel that the woman would be approachable. And so, as she accepted her offer to share a cup of tea, she asked if she could shed light on the mysterious matter of Shirlianne's mother. She said she realized it was a delicate subject and would understand if she did not want to confide in a new employee.

Leah Frost had been impressed by the extreme efficiency of the new employee. Leah herself was a "no nonsense," down-to-earth sort of person, who would describe the younger employees as "all gussied up in their high heels and brilliant nail polish." She, however, was for the most part good-humoured, and they all respected her for her knowledge and good sense. Actually, she reminded Cindra of Phyllis Pindar in a lot of ways, and the young girl sensed that Miss Frost trusted her. She had not been deluded by this feeling, since the older woman began to tell the story of Cameron Brent's deceased wife.

First she explained, "I can see, Miss Gold, that you have a kindly sentiment towards little Shirlianne, just as I have. You know she always stops to see me before she goes upstairs to see her father, but the poor little girl, not too many are that friendly towards her, including her paternal grandmother, and both of her maternal grandparents."

"But she is such a delightful little girl." Cindra came to the immediate defence of the little dark-skinned charmer. She was infuriated by the unkind prejudice.

Leah Frost continued, "Well, Cameron Brent has been ostracized by most of his relatives and friends for deciding, at her birth, to keep the infant."

As the story unfolded the prim young secretary gave ear to it with keen interest.

The older woman related how Cameron Brent had, as a precocious young student, gone into the study of medicine. It was funny how the woman explained it; "You see, Cam's mother used to listen to a radio program called 'The Young Dr. Brent,' and she is such a one to be influenced, she just decided that that was what she wanted for her oldest son. Well, he knew he wanted to become a doctor, even before she suggested it, but he was one to humour her; he just adored her, you know, so he let her think it was her influence."

The younger woman was wishing Miss Frost would get to the explanation of Shirlianne's mother, but she realized that the woman must tell it her way, so she listened patiently with an attentive ear whilst the whole story evolved in a roundabout fashion.

"Cameron had completed his premeds, and, indeed, with honours standing, and he was ready to go into his preclinical years, when his medical training was interrupted by a stint in the navy, as an officer. He was very handsome in his uniform. During his time at the university he had met Sylvia Glendon, a fair-skinned, dark-haired beauty. He met her at one of his mother's soirées; they were infatuated with one another and were married, which certainly pleased his mother—some say she'd planned it." Miss Frost poured herself another cup of tea, her mouth having become dry from talking, then she took up the story again. She related how John Brent's printing business was in need of management help, as his assistant manager had died, and the establishment seemed to be going downhill, so Cameron left the study of medicine and the navy, going into the Brent Printing and Publishing Company in the position of his father's assistant manager. The woman explained that it was a job for which he seemed well qualified, as he had shown interest in his father's business even as a child.

Cindra's curiosity was brimming over as she waited for the facts that were the point of the discourse.

Meanwhile, Leah Frost changed her position in her chair, then continued with the lengthy tale. "Sylvia became pregnant, I don't think she'd planned on that. Anyway, I can remember one night at my cousin Phyllis's house, Sylvia was discussing names; she said she felt that the child would be a girl and they would name her Shirley. I really think she picked it because of the dear little child movie actress we all like so well. That name is very popular. Anyway, the night the babe was born Sylvia's parents and Cameron and his mother were there at the hospital; John Brent was at home in bed nursing a cold. Phyllis asked me to go with her; I had been there for supper, you see. Well, there seemed to be a commotion taking place in the delivery-room. Two doctors rushed by the waiting room into the delivery room, and a young student nurse had come out of the delivery room, rushing by in the other direction, she had the most frightened look on her face. Cameron was pacing in the waiting room, vowing he'd never have another child. One of the doctors came into the waiting room, looking very discouraged and announced to us that Sylvia's heart had stopped when the baby was born, and that all attempts to save her had failed—she was dead!

We all stood there in disbelief. Sylvia's mother was sobbing; Cam went white as a sheet."

One could see that Miss Frost, on retelling the tale, felt again some of the emotion that must have been going through the little group that night. She looked at Cindra, and she appeared to be almost dreading to tell the rest, but she went on. "One of the doctors came out shortly afterwards and told us the baby was dark-skinned! Well, you can imagine what a stir that caused! My cousin said they must have gotten the babies mixed up; she didn't realize the absurdity of her remark. Also, we heard afterwards that the student nurse who had run out had been there, just observing, in preparation for her required stint in obstetrics, in her nurses' training course, and when she saw the head being delivered she thought the baby was dead! It was all so very awesome! The grandparents there all agreed the child should be adopted out, but Cameron, having recovered somewhat from the shock of his wife's death, when he held the little bundle in his arms and looked into her half-open eyes, said, 'Little one without a mother, you will be my only child and I will love you.' Those were his very words, and he's certainly loved and nurtured little Shirlianne."

The young secretary could not help asking if there were any doubts about Cameron Brent being the father of the child.

"Yes," Miss Frost went on, "that possibility was queried at the time, but Sylvia's father, anxious to defend his daughter's reputation, confided that back in his ancestry there had been a scandal in the household, but things were covered up and nothing had shown up in the lineage until now. Mrs. Glendon said that at the time of her betrothal her husband had told her of this, and so she confirmed the fact."

"Is Cameron Brent's mother's name Phyllis?" Cindra queried, rather astonished.

"Yes, she was Phyllis Gale, and she and my mother were cousins." The older woman paused after answering the question, then continued, "Cameron's chauffeur and his house maid, Clarisse, are husband and wife. They've been married for some years but remain childless, so Clarisse was thrilled to have an infant to look after. She was a little hesitant at first when she saw the baby, but when she saw how adamant her employer was about raising the child, she gave him the help he needed to care for the tiny infant, so she and Raoul have grown very fond of the little girl."

Miss Frost wondered at first if she should have told so much. She considered herself in a rather precarious position, as she valued her good relationship with Cameron's mother, whom she genuinely liked, but she also felt great compassion for Cameron and his charming little daughter. She was heartsick that the mother and son's relationship was so strained because he had kept his child. However, the older woman wanted to encourage the young secretary's interest in Shirlianne. She was fully aware of how much the little girl needed caring friends, especially now that she was getting older and becoming more perceptive about the situation. Also another concern was rearing its head. Phyllis Farrell, Cameron's fiancée, was not too receptive of the child, and Leah Frost rather suspected her cousin of pushing for that alliance in hopes of having the child go off to a boarding school or something like that. She knew her cousin was a very determined woman and that the estrangement from her eldest son was a real thorn in her side.

The young woman's heart went out to the little girl and she muttered, "The poor little thing; she's such a loving child." She vowed then and there that she would help out whenever she could. She then asked Leah about the child's name. The woman obligingly told her that the couple, before the baby was born, had chosen Anne for her second name, and since Cameron was not very fond of the first name, he had combined the two names. Both of the women agreed that it was lovely and really suited the little girl.

A soft bell announced the end of the lunch break. As they left the staff lounge together, the older woman told the younger one, "The rest call me Lee." Reciprocally, Cindra asked Leah that she use her first name too!

Before she left for home that afternoon, "Miss Prim" asked her boss if he would mind if she took his daughter to church with her on Sunday. Cameron Brent laughed.

"So that is what my little pixie has been talking about. Actually it would work out well for me, I have to drive my fiancée to Kansas City on Sunday. One of her relatives died, and she must go there on Sunday. What time is the church service, Miss Gold?"

The prim secretary wondered what her boss's religious persuasion was, if any. She thought it was odd that he did not ask what hers was. Oh well, some people just do not bother with religion, and she thought of her friend Phyllis as a case in point.

"It's at eleven o'clock." She felt obliged to tell him where, so she added, "at Christ Church Episcopal Cathedral, downtown. If you're going to be away, Shirlianne could come back to the apartment with me for lunch, if it's alright with you."

"Now I hope it will not be inconveniencing you people; it is very nice of you to offer." Cameron Brent spoke with perfect grammar. He made it obvious that he did not want to impose, but he did feel relieved at the prospect of his little girl having a bit of a change, especially when he would not be with her all day.

Cindra, for a brief moment, wondered if she had done the right thing. She must get her practising done. But she, watching her grammar too, answered, "That will be fine. Shirlianne is such a little grown-up."

It was arranged that Raoul would drive the child to the apartment on Chestnut Street, and after picking up the secretary, would take them to church in the limousine.

The prim young businesswoman had a few qualms when walking home that afternoon. When she had first spoken of her boss's little girl to her benefactress, she had neglected to mention the colour of her skin. Afterwards she figured it was just as well, that once Phyllis spoke with the child, it would not matter at all. Still she could not help wondering how accepting she would be of the little girl.

Chapter 16
Auntie Phyllis

Sunday rolled around and before church time the shiny black luxury limousine drove up to the Plaza Apartments. Cindra was ready and watching for it, so, with a farewell word to her living companion, she walked briskly to the motor car, responded to the good morning greeting of the chauffeur, then slipped through the door he held open for her.

"Oh, Miss Gold, isn't this fun! See what my daddy gave to me to give for the church!" The little girl opened her small purse and showed her companion, who had just barely the time to sit down, a five-dollar bill. The child first had to reveal her offering to the church, then her two little arms were around Cindra and she was greeting her joyously.

The young woman looked at the child; Shirlianne was dressed in a frilly pink dress, and a petite pink straw hat, and she confided to her friend, "At last I can wear my white gloves." She settled back on the seat and proudly displayed her gloved hands.

Cindra duly admired the gloves as well as the rest of the little one's outfit. She told her little charge how nice she looked and saw, according to the smile it evoked on the face of the child, how pleased she was.

Arriving at the front door of the church as the bells peeled forth their call to the faithful to worship, the prim young lady and the little girl alighted from the limousine, the door of which the chauffeur held open. A few spectators paused before entering the church and took notice of the unusual scene, especially of the appearance of the prim, fair beauty and the little girl with the bronze-coloured skin. Raoul gave the instructions that he would be back in an hour to pick them up. With that he left and the two worshippers walked up the steps into the large stone edifice, the young one with her eyes agog, taking in the gothic grandeur of the magnificent old cathedral.

After genuflecting before entering the pew, Cindra, having put down the padded kneeler, knelt to pray. She felt the small girl kneel close beside her, and out of the corner of her eye she saw two tiny gloved hands pressed together in a prayerful attitude, and a beautiful little bronzed face turned upward. Perhaps the child will not mind sitting so long, she thought. That consideration had been somewhat of a concern to her.

The anxious woman need not have worried. Shirlianne occupied the time by staring at the beauteous stained-glass windows, through which the bright daylight shone, at the reredos back of the altar with its central figure of the crucified Christ, and at the women's hats, of which there was a vast array. She was intrigued by the hat that covered the head of the lady sitting in front of her. It had long wispy feathers around the brim, and one hung down at the back. At one point Cindra had to nudge her, as she had leaned over and gently touched the soft feather. The little girl shrugged her shoulders, covered her mouth with her hand, and smiled mischievously, snuggling close to her companion.

Raoul was waiting for them at the end of the service. The short drive home seemed to take no time; the prim young woman sat pensively, absorbed in the thought of the meeting between her benefactress and the bronze young child sitting beside her. How she wished now that she had told Phyllis. She only half heard Shirlianne, as the little one chattered on about her experience at church, so great was the persistence of her feeling of thoughtlessness.

The two church goers walked in the door of the apartment. Phyllis came running out of the kitchen, gazed at the child, then drew back a bit, a look of astonishment on her face.

The little girl, being a sensitive child, ran over to the sofa and hid her face in a cushion, exclaiming, "My daddy likes me anyway." There were tears in her eyes when the older woman went over to her and lifted her up in her arms. But when their eyes met a kind of bonding took place that secured a strong friendship between the two individuals, and that was to grow stronger as time went by.

"Just look at that; you've knocked your hat all askew!" Phyllis thought this bit of frivolity might soothe the hurt feelings of the child, and it worked. The little one laughed. She removed her hat and her soft, black curls cascaded down around her face.

"Oh, what pretty hair, and what a lovely dress! Let me see it." The wise woman seemed to know just what to say.

The child ran to the centre of the room and, in ballerina fashion, turned slowly around so that her admirer could get a good look at the frilly garment. She made this movement so gracefully, her little arms held out, that the two women exchanged glances, both impressed by the daintiness of the child.

Shirlianne quite forgot her initial meeting with the older woman. Perhaps the suggestion Phyllis gave her that she should call her "Auntie Phyllis" had helped, and the latter was glad she had proposed this. She suspected, by the child's query as to what an "auntie" was, that she was not accepted by her relatives.

Anyway, the youngster, propped up on a couple of cushions, ate the luncheon meal with her two friends, chatting freely, and endeared herself to them with her precocious and sparkling conversation. She said she had told her daddy that she would be on her best behaviour, and that she would help out at Miss Gold's wherever she could.

"Now, Shirlianne, Miss Gold has to do her music practise, so how would you like to help me clear the table? After we wash the dishes we'll make some cookies." Phyllis figured the child might like to help her, and she was right in that thought, judging by the response.

The child clapped her hands, "Oh goody, I love cookies, and so does my daddy."

Phyllis laughed at the little hint the child had given. "Yes," she said, "you can take some home to your father."

The older woman was enjoying the company of the little girl, who was very responsive to the woman's tutoring;

she learned quickly, and she was turning out to be quite a help. Thus several batches of cookies were brought into existence, Shirlianne being instructed in making faces on some, with raisins for eyes, glacé cherries for noses, and candied peel for mouths. What a good time they had!

Earlier that day Phyllis had invited Mr. Serenity down to the apartment for afternoon tea, so at the designated time he appeared at the door for tea-break. Of course the little girl was the focal point of the conversation. John Serenity, in his gracious manner, revealed that he too was delighted with the child. The four friends had a lovely visit, but no one enjoyed the gathering more than the little girl. When Mr. Serenity left, he bent down and embraced her. Cindra thought how touching it was, and she, on reflecting afterwards on the gesture, figured that he too had found a replacement for loved ones, a replacement for the grandchildren he no longer saw.

When the Cameron Brent household was contacted, Raoul answered the phone, and he informed Miss Gold that his employer was not expected back until late that night. When he was asked if he thought it would be alright if Shirlianne stayed for supper and he picked her up around eight o'clock, he agreed to the plan, and said he would tell his wife. There was no one happier with this arrangement than Cameron Brent's daughter. She was in ecstasy, especially because her dear Miss Gold had promised to play the piano for her after supper.

Thus, it was a felicitous little girl who walked into the musician's room after the evening meal that night. Miss Gold had promised her she would play some children's pieces. When she described one, saying it was about five little babies born at the same time, to the same mother, and there was a lullaby written about them, the child was fascinated by the story and wanted to know where these babies lived. Miss Gold explained that they had been born some time ago, and they lived in Ontario, Canada, where she used to live. Then Miss Gold sang the song. She was asked to repeat it, so delighted was Shirlianne at hearing about the "fifty toes," the "fifty fingers," and the "fairy that lingered." To grant the child's wish the pianist taught her the song. The latter discovered that the little one was musical and could carry a tune well, as she was humming the lullaby after the mini-concert was over.

Mr. Brent's chauffeur was punctual, arriving at the Pindar apartment as the clock began to strike eight. Shirlianne was ready. She had to hug both of her friends before she left with Raoul. The child clutched a fancy tin box filled with the homemade cookies in her hands, and, as they walked out to the car, she could not wait to show the chauffeur what she had helped to make, so she opened the tin and offered Raoul a cookie.

Chapter 17
A Visitor from Canada

Life was going on. Not as Miss Janes would have liked it, since she had only had the one date with Robert Brent. Of course, he had been away in Europe on a business trip and had not yet returned. Cindra would not want to admit it, even to herself, but she did miss seeing the handsome, dashing young man as he went about his business duties in the office. And she was pleased with the way things were going as far as her affairs were concerned. Her music teacher seemed to be very pleased with her progress. The lady did not express this in so many words, but there was a strong indication of it in her attitude towards her pupil. The young secretary naturally still had, at times, longings for her home and kin, but her father's book, with its bits of philosophy, scripture, prose, and verse, were her mainstays, along with the church services she attended, as she found the sermons of the priest progressive and most enlightening.

Then there were the luncheons. Now, about twice a week, the prim secretary accompanied her boss when he hosted these gatherings, for certain businessmen and prospective clients. Cindra, basically a shy person, surprised herself at these affairs. Perhaps it was the disguise of "Miss Prim" (and she had found more ways of making her prudish appearance even more exact) that made her feel so self-assured, or maybe it was that she was there, fulfilling the job of taking notes, and therefore felt important, or perhaps it was a bit of both. Whatever it was, she did sense that she was part of a team, and was able to contribute, with assurance, to the overall purpose of her employer's business ventures. There happened to be one of the businessmen in particular who began showing an interest in her. She was glad that her employer would tolerate no exploitation of this sort of his employee. Cameron Brent conducted these luncheons in a strictly businesslike fashion, for which she was very grateful. Confidence was growing within her, and she felt every inch a career woman in both aspects of her life endeavours—in her job and in her music.

Shirlianne's visits to the apartment on Chestnut Street were becoming more frequent. Cameron Brent had requested that his little girl continue to call his secretary "Miss Gold." Since the young lady was in his employ, he preferred this formality. Indeed, he had had to tell Shirlianne she must not refer to her beloved Miss Gold as "Cindra," which she had started to do at home. However, in reference to Miss Pindar, he said he liked the title of, "Auntie Phyllis," which the woman had suggested to the child, and he quite understood why his daughter preferred to use just the appellation "Auntie."

Mr. Brent was very pleased with the tin of cookies his child had brought home, especially since she had had a hand in making them. In appreciation there was delivered to the Pindar apartment a huge wicker basket filled with delicious fruit, with a box of mixed nuts, and a box of chocolates tucked inside. On the little card that accompanied the gift was inscribed: "THANKS FOR THE COOKIES,—Shirlianne and Cameron Brent." The two ladies were thrilled with the thoughtful present, and they could hardly wait to express their appreciation to the little girl when they would see her on her next Sunday's visit.

Cindra looked forward to these Sundays with great anticipation. Shirlianne, of her own volition, would go to church with her, and the young woman was glad to have a companion. The fair-skinned maiden and the dark-skinned little girl got over the hurdle of what to do about walking to the cathedral unescorted through a kindly offer of John Serenity. He said he would enjoy escorting the "two beauties" to church and pick them up again for the stroll home. Our heroine had been concerned about not getting her Sunday morning exercise, with Raoul driving them to church. So the young woman was very grateful to John, and the three of them would set out together, even in inclement weather, for their aforementioned destination.

However, right at the outset, Mr. Serenity made the terms clear: "Don't expect me to go in to the service with you, it's just not my cup of tea. I have friends downtown I can visit." The dear old man explained that he had nothing against church people; he obviously did not want to hurt the feelings of "Little Miss."

The small girl would then spend the afternoon with Auntie; that was how the child would address Phyllis, not "Auntie Phyllis." The two women both surmised, as did Cameron Brent, that because her father's fiancée had that same name, she was reluctant to attach it to the older woman whom she adored. It was becoming quite obvious the youngster was not fond of Phyllis Farrell. The two women had both noticed the anguished look on the little girl's face when she was introduced to Phyllis Pindar and the disappointed note in her voice when she remarked, "That's my daddy's fyon-say's name!"

Sometimes they would make fudge or bake cookies. Shirlianne had to laugh when on one occasion Auntie popped some corn in the wire mesh corn-popper with the long handle. She was fascinated at seeing the kernels of corn burst into something four times their size. "Oh Auntie, they look like little flowers," was her remark.

Mr. Brent on his part was pleased at how happy and content his daughter had become. He confided to his secretary that his little one had taken one of the small tables in her room and set up an altar. She had spread a white cloth, which Clarisse had given to her, on the table, and set upon it a picture of Jesus that came from a church folder. He related how the little girl said that that was where she and her dollies said their prayers to Jesus.

Cindra wondered if her employer was in favour of this, but his tone was one of satisfaction and pride, and she could see that he did not disapprove of his daughter's budding religiosity. She knew he was not totally without any religious convictions, as Raoul told her Mr. Brent had seen to it that the infant was baptized in a church in Ladue, explaining that his wife, Clarisse, and he were the godparents.

There was also something else "Miss Prim" had looked forward to with increasing expectation, her mother's visit to St. Louis. Mrs. Gold's daughter Madge and her husband had paid for the trip. Madge had revealed, in a letter to her sister, that their mother needed to get away for a change.

The visit had gone well. Phyllis Pindar especially enjoyed it. And Shirlianne Brent found yet another friend. Mrs. Gold described the little girl as "the cutest thing."

The visitor from Canada had even visited her daughter's workplace. Mr. Brent, Sr., had had a long chat with his deceased friend's wife, and he took the lady out to lunch at the Missouri Athletic Club, where the Brent men were members. John Brent had explained to her it was where he took her late husband, when he was in town on business. Cindra's boss had been at the club that morning exercising and swimming, so he joined the couple and had lunch with them.

Cindra's mother had had to tell in detail about both the elegant surroundings and the fine meal to which the two men had treated her. She had been most eloquent in describing it all to her two eager listeners that evening at supper. And she had nothing but praise for the two men. Her remark was, "They treated me like a queen."

But the time had gone so fast, and now the visit was just a memory The young musician was somewhat disappointed that her mother had not been more enthused about the progress she had made in her music, but then she knew her mother to be undemonstrative, so she salved her feelings by the remembrance of past incidences.

Chapter 18
A Birthday Party

One sunny, fall afternoon Cindra's boss, having finished dictating a letter to her in his office, proposed a request: "Could you and Miss Pindar come to Shirlianne's birthday party on Sunday afternoon, Miss Gold? My fiancée is going to be away for the week-end, and I would like to have more than just her and myself at the little celebration I am planning for her." Before the secretary could reply, he continued, "You and 'Auntie,' as she calls her, have been so good to my daughter that I would like to show my appreciation in this small way."

"Could I let you know tomorrow, Mr. Brent? I'll ask Phyllis about it tonight." The prim woman would have answered yes right on the spot, but she had to consult with her benefactress to see if she approved. "If so, could Shirlianne still come to church with me in the morning?" Cindra knew how much the child liked to go to church with her, and that she would especially want to go on her birthday.

"That poses no problem. Raoul can bring you to the house after church, and you can have lunch as well with my daughter, if you like; I will be at the Athletic Club in the morning. I have arranged to have lunch there with a business associate, so I will be back at the house in the afternoon." As usual her boss was precise in his plans.

Cindra had a concern and she voiced it. "Do you have a piano, Mr. Brent?" She knew she had her required hours of practice to fit in, and she counted on Sunday afternoon to help achieve this, so she explained her plight to her boss.

"Yes, Miss Gold, there is one in the drawing room. I will get it tuned for you; it never does get used." Then, in his businesslike manner, he started looking in the telephone book for a piano tuner whilst stating, "You may go, Miss Gold. Please type that letter right away, and get it in the mail this afternoon."

Before "Miss Prim" had left the office and closed the door, she could hear her employer on the telephone, arranging to have his piano tuned.

The prim secretary, as she typed the letter, thought to herself, *He sure does get things done!*

That evening at the supper table Cindra told her companion about the invitation to Shirlianne's party. The women had known about the pending birthday of the child, and Phyllis, with a little help from her young charge, had made five little cloth baby dolls for a birthday present; one of the dolls she had fashioned out of brown cloth. The dresses and bonnets were trimmed with ribbons and lace. The huge wicker basket, which had been sent to them from the father and child, she had fashioned into a bassinet. When the pillow was in place and the dolls laid upon it, it was a picture! The women were proud of their handiwork and hoped that the child would be pleased with the gift.

Miss Pindar was not so sure they should accept the invitation. She explained to her friend, "We don't belong to high society—they live in another world, Cindra. Besides, he is your employer, and I believe it's not wise to mix the two."

The young woman was not in agreement with her benefactress. She reasoned that it was just a private party to which they had been invited, and not some glamorous affair. However, she kept her peace, and later, after she had finished her music practice and Phyllis had finished her evening chores, the latter, before she retired, told Cindra she thought they should go the function, as she would not want to disappoint the child.

It did not take long for Sunday noon to roll around. The two women and the little girl, who had come for church, were soon on their way to the Cameron Brent estate in Ladue, in the luxury limousine. They were chauffeured, of course, by Raoul, who had placed a large, tissue-wrapped package in the backseat of the motor car before he had assisted the ladies into the limousine. The child's eyes opened wide when she saw it being carried out, and she exclaimed, "Oh, what a big thing."

"Well, that's for a certain birthday girl," was Phyllis's remark.

"That's me!" As she spoke, Shirlianne snuggled close to Auntie, and there was an air of excitement passing through the three people; for the child, it was the wonderment of what was in the large package, and for the women, it was the anticipation of seeing the little girl's response when she unwrapped the gift.

The three were each absorbed in their own thoughts as the black limousine left Saint Louis proper, sped along the highway, and without much time having elapsed, entered the city of Ladue. The child was thinking of how this was "heaven," a party with her daddy, and her wonderful friends; the older woman, whilst viewing the magnificent homes in the upper-class area, was pondering to herself how being rich in worldly goods is no insurance of happiness; and the younger woman was dreaming of the day when she would be launched successfully in her career and living in just such a beautiful mansion as one of these.

They were soon walking up to the front door of the estate. A formally attired butler answered the ring of the door-bell, and they were ushered into the reception area of the magnificent dwelling. Raoul followed with the huge parcel in his arms.

It seemed to the two women that there were servants

all over the place; one took their wraps, one took the package from the chauffeur and disappeared with it; another was about to lead them into the dining-room, when Clarisse appeared.

"I'll see to the guests, Suzie; you get the lunch on the table, please." Clarisse had been instructed by her employer to act as hostess until his return, and she was following his orders.

After greeting the two guests, Clarisse first showed Cindra where the piano was situated, another instruction given to the "appointed hostess" by Mr. Brent. Then she had the women follow her through the dining-room, the enormity of which greatly impressed the two ladies, and out through some beautiful french doors to a patio, where was lavishly set up a white, wrought-iron, plate-glass table, with dishes of salads, fresh fruits, and miniature buns in a warming basket. Clarisse spoke in her droll manner. "Mr. Brent thought that being it was such a nice sunny day, you ladies might like to have lunch outside. I'll get your coats, if need be."

The women assured her that that was not necessary, nor was it: the table was in a sheltered spot, and the afternoon sun was very warm, as it so often is in Missouri in the fall of the year.

Shirlianne came hustling out to the table, informing them, as she approached the group, that she had been washing her hands. She went to her chair, and when she was settled properly on it, she leaned down, turned a knob, which projected out from the frame of the seat, and elevated its height, until she was on the same level as the adults. The conversation centred around this occurrence for a while, Clarisse informing them that the father did everything he could to make life comfortable for his child.

The two guests agreed heartily that it was a most enjoyable meal. The setting could not have been more beautiful. The immaculately maintained garden was showing off its roses and fall flowers of every hue; the perfectly manicured grass, with not the trace of a weed, looked like a vast green carpet. There was a walkway, which Cindra thought looked like marble, with steps where the lawn was terraced, and this led down to a swimming pool whose water gleamed in the sun.

After the repast Phyllis was the first to break the spell of complacency that had claimed the little group. She said, in her assertive way, "You must get to your practice now, Cindra."

The young musician assented in a tone as though her thoughts were not going along with her words; however, she followed through with the spoken agreement and headed off to the drawing-room to work at her music.

"Auntie, would you read to me?" The little one had eased her chair down and had gone over to her friend to make her request.

Clarisse, having summoned Suzie to come and help clear up the table, heard the child's entreaty and said, "Shirlianne, dear child, don't forget the magic word."

"Oh yes, Auntie, 'please.' "

Auntie agreed and she and the child went upstairs to the latter's bedroom, and she felt she had entered into a fairyland, so bright and pretty was the decor. Most impressive, though, was the cream-coloured book-case, which matched the rest of the furniture and stretched along two sides of the large room. The shelves were not full, but they certainly were not empty, either. The child went to one of the shelves and selected a book; it was one of the "Bobbsey Twins" series. She explained her acquisition of such an array of tomes. "My daddy brings me back some books when he comes back from when he travels. See these ones, these ones were my best ones when I was a little girl." She went over to a little group of volumes and chose one from it, "See, here's one." It was one of the "Noddy" series.

"My daddy reads to me here." And Shirlianne scrambled up onto a comfortable-looking lounge, having removed her shoes.

The woman thought to herself, *No wonder you are such a precocious little one, your father is certainly responsible for that,* and she too removed her shoes and eased herself into the supportive back of the recliner lounge. The two people were soon engrossed in the adventures of the Bobbsey Twins.

Meanwhile our heroine was lost in her world of music. Having entered the huge drawing-room, she approached the piano. It was a shiny, mahogany grand piano with the name Steinway embossed just above the keyboard in gold letters. Cindra sat down on the stool, adjusted it to her liking, and began to play. Fantasy then took over! The drawing-room was an ideal setting for a concert: there were maroon velvet drapes at the windows, not fully drawn, as it was daylight, so that pure white sheers were visible, covering the sashes between. The musician imagined her blond hair released from its tight knot at the back of her head and arranged in a soft bun at the nape of her neck; her dark silk tailored dress had become a black velvet evening gown with long sleeves and a low neck-line. Her imagination went still further and the gilded Louis the XIVth chairs, scattered about the room, increased, and were occupied by attentive listeners. The piano keys came alive under the soft touch of her skilled fingers. *What a magnificent instrument!* was the theme that kept running through the young lady's mind.

The hours went by so fast she did not even hear Mr. Brent come into the room. He stood for a while, listened to the young virtuoso, and was duly impressed. "Miss Gold, I am sorry to interrupt you, but it's time for the birthday supper." The man spoke gently. He continued, "You do play beautifully, I can understand why you are planning a career in music. The piano tuner came and worked on the piano. I hope it's satisfactory."

The lady thought to herself how relaxed her boss seemed compared to when he was at the office; she answered his question by saying that it was in perfect tune and an excellent instrument on which to play. After gathering up her music and putting it away in its cloth case, she preceded him out of the drawing-room. Then together they entered the dining-room, where were already seated at the table her benefactress, the child, Clarisse, and Raoul.

The little girl was a great one for putting everyone at ease. "My daddy said I could invite you all to my party, and he's the bestest daddy in the whole world!" She spoke in a serious tone, then without anyone prompting her, when her food was given to her, she put her hands together in a prayerful attitude and said reverently, "Thank you, God, for this food, an' for my daddy, an' for my friends. Amen." All eyes were focused on her with admiration, the little girl's grace having been so spontaneous and matter-of-fact.

Phyllis especially enjoyed the delicious meal. She thought how nice it was to have a respite from her usual Sunday duties, even though the visit of the child was making Sundays much more pleasant for her. She was completely unaware of how Clarisse was missing the youngster, though the woman said nothing, as she knew that the little one was very happy with her new friends.

It was a traditional celebration with cake and candles and all, and a happy little girl smiling broadly when the birthday song was sung. The festive mood continued as the joyous group left the table and gathered in the drawing-room for opening of the gifts. The child chose to leave till the last the unveiling of the tissue that wrapped the large package she received from her new friends. Then there was a squeal of delight: "Oh, Daddy, see my quin-tup-lets, oh my beautiful quin-tup-lets, and one is just like me!"

Shirlianne requested that Miss Gold play the "Quintuplet's Lullaby," so her musician friend, only too happy to have a chance to play the magnificent instrument again, complied with her request, and they were soon singing the poetic song, which at its end received so much applause from the little audience that they were obliged to give it an encore.

Shortly after the music had stopped, the butler entered the drawing room and summoned his employer to the phone. It was a phone call from Mr. Brent's fiancée, and afterwards he informed them he was leaving for the station to pick her up as had been prearranged. Since the two guests said they must leave, and the station was in the vicinity of their apartment, he drove the ladies home. On the way there he expressed how very grateful he was for all they had done for his daughter.

Chapter 19
A Guest for the Weekend

Winter will soon be upon us, was what Cindra was thinking as she walked to work one blustery November day; it seemed to her there was snow in the air, and she wrapped her scarf tighter around her neck. She missed her companion walking with her. Miss Pindar had the day off, and the young girl could see her now in her mind's eye, knitting the various items that she was making for Christmas presents. The cold snap was chilling her and causing her to feel even farther away from the house and the loved ones she had left. She entered the building that was her workplace; the warmth of it seemed to dispel the gloom, this process being helped further by Leah Frost's cheery greeting.

Then later that day storm clouds gathered in the office as well. Phyllis Farrell had gone into her fiance's office and it was not long before she could be heard emitting derogatory remarks in a shrill tone. All the employees in the outer office were pricking up their ears, trying to make out what was taking place. It was not long before Mr. Cameron Brent's office door opened and the couple walked out as though nothing had happened, the heightened pink colour of Miss Farrell's face being the only indication of the rancour that was heard moments before. They talked amicably as they walked to the elevator, then Phyllis Farrell bade her companion good-bye, got on the lift, and disappeared.

Cindra's boss, on passing her desk, asked her to come into his office. He appeared his usual calm self. He explained to his employee just what had caused his fiancée to become so irate: he had suggested they take his daughter with them on a little trip they had planned for the coming weekend, and Miss Farrell would not hear of it. He said he was sorry there had been a disturbance; he was aware that it must have been heard by the employees.

It was hard for the prim secretary to hide her dislike for Miss Farrell. If she would only give the little girl a chance, she thought, and try to be friendly with her, but then she searched her feelings further. She noticed how people stared when they saw Shirlianne with her, and she thought in all fairness the poor woman probably could not handle that.

"Mr. Brent, how about letting Shirlianne come to stay with Phyllis Pindar and me for the weekend? She's no trouble, you know, and I think she'd like that." The secretary spoke assuredly this time, knowing her benefactress would be thrilled to have the child stay with them.

Cindra's boss assured her there was not the problem of someone to look after his child, as Clarisse was always there, but he would like to have had her along on the trip. He told her he did not want to impose on them, and they had done so much already.

Cindra was not giving up on the idea, she recalled that her living companion had the day off, so she phoned her. Phyllis was very pleased and informed her she had been hoping the little girl could stay with them sometime.

Mr. Brent seemed relieved when his secretary told him she had contacted her benefactress, who said she would be delighted to have the child stay with them. The prim woman also revealed to him the fact that she had left a nephew in Canada, whom she missed very much, and his little girl was helping to fill that void.

Thus it came about that Shirlianne spent a weekend with her beloved friends. The older woman was teaching her to hand sew, at the child's request, and though the workmanship was extremely juvenile, the end product of pillows for her dolls gave her a sense of accomplishment and pride. The younger woman would have her come into her room after supper, and she would play for her and teach her songs. This the child liked very much.

On Saturday evening the youngster sat in a chair beside the piano. Cindra was leafing through some sheet music and Shirlianne caught a glimpse of the coloured picture on the front of the folder enclosing one of the pieces. She asked to see it and when she did she exclaimed, "Oh, that's Jesus in a garden. Oh, what pretty flowers!" The same figure in a white robe, and His arms outstretched, she had seen on different pamphlets at the church; she knew exactly who it was. She held the folder up and tried to make out the title of the song, "In A Mo-na." She was having trouble with the big word. Her father had been teaching her to read, and lately so had Miss Pindar. There were some familiar large words she knew, but this was a new one.

Her musician friend came to the rescue and helped her pronounce the word, *mon-a-ste-ry* by breaking it up into syllables for her. She already knew the word, *garden*, and proudly spoke it aloud with gusto; then the child touched the piano player's arm excitedly, requesting, "Oh, play it for me!" and adding hastily, "Magic word, 'please'." Cindra had to laugh at that, she recalled Clarisse's reminder to the child when once before she requested a favour.

The pianist thought it was a rather wistful tune for a little one, but she complied with the entreaty, as her young listener was looking at her so earnestly. To the musician's surprise the child was very touched by the melody, which she herself would assess as soul-stirring. She was not sure whether it was the tune or the picture of the Lord with the flowers that had captured the little girl's heart, but she was very quiet, and as the final note was struck, the artist turned around to her captive audience and saw a most angelic look on the child's countenance.

The little one got down from the chair and put her arms around the young lady at the piano. She seemed troubled and spoke very seriously: "The priest at the church says we're to love everybody, don't he?"

"That's right, dear child." Cindra looked into the sad eyes of the little one. She wondered what was causing her anguish.

"Well, I don't love my daddy's fyon-say, I don't like her, I jus' don't like her, and she don't like me!" The child's grammar seemed to be deteriorating with her upset emotions; her grammar was usually quite good for a child her age. She went on. "I prayed about it and God din't answer my prayer, she still don't like me."

Cindra tightened her arms around the child who was feeling so rejected by the woman who was to become her mother. "You have to be patient, Shirlianne, it's something we all have to learn." Noting the questioning expression on the little one's face, she added, "That means we go on with our prayers, no matter what."

The musician felt a bit of frivolity was needed at this point, so she started to play "The Quintuplet's Lullaby." Well, that did the trick: Shirlianne climbed back on her chair, and was soon singing happily along with her friend.

The weekend had passed very quickly. It was the child's father who picked her up on Sunday evening at the Plaza apartment. He explained that his fiancée had stayed with the friends they were visiting, so he had come back alone. Shirlianne proudly showed him the pillows she had made for her dolls. The man, on seeing the handicraft of his child, lifted her up high and proclaimed, "So now you can sew shirts for me." He was laughing, and so were the others.

"Oh Daddy, you're so funny!" The little girl was tickled by the absurdity of the remark and hugged her father as she was lowered to hugging level.

The two women were touched by the loving bond that existed between the father and his little girl and the spontaneity with which it was shown.

Fond good-byes were said and it was not long before

the father, with his daughter, was driving back to their home in Ladue. Shirlianne seemed very pensive, which caused her father to remark, "A penny for your thoughts, little girl."

The child looked at her father and blurted out, "I wish Miss Gold could be my mother!"

Shirlianne was taken aback by the abruptness of her father's reply. "I do *not* want to hear you say that again, Shirlianne!"

The child was not giving up, "Well, what about Auntie?"

The father laughed inwardly; he thought of how age difference did not mean much to a child. However, he said quite seriously, "Phyllis Farrell is going to be your mother, so please, Darling, try to get along with her. I want to see you both happy."

The little girl said nothing, but she clutched the brown paper bag with the pillows closer to her. It seemed to be a liaison between her beloved friends and her, and it sufficed, at the moment, to soothe her.

Later that evening, after her father had helped her place the handmade pillows in her dollies' crib, and had said good night and left her room, she got down on her knees beside her bed and prayed. "God, don't let Miss Farrell to be my mother, magic word 'please.' "

Chapter 20
A Suggested Solution

The year passed by so very quickly; it was summer again and Cindra reminisced about the year's happenings on her walk to work this beautiful morning. Her living companion had had to go early to work this particular day. There was some sort of important meeting taking place, the older woman had told her, so the prim secretary was alone with her thoughts. She recollected how Christmas had not been so lonely. She had missed her family, of course, but there was her dear benefactress, there was kindly Mr. Serenity, and there was Shirlianne! The precious little girl had been so thrilled with the hat and mittens Auntie had knit for her that she refused to wear anything else on her head and hands! They were fashioned from red wool, a colour that clashed with some of her coats, so Auntie got busy and knit another set in a neutral colour that would go with everything. Well, you would have thought she had given the child the moon!

And her boss had given such a generous Christmas bonus to her, along with a caution not to discuss it with the rest; he said they would not understand, that they were unaware of the number of times his little girl visited at the Plaza apartment, and he said it was in appreciation for all they had done for Shirlianne. The young woman recalled how much the extra cash had helped out at the Yule-tide season.

Memories continued to flood back. She would never forget the day Robert Brent approached her at her desk at work and asked if she would go to the office Christmas party with him. When he added that it would be at the Missouri Athletic Club, she was sorely tempted. He stood there so straight and tall, and he was so handsome; however, she had to decline regretfully. There were several reasons: First, she did not want to give away her "disguise"; second, she knew Jane Janes was hoping he would ask her; third, she knew he tended to over imbibe "spirits"; and last but not least, she knew her benefactress would object strenuously. It was a tough decision, requiring courage and self-discipline—courage to refuse him, self-discipline to deny herself pleasure. As it turned out Robert still did not take Jane to the party.

The young girl mused on. She recalled how at the beginning of the new year Clarisse made it known to her employer that she missed his daughter being away every Sunday, and she requested she be allowed to take Shirlianne to her church, which was a Baptist church, every other Sabbath. Cindra chuckled to herself when she recollected what her boss told her Clarisse had said about the Episcopalians: "They don't know if they're Catholic or Protestant!" And she could imagine the words being enunciated in the good housemaid's droll manner. The secretary and her boss had both laughed about it; they had agreed the woman was quite definite and bigoted in her religious views, but she was a good-hearted soul, and the exposure of the child to different systems of faith would not hurt her. When she was older she could decide for herself. Cindra was aware of her boss's gratitude for his household employee, as he had told her before that he would never forget the help and support the woman had given him during the infancy of his little daughter's life.

At midwinter her boss had made a business trip to Toronto, Canada. She recalled how amazed she had been to hear that his journey by air in a Douglas DC-3 had taken only a few hours, whereas her train journey from the same area in Canada had taken several days. How she would love to have gone on that trip, to fly in an airplane. The thought of it still gave her a thrill, but she knew it was just for people with a lot of money, and *that* she was not! Her boss told her he had taken a taxi to Belleville and had visited her mother. Mrs. Gold was overcome by his charm and attentiveness. He had fêted her at some very swank restaurants in recompense for his overnight stay. He had said it was a gesture of appreciation for the clever daughter she had parted with when she let the girl go to Saint Louis to study music. Cindra's mother had written to her telling her these things. In the letter she described how he had said he would be eternally grateful for the interest that the concerned secretary had taken in his little daughter. She also called to mind something else her mother wrote about, and it was to tell her Mr. Brent said she had become a very valuable asset to the Brent Company.

The young lady reminisced on about how the Lenten season had meant so much to her that year. She was only halfway through her father's memo book, as she had concentrated on the reading material she obtained from church during the penitential time leading up to Easter. The time had passed by so quickly!

Then, returning to the present, she remembered the words from the treasured book, which she had read last night before she settled to sleep. Her father was always appreciative of the legacy contemporary mankind had been left by others in art, music, science, literature, and so on. He had written down an inscription, which he noted was from Dallas University, and which she thought worth committing to memory: "We have all warmed ourselves before fires we did not build, and drunk water from wells we did not dig." What a philosopher her father was, she mused, he certainly had sought out and enjoyed the finer things of life!

As she approached her workplace on this bright summer morning, she offered a little prayer of thanksgiving; she felt in tune with all of nature. She was more than pleased by the way her musical ability was developing, her career in music was forming brightly and vividly in her imagination, spurred on by the successful way her lessons were going. Surely nothing could interfere with the joy of this day!

How mistaken she was! Later in the day Mr. Brent called her into his office to take some dictation. It was to send for application forms to several boarding-schools for Shirlianne. The secretary felt a cold chill come over her; she thought to herself that Phyllis Farrell must have cast some sort of spell over the poor man. She had to calm herself inwardly to hear what he had to say about the plan. It was obvious that her boss sensed her negative reaction to the project, even though she had said nothing. He explained, "One has to apply early to these schools, Miss Gold. Shirlianne will be six years old in another year and she must start her schooling."

The prim secretary knew her boss and his fiancée were planning to get married the following spring, and she was aware of Miss Farrell's sentiments towards the little girl. She could just imagine how devastating the thought of separation from her father would be to the child!

Cindra had grown to love the intuitive little one whose insight, the young woman had discovered, was remarkable for a child her age. It was Shirlianne who had helped her conquer her homesickness—she would always feel indebted to her for that. Her heart went out to the little girl. Well, it would not be for another year, and the young woman consoled herself with the thought things could change in the interim. She did not know at the time how right she was!

It was a sad "Miss Prim" who sat down to her typewriter in the outer office to type the letters to the various schools requesting application forms. But the question that was foremost in her mind was, Would the child be sent to a coloured school? She was interrupted by the appearance of two women who stepped off the elevator and made their way towards Cameron Brent's office. What a comely pair they were! Cindra recognized Miss Farrell, but the other lady she had not seen before, and judging by her demeanour, Cindra surmised she was the wife of Mr. Brent, Sr. She was the perfect stereotype of a wealthy man's wife, thought Cindra. Though she was a little on the plump side, it seemed to add to her attractiveness; she carried herself with queenly ease and grace and with such assurance, as though the world had been made for her. The two women were dressed in the height of fashion, of course!

A few minutes after they disappeared into Cameron Brent's office, Cindra was summoned in, and it was with sang-froid and poise that the man introduced Miss Gold to his mother. Mrs. John Brent smiled condescendingly, looking at the prim young woman in a manner that bespoke one who was used to dealing with servants. However, the younger woman felt no intimidation, whether any was intended or not, no doubt because her father had instilled in his progeny the belief that they were as good as anyone else, and that it was not great wealth that made the person. "Miss Prim" smiled back perkily and uttered a "glad to meet you" with sincerity. She felt the greatest urge to curtsey, and smiled to herself later on recall of the incident.

There were some beautiful rings on several fingers of the older woman's perfectly manicured hands, but the large diamond on the ring finger of her left hand caught the employee's eye. She had never before seen such a huge "rock."

Cindra sensed her purpose for being there was over, so she headed for the door, and on her way out she heard Phyllis Brent say to her son that they had come in to see his father and they thought they had better drop by to see him.

As the secretary returned to her outer office desk she could not help wondering if her boss's mother had patched things up with her son. He certainly seemed to be overjoyed at his mother's visit, and in the light of what Leah Frost had told her, she figured this must be the case. Perhaps it was because the man was planning to send the child to boarding-school. Miss Farrell would undoubtedly be pushing for that. Then Cindra came up with an idea. She was glad that her boss called her into his office after the two women left. Before he had time to give the young lady the assignment he had for her, she blurted out, "Mr. Brent, I have an idea that could solve your problem of schooling for Shirlianne."

"Well, let me hear it, Miss Gold. I really would welcome an alternate suggestion."

The prim secretary was pleased her boss was at least willing to listen to another course of action, so she divulged her notion. "Mr. Brent, what about getting a private tutor for Shirlianne?"

"You know, Miss Gold, I never thought of that. By Jove, it just might be the solution!" And he added as an afterthought, "Finding an appropriate school would be difficult."

Still, the man did not cancel his order to send the letters requesting applications, so Cindra, having returned to her typewriter, settled herself and completed that task, consoling herself with the thought the letters were only appeals for forms for applying to the different schools, nothing determinative. The fact her boss gave such positive support to the solution she suggested served as sufficient consolation to put her mind at ease.

Chapter 21
A Lost Child

Another weekend with Shirlianne as their guest, and how the two women in their Plaza apartment had looked forward to it. She had come on Friday evening. Raoul brought her in the limousine, and with her quintuplets, as Phyllis Pindar had requested. The latter had told the little girl on the phone to bring the five dolls; they would make summer dresses for them. Shirlianne was ecstatic when she entered her friends' home; the chauffeur, on the other hand, was feeling a little conspicuous, as he carried in the huge bassinet with the dolls. Well, he would be the first to say that he and his wife would do anything for the child whom they adored.

In the bustle of packing the bassinet and the little one's overnight case into the vehicle, the bag with the pyjamas had been forgotten. Clarisse discovered this early the next day, and since Cameron Brent and his fiancée were passing through downtown Saint Louis, on their way to Illinois, the gentleman, instead of detailing his chauffeur to deliver the nightclothes, said he would drop them off on his way through the city. Thus it was that Saturday morning Cameron Brent appeared at the apartment door of Miss Pindar. It was Cindra who answered the ring of the doorbell, her magenta gown draped softly around her lithe body and her golden hair flowing down past her shoulders. The man, on beholding her, stammered a greeting. He was somewhat startled; he had not seen the young woman out of her "Miss Prim" image before, and he was visibly moved. After handing the little bag to the fair lady, he left abruptly, somewhat embarrassed at his spontaneous reaction; he had not even thought to ask to see his child!

The fair lady, on her part, was disappointed that her disguise was divulged. Oh well, she would not let that happen again; her hair would go into its top-knot bun first thing in the morning. With that decision made, she gave no other thought to the incident. It was to be different for the man who saw her!

The week-end was a thrilling one for Shirlianne: She helped sew clothes for her favourite dolls; assisted Auntie in making some chocolate fudge, in preparing a lemon pie; and sang some favourite songs with her precious Miss Gold after that lady had finished her required practice hours on Sunday. She also had a nice little visit with Mr. Serenity, who let her sit on his lap while he read to her the story of *Black Beauty.*

Our heroine and her benefactress walked to work side by side the next morning. It was a glorious summer day, the sky ever so blue, and the birds were full of song. It brought to mind for Cindra what her father used to say when he heard the birds singing thus: "The birds are singing their Psalms."

Phyllis informed Cindra she had a theatre date with her gentleman friend this evening, she said she had forgotten to tell her about it before. Then her musician friend related to her that she had composed a little nocturne when she was at the piano on Saturday afternoon, and she was anxious to play it for Miss Grace at her lesson the following night.

Both women recalled little instances that had happened over the week-end, loving incidents concerning their small guest. Both of them confessed that these occurrences endeared her to them even more. Auntie told how she had fallen asleep on the chesterfield on Sunday after lunch whilst reading to the child; Shirlianne had removed the heavy book from her chest, drew up a chair close to the sleeping woman, and amused herself by looking at a picturebook until the sleeper awoke.

The pianist also told a little story of how the child had come into her room on Sunday afternoon whilst she was practicing and had left a little plate of chocolate fudge on the table beside the piano. Along with it she had set down a glass of water. The little one had explained to her afterwards that candy always makes the candy eater thirsty.

Cindra took delight in the brief walk with her friend. She thought to herself how fast the time went by when one was enjoying oneself. She was soon at her desk in the outer office, getting set up for the day's work. It was not long before her boss and his fiancée stepped off the elevator, the latter looking very glamorous in a cerise silk summer dress, with a large white straw hat, white shoes, and white gloves to complete the ensemble. What a handsome couple the man and his future wife made! And they seemed to be in very good spirits. Morning greetings were exchanged between the employer and his employees, then the couple disappeared into the man's office. Sometime later Raoul stepped off the elevator, nodded a friendly greeting to Miss Gold, and went into their employer's office. Soon he emerged with Miss Farrell, who had him hold open the door of the lift for her and had him stand a few paces behind her in servile fashion as they descended to the ground floor.

The prim secretary was summoned to her boss's office. He explained that there was some important correspondence he had neglected to do on Friday afternoon, so they had to get right at it. That was why Raoul was summoned to come and pick up his fiancée. The stenographer was soon back at her typewriter, eager to get the neglected letters on their way.

It was midafternoon when the prim secretary answered the phone. It was a tearful Clarisse on the other end of the line asking to speak to Mr. Brent, saying that she could not find Shirlianne anywhere. Cindra immediately transferred the call to her boss's office. Before long the man hustled out of his office, informing her that he was going home to see what had happened and that he would tell her when the child was located.

The afternoon dragged on for Cindra. She found it difficult to concentrate on her work. She did manage to complete it before the day's end, but it took much longer than usual, and her nerves were on edge when she hustled home that afternoon. She had expected to hear from her employer that the little girl had been found, but no word had come. She would like to have phoned, but she did not want to tie up the line to the home in Ladue in case it was needed—what if the child had been kidnapped? Oh, what disturbing thoughts were going through the young woman's mind. She finally had to take hold of herself and try to think rationally. Surely the little girl had fallen asleep in some hidden corner of the huge mansion. *Oh, dear God, please let that be the case!* She remembered the little discussion she had had with Shirlianne about prayer, and she felt a pang of love tear at her heart at the rememberance of it.

Phyllis was at home when the anxious young woman arrived there. She expected her benefactress to give her news of a phone call from Mr. Brent, but instead she found herself relating the story of Shirlianne's disappearance to her benefactress. Now two people were nervously awaiting a phone call in that Plaza apartment! And a call came shortly from Cindra's boss, but he was phoning purposely to see if perhaps the child had somehow found her way to their apartment; so the little girl had definitely disappeared! The worried man told them the police had been informed earlier, and now a concentrated search was being made for the missing child.

Neither of the two women felt like eating their supper; they did so automatically, not with the purpose of satisfying their hunger, but for something to do whilst they waited for news.

The older woman's gentleman friend had come early for their theatre date and helped her with after-supper clean-up by drying the dishes. Cindra did not fare so well; she tried to practice, but was unable to fully concentrate.

Phyllis felt like cancelling the theatre date; however, before the planned time they were to leave, the telephone rang. It was Raoul informing them that Shirlianne had been found by the police and that she was unharmed. He said Mr. Brent was just getting the details now and told him to tell them he would phone later.

The Pindar household was much relieved and things carried on as originally planned.

Meanwhile at the Cameron Brent household it was a different story. The police told the anxious father they had found his daughter wandering around the Country Club Golf Course in the Ladue area. She was thoroughly lost, they said. She was carrying a small suitcase, with a few clothes packed therein and was clutching a doll wrapped in a blanket. One of the officers said she told them she was running away from home, and she would not tell them her name, however, he said they were quite sure it was little Miss Brent, as she fit exactly the description they had been given.

Forms had to be made out and papers signed before the police could leave. Shirlianne clung to her father the whole time. It was apparent she felt sorry that she had caused him such trouble.

Phyllis Farrell had been there all day. Raoul had taken her to the mansion after picking her up at the office that morning, as she was to have dinner with her fiancé and his daughter. The plan was that through the day she would try to get better acquainted with Shirlianne.

The child was still clinging to her father when the policemen left. It was Phyllis who spoke first:

"What were you thinking of by running off like that and scaring us half to death? You should be punished, you're a naughty little girl!" The woman's tone of voice was anything but kind.

The child began to cry and started trembling involuntarily. The father held his daughter closely. He looked at the angry woman incredulously. How could she berate the child when the little one was so obviously troubled and upset! However, he spoke to the indignant woman without rancour in his voice.

"Phyllis, please, don't be harsh with my child. You can see she is very upset."

It was then that the child recovered enough to speak, though she was still trembling, "Oh, Daddy, your fyon-say said I had to go away to boarding school; couldn't I just live with Clarisse and Role in their rooms and she wouldn't have to see me?"

The words of his little daughter cut him like a sword! He was sorry she had been told so bluntly about the possible plan that was being considered for her schooling. He decided then and there that that was the end of that plan!

The troubled man thought it would be best if his fiancée went home at this time. He wanted to be alone with his little daughter and comfort her. The woman left with feathers somewhat ruffled. She was not happy with Cameron's last remark. He had said, "I should have told you, Phyllis, I am planning to have a private tutor for Shirlianne. Had I done that, this wouldn't have happened."

Chapter 22
A Nice Diversion

Neither father nor child were able to eat much at the late supper meal they shared. Whilst Clarisse helped Shirlianne get ready for bed, Mr. Brent phoned the Pindar apartment as he had promised, and he explained to Miss Gold just what had happened. He then sat at the bedside of the little girl, trying to get her interested in her favourite storybook. But the child became increasingly restless; she was developing a fever. It was then the man phoned his family physician, and before long Dr. Robertson was examining the child. His opinion was that she had been shocked by the news Miss Farrell had given her, and also badly frightened by being lost, and this was an adverse reaction. He prescribed an antipyretic for the fever and a very mild sedative. The little girl was familiar with "Dr. Rob." That had been his nickname from way back. He himself felt it made him seem more like a friend to his child patients; it certainly had worked with Shirlianne, that and his little black bag, which held, besides his examining instruments, balloons and small trinkets that he knew would appeal to a child and put him or her at ease whilst he was doing his examining. Before Dr. Rob left her room, Shirlianne managed a smile for him and a polite "Thank you" for the Mickey Mouse balloon he had given her.

Cameron Brent spent the night in an easy chair beside his daughter's bed. He did not get much sleep, but he was glad he had kept watch, as the child's temperature had fluctuated and was kept under control only by the administering of the medication as prescribed by the doctor.

The following day the child's father knew he had to get to the office; there was important work to be done and certain clients with whom he was to meet. He arranged through the nursing registry for a registered nurse, a Miss Conklin, to look after his child. He also phoned the Pindar apartment and made arrangements for his secretary to spend the day with Shirlianne. He said Jane Janes could handle her work for the day. He explained that he did not want to leave the child alone with the nurse, who was a stranger to her; Clarisse, as it happened, needed the day off. He went on to say his daughter asked him if Miss Gold could come and play the piano for her, so he had set up a cot in the drawing room where she would be near the piano.

The budding pianist was thrilled with the idea of such a break in her daily routine. However, her benefactress took a dim view of it, even though it was for their beloved Shirlianne. But Cindra was happy at the thought of another chance to play on the magnificent Steinway piano. As an added bonus she could chalk up more practice hours for her lesson that night.

It was a grateful young woman whom Raoul drove to the Ladue mansion that day. She could hardly wait to see her dear little friend who had been through such a miserable ordeal. And there sat the little one, propped up with pillows, on her cot, anxiously waiting for her good friend. They were soon hugging one another.

Shirlianne was sobbing. "Oh, Miss Gold, I wish you were my mother!" The child looked at her with adoring eyes. "But Daddy says I mustn't say that; he says you are going to be a famus pyan-ust, and we'll go and hear you an' we can say, 'We know that famus lady pyanust!'"

The pianist could not help laughing at what the little girl said. She held her closer and felt her feverish little body. To comfort her she stated, "Don't cry, little one. You're safe now and your daddy is not going to send you to boarding school."

Hearing those words from her dear Miss Gold was reassuring to the child.

"Now you must drink plenty of fluids to get well."

The child looked at her as though she found what Cindra said incredible. "You know, my daddy said that too!"

The fair-haired pianist began by playing for the child

the little nocturne she had composed, and when she told her she had named it "Nocturne for Shirlianne," the little girl was delighted.

She then divulged a secret to her favourite lady. "I took my quintuplet 'Cindra' with me when I ran away, so I wasn't so scared. She reminded me of you!"

The young woman was touched by the confession of the little one. She could see the child was beginning to feel better, as by this time the kindly nurse had administered more medication to her patient and had made sure she drank the fluids she had brought her.

At lunch-time the three people had a meal together. Suzie and the rest of the servants were fussing about, carrying out Mr. Brent's orders that they be looked after royally. Shirlianne was weak, but with the help of Miss Conklin she was able to join them at the plate-glass table out on the patio.

During lunch Cindra tried to think of something that might spark the child's interest and imagination. "Shirlianne, what about giving your house a name?" As she said that she could see the child was interested.

"Yes, it'll be fun, Miss Gold, but I wouldn't know what to call it!" The child sensed that a house would not have a regular name like a person.

The young woman explained to her that at the front of the house there were huge columns, and having answered the child's query as to what columns were, she suggested they name the house the Columns.

The child seemed satisfied that the appellation was appropriate, as she uttered a statement that made the two adults seated at the table laugh. She said, "So now we're living at the Columns—I think Daddy will like that!!"

After lunch the child refused to go upstairs to bed, which had been the nurse's suggestion. She said she would sleep on the cot in the drawing room whilst Miss Gold practised. And that she did, feeling safe and secure, lulled by the musician's notes. The artist played very softly to achieve that effect.

The young woman played on into the afternoon, her nimble fingers flying over the keys of the magnificent instrument. She felt she was in seventh heaven, if there was such a place. She felt her soul was soaring high in the sky; with the swallows she could see through the french doors, which opened to the sunny outside. Now she was playing to a huge audience in a large hall. Yes, it was the Kiel Auditorium, and she was appearing as a guest artist. How this fantasy stimulated her! She felt a joy within herself greater than she had ever felt before. At the imaginary ending the applause was deafening; however, later on, when she did finish her practising, she heard the enthusiastic applause of two tiny hands clapping their appreciation and approval. As she saw the delight and happiness on the little girl's face, it meant more to her that day than if her fantasy had been reality. The fact the ailing child took such pleasure in it was enough for her. Shirlianne had remarked, "I love you, Miss Gold, you're the bestest pyan-ust in the whole world."

When the pianist left for home that afternoon she felt satisfied that the little patient was recovering nicely. Miss Conklin, before she left, checked the child's temperature again and said it had been stable all afternoon, so she felt quite comfortable leaving her patient in the care of the concerned Clarisse, who had returned. She could see the woman was very willing to take the responsibility. The domestic said, as she so often did, "Why, she's like my own child."

During supper at the Pindar apartment, Mr. Brent phoned his secretary to thank her for staying with his daughter. He said the child had told him about the "Nocturne for Shirlianne," and she had hummed it for him. He also informed her that the child's appetite was back; she had said she was so hungry she could eat a horse, and when he replied he hoped it was not "Black Beauty," she went into a fit of laughter. She was back to her happy little self. He wound up the conversation by expressing his heartfelt gratitude for her help and concern.

It was an eager student who went to her piano lesson that evening, and it was a very pleased Miss Grace who listened to the piece of music her creative pupil had composed; the teacher did not say much, but Cindra could tell the woman was impressed.

Chapter 23
An Estrangement

The young secretary was back at her desk the next morning. She had a strange feeling as though she had been away from the office for much more than a day. However, Jane Janes filled her in on what had transpired the day before and informed her there was only one bit of correspondence left to be done; it was not a matter of any urgency.

A few minutes after her boss arrived he called her into his office. He asked mischievously that she file any admission forms coming from boarding schools in the wastebasket! He again thanked her for her compliance to his request to stay with his little girl and told her she was mostly responsible for Shirlianne's speedy recovery. She assured him it had been a great pleasure for her, and profitable too, as it was extra piano practice for her last evening's lesson.

Work proceeded as usual, the boss dictating some letters to his prim secretary, when a startling occurrence happened—the door suddenly opened and a very hostile-looking Miss Farrell entered. She slammed the door behind her, then braced herself against it, thus barring access for anyone to exit. She emitted her words in an explosive manner directed at her fiancé.

"We had it all settled that Shirlianne should go to boarding school, and now you've given in to that spoilt child." Before the man had a chance to intervene, she turned towards Cindra, and, pointing an accusing finger, she continued, "I'll just bet it was your idea. I'd thank you to keep your nose out of our business."

Cameron Brent, in his usual unruffled manner, got up and approached the angry young woman, whose rapid respirations were causing her chest to heave. He took her arm gently and led her to a chair. He dismissed his stenographer, giving her an understanding look. He could see that the caustic words had bothered her. As she left he told her he was going to take his fiancée out for a cup of coffee, and he would be back later to finish his dictation.

The prim secretary was glad of her own coffee break. Being with her working associates helped to restore her self respect and get a proper perspective on the accusations her boss's fiancée had made. She reasoned that finding an appropriate boarding school for the little coloured girl would be well nigh impossible. Why on earth could Miss Farrell not see that? She could not have realized how adversely the thought of the boarding school had affected the child.

Back at her typewriter the young typist was very pensive. She thought of her boss. What a gentle man he was.

She had developed a great respect for him; he had such patience and such an air of suavity about him. And what a challenge he had to face when he decided to raise his infant daughter. That decision had almost completely alienated him from his mother, who had refused to see or go near the child after viewing her in the hospital at the time of her birth. And he gave such love to the babe who cost her mother her life!

Cindra continued with her musing; what a fool Miss Farrell was! Did she not know she would be shown that same self-sacrificing love? Usually women had better insight than that, a kind of intuition, a sixth sense. Well, if she kept up the same tactics she would lose the man she loved! What a pity! He was such a good catch! She just did not know what the woman was thinking of. Oh, Miss Farrell looked so beautiful this morning in her lemon-coloured dress, which fit her body perfectly, and her spiffy large-brimmed hat to match. Cindra had quite forgotten the sarcastic words she had thrown at her earlier, and only wished she could talk to her and try to get her to see just what she was doing.

On her boss's return she presented him with her idea of she, herself, talking with his fiancée to try and persuade her to accept their view as regards his little girl. But her boss, though touched by her caring and concern, said he thought it would be to no avail, as he was sure her mind was made up concerning the matter. He did not divulge to her the trouble he had with Phyllis in the restaurant when they went for coffee. She had made a horrible scene, which put him right off. Eventually it was to sever their relationship, though he did not fully realize it at this time.

As he resumed his dictation to his secretary, he began seeing her in a different light. The vision of her in her magenta gown came back to him, and the remembrance of her long golden hair framing her lovely face was stirring up in him certain feelings that he tried to suppress, partly because of their age difference, but mainly because the golden-haired beauty was aiming for a career in music.

And so, things started to change around the office. Cameron Brent was not there as often, and when he was, it was only to look after the bare necessities. He was trying to avoid too much contact with his secretary. He knew he was falling hopelessly in love with her against his better judgement; much as he tried, he seemed powerless to prevent this entanglement of his emotions, especially with his little daughter's attitude towards the young woman, which tended to fan the flame!

Cindra, on the other hand, was sure the engaged couple would soon straighten things out and carry on with their wedding plans. She presumed the two people were continuing their relationship, quite unaware that they were estranged.

True it is that Phyllis Farrell had been trying to patch things up between herself and her fiancé, but she was unaware of the metamorphosis that had taken place in Cameron's emotions, and the phone calls she made to the home in Ladue remained unanswered, much to her chagrin.

The prim secretary carried on with her work and kept the office running efficiently. She would certainly admit she missed her boss's presence in his office; he was there now so rarely just taking the time to do the required dictation and to give any instructions concerning the day's work. The rest of the day he would spend entertaining prospective clients at the club, or taking his little girl on outings, much to the little one's delight. Between her father's attention and her visits to the Pindar apartment, Shirlianne was a happy child again, and her father vowed to keep her that way.

But the eldest Brent son found his scheme was not working. He was missing the day's contact with his secretary, and he had proved to himself the truth of that old adage, Absence makes the heart grow fonder. So, within a few weeks he was back to his usual routine. He found there was something soothing about being around Miss Gold, despite the yearnings of his heart, and he could hardly keep his eyes off her as he observed her going about her work.

The fact Miss Farrell was not making visits to the office was becoming apparent to all the workers, including Miss Gold. Also, the latter had been told not to put through any phone calls to her boss from Miss Farrell. He explained he could not have a wife who refused to accept his child. The prim secretary was not surprised. She could not help feeling sorry for the attractive older woman, but she did sympathize with her employer; she figured the poor man had come to the end of his patience, as far as Phyllis Farrell was concerned.

Chapter 24
A Forced Decision

Cindra was enjoying the business lunches to which her boss had her go, in her capacity as note-taker for the business dealings of the different clients. He was very attentive to her and protective of her, especially against the clients who would pay her particular attention and sometimes ask her out on dinner dates. He made sure these occasions were kept on the strictest business terms.

The prim secretary had not told her benefactress of Cameron Brent's split with his fiancée. She knew the good woman felt very strictly that the office was for business affairs, and that alone. Secretaries should not concern themselves with their employer's private affairs. She was aware Phyllis Pindar had made an unprecedented concession by allowing Shirlianne to visit, but she had taken to the little one so specially, and the same little one had brought so much pleasure into their lives that she was sure Phyllis did not regret it.

On the rare occasions when Raoul was busy and could not deliver or pick up the small child for her routine visits to her adored ladies' apartment, her father would be the substitute for the job, and it was at those times when the older apartment dweller began to notice Cameron Brent's attitude towards her charge.

After one such occasion Phyllis remarked to her young boarder, "My dear, have you noticed the way Mr. Brent has been looking at you? He never seems to take his eyes off you, and I don't like it!"

"Oh, Phyllis, you're imagining things." The young girl uttered a flippant little laugh and went into her room to do her piano practise.

However, she wished her benefactress had not made such a remark. The next day at the office she became conscious of her boss's soft, kindly eyes focused on her frequently, and with such fervour it was stirring within her ambivalent feelings—on the one hand those of uneasiness, on the other, those of pleasure. But her female vanity surfaced and the feeling of pleasure predominated. To be admired by such a distinguished gentleman did wonders for her ego and made her feel rather special. She so wanted to get rid of her "Miss Prim" garb and present herself as being more attractive, but her female vanity was not as strong as her self-discipline, and the prim image prevailed, though the fantasy was delightful to the young woman!

Summer eased into fall so gently that year. Shirlianne's birthday had come and gone, there had been the usual special celebration, this time at the Pindar apartment, with the father invited to the simple repast. Cameron watched his manners and played a very low-key role. He had sensed Phyllis Pindar's enmity towards him, especially since he told her of his break-off of his engagement to Miss Farrell. He knew she was very protective of her beautiful young living-companion and would be averse to any suitor, even more so of an older man. He managed to keep his emotions subdued, so the suspicious woman became convinced she had been imagining things. Thus he was, so to speak, in her good books again.

Then winter made an early approach, as though to balance out the late overture of fall. Cameron Brent was celebrating Thanksgiving Day by having a party at his cottage in the Lake of the Ozarks region. Robert Brent had surprised Cindra by inviting her to go with him to the affair. The poor young beauty was reticent in asking her benefactress about attending the holiday celebration. She had been invited to go out with Phyllis and her gentleman companion, though the girl had not yet made a commitment to that event.

It so happened an unexpected occurrence decided the outcome. The budding artist had spent the week-end before the holiday practicing on the melodious little "Dove," and so intensely that when she emerged from her doorway on Sunday evening, she collapsed in a faint at the feet of her older companion, who immediately ran for the smelling-salts. The pungent aroma of the olfactory stimulant quickly revived the young musician, and it was then and there Cindra got Phyllis's sanction to go to the holiday celebration at the Lake of the Ozarks, the latter reasoning that her charge needed a complete change, so when she was told of the pending event she gave her whole-hearted approval.

But after the prim secretary had accepted Robert Brent's invitation, she started to get qualms about it. She thought of what a hard drinker he was, and if it had not been for the fact her boss would be there and she would be with Shirlianne, she would have changed her mind and told him she was not going!

Chapter 25
An Unfortunate Incident

It was early in the morning of that fateful Thanksgiving Day when Robert Brent, in his exclusive black sedan (his jaunty yellow sports car having been stored for the winter), drove up to the Pindar apartment. The air was chill and there was a hint of snow in it. This was the first time Phyllis had met the younger Brent son and she noted what a superbly handsome figure of a man he was. She conjured up visions of a very spoilt, rich young man and she began to have second thoughts about allowing her charge to go on the outing, but there was not much she could do now except to request that the young man bring the girl home at a reasonable hour.

Before leaving Saint Louis they picked up two more girls, Jane Janes being one of them, and a young man, all employees of the Brent Company. Cindra's mind was put at ease by this development; she smilingly recalled an old adage of one of her aunts, who used to say that there was "safety in numbers."

The conversation was animated and jocular on the way to the cottage. Our heroine began to relax, so her quips and remarks were just as witty as those of the rest.

The rustic nature of the country-side appealed to Cindra, and she was enjoying the trip into this unfamiliar territory. She had no idea it was so far, and she speculated she would be arriving home at a very late hour. She wondered why Robert had not explained this to Phyllis. Well, they would probably differ as to what constitutes a reasonable hour! They encountered some snow on the way, but when they turned onto the spur road leading to the cottage "Miss Prim" observed that there had been a greater snow-fall in this area, and it had piled up to a considerable depth on the ground. She could see Robert Brent was a cautious driver and she was glad of that, as the road wound up and down some hills. It was obvious a snowplough had been engaged to clear the road, and when they arrived at the dwelling there was a ploughed clearing for the cars as well.

Among the parked cars the secretary recognized her boss's large shiny black sedan and his limousine, which would indicate that Raoul was there and most likely Clarisse as well. Before the motor was turned off, a little figure emerged from the huge cottage dressed in a winter jacket and rubber boots; she ran towards her uncle's car. Her uncle, having come around to the other side to let the ladies out, swooped the child up in his arms; she was squealing with delight! Shirlianne could hardly wait to see her darling Miss Gold and was most concerned when she saw her favourite lady was not wearing boots. However, her uncle went to the trunk of the car and came back with everyone's winter foot-wear. It so happened the owner had phoned his brother very early in the morning informing him of the premature snow-fall and to let his guests know about it before starting out. As soon as Cindra had pulled on her overshoes, she got out of the car, and the young woman and the child hugged each other.

"Oh, Miss Gold, Daddy said you were coming and I couldn't hardly wait!" The child hugged the young woman even tighter.

By this time Cameron Brent had arrived on the scene to welcome his guests. He thanked them for coming, then took his secretary's arm to escort her to the house. Shirlianne, meanwhile, hung on tenaciously to her other arm. The little procession wended its way through the snow to the house, the couple with the child in the lead, Jane Janes on the arm of Robert Brent, and the other couple, arm in arm, bringing up the rear.

What delicious aromas accosted their nostrils as they walked through the front door of the house! The mouth-watering smells were a mixture of turkey, dressing, cranberry, and pumpkin pie spices. After wraps were shed, the group was ushered into a large sitting-room, where they were joined by another, larger group, who were likewise all employees of the Brent Company, so that introductions were unnecessary. Mr. Brent, Sr., was there; he apologized for the absence of his wife, saying she was at home suffering with a migraine headache. However, most of them knew Mrs. John Brent was not accepting of her eldest son's little girl. As a matter of fact, they would have been very surprised to see the elegant lady there. Her son-in-law, Jeremy Beck, an employee, was amongst the group, accompanied by his wife, Nancy, Cameron Brent's sister.

All were invited into a large dining-room to partake of a buffet luncheon. Because of the guests' long trip in the wintry weather, brunch was served a little later than planned. The people formed a line, having received from the host explicit directions to help themselves to the tempting dishes that were spread out on the long tables stretching almost the length of the room on both sides.

The servants were buzzing about bringing in the last-minute edibles. Cindra knew several of them, and she had a few words of greeting with Clarisse, of whom she had become very fond. There were cold cuts of meat, salads of every description, and condiments galore; the prim secretary could not help thinking of how extravagant it was, especially when she looked over at the dessert table. What an array of sumptuous-looking sweets! And she mused to herself that this was only lunch, as Clarisse had told her the turkey dinner would be served around six in the evening.

As Cindra observed the men (chiefly) piling their plates with food, she was perplexed by the fact they were so trim of figure, with only one or two exceptions, and she was certain it was due to the sports activities in which they were involved at the Athletic Club. Anyway, the food looked so appetizing she found herself, as well, taking larger portions than she normally would.

The young lady could not help but think back to her mother's table at home, how every morsel was thought out. Her mother served nourishing meals in which there was enough food for each family member to get their fair share, but there was never anything left over. Well, there would surely be lots of food left over here. She even doubted the servants could eat the rest.

Luncheon over, the folks sauntered back to the tastefully decorated sitting room, where coffee and drinks were to be served. Cindra had not noticed it before, but there was recessed off from the sitting room a little alcove where the alcoholic beverages were being concocted. Robert Brent, as one would suspect, took over as bartender and the drinks flowed freely. The prim secretary decided not to imbibe any further; she had had a little white wine with lunch and it was enough for her. She felt very relaxed and was enjoying the whole thing. Her boss showed her his usual kind attention, and Shirlianne had sat beside her at lunch, being her charming little self and emitting funny remarks that made her laugh. The precocious child really enthralled her.

There were several requests for the budding pianist to play the upright piano that stood at one end of the sitting-room, so she said she would if Shirlianne would sing a song. The latter stood confidently by the piano, and after repeating to her audience the little account of what Miss Gold had told her about the quintuplets in northern Ontario, she sang their lullaby to the willing musician's piano accompaniment. The child made quite a hit and one could see the look of pride on her father's face, and if one was very discerning, one could also detect his look of adoration for the lady pianist.

There being such a surprise snowfall, it had been arranged on the phone, when Cameron Brent got in touch with his brother, that those who wanted to could go snow-shoeing; Robert had brought the three pair of snow-shoes he owned, and they figured there were enough pairs of them, counting those which were already at the cottage, to outfit any of the guests who wished to indulge in the sport. There was an aura of excitement in the air as the participants fastened the strung frames to their boots. "Miss Prim" had never indulged in the sport and could hardly wait to get outside to try out the odd-shaped footgear.

They were ready to set out when the homeowner received a phone call from a not-too-distant neighbour requesting he come to see him right away, as he needed some advice. Thus the little group went on ahead, at the host's suggestion. Cameron said if he was not too long he would try and catch up. He knew their pace would be slow, as most were novices.

Before they went very far, Cindra, not being much of a sportswoman, became tired and said she was going back. Robert figured his brother would be joining them, and since they could still see the house in the distance, the young woman was able to convince him that she could make her own way back.

It was a lovely sunny afternoon, and the snow glistened brightly. Nearing the cottage, the returning snowshoer heard what sounded like a kitten meowing. The faint sound seemed to be coming from a roadway that ran behind the cottage. Cindra detoured on to this road, unaware of the deep ruts and rough terrain the snow concealed. The snow was beginning to melt, but Cindra was off her guard to any dangers that might lurk in her path, so intent was she in discovering just where the urgent animal sounds were coming from. Suddenly she lost her footing; her left foot, with the awkward snow-shoe, was wrenched from under her, causing her to fall. Simultaneously there was an excruciating pain in her left ankle, and her head hit the soppy ground with a thud. Whether it was the severe pain in her ankle or her head hitting the ground that caused her to lose consciousness for a moment was hard to tell. Anyway, the next thing she knew she felt someone's mouth being pressed against hers, and, opening her eyes, she could see it was Cameron Brent. In her dazed state she could feel him removing the snow-shoes and splinting her injured left leg, then gathering her up in his strong arms and carrying her to the cottage. She was fully conscious as the dark-haired man laid her gently on a sofa.

Shirlianne stood by, wailing and crying. "Oh, my darling Miss Gold! What's wrong with her, Daddy, is she dead?" The young child was almost hysterical.

"No, love, she has had an accident and has injured her leg." The father spoke calmly. "You go and ask Clarisse for an ice bag for Miss Gold's ankle."

By this time the accident victim's left ankle had begun to swell, which made the site of the leg injury identifiable. There was no misalignment of bone, so the concerned man considered there to be no fracture; however, he knew she must be taken to hospital, where an X-ray would give a definite diagnosis and she would receive professional treatment.

Since the host had taken a good many of his household staff to help with this celebration at the cottage, it was decided Clarisse could be spared to accompany Raoul and Cameron in taking the injured woman to the hospital. Cameron, by what training he had taken in medicine, knew his secretary's vital signs should be checked periodically, as he deduced her head must have struck the ground, which would account for her unconsciousness.

Shirlianne's father explained to her just what was going on and that she could help her dad and Miss Gold best by being a brave little girl and staying at the cottage to help entertain the guests, whom he would have to desert. This seemed to appeal to the conscientiousness of the child, as she desisted from her requests to go with them and promised, "Daddy, I'll stay here and help to be good to the guest-es, but don't let anything bad happen to Miss Gold."

"Well, my love, I know I can count on you to be a good hostess." Cameron Brent knew his little daughter thrived on praise, and he never missed an opportunity to commend her. He then reassured her he would take good care of Miss Gold.

The injured young woman had fully regained consciousness and had enjoyed the strong cup of tea Clarisse made for her. She was all apologies for the disrupting occurrence and firmly insisted, "I've just twisted my ankle a bit. The ice has made it feel better already. I'm just fine and looking forward to that turkey dinner."

Cameron Brent looked at her. He felt remorse at having suggested the group go snow-shoeing, and more so at the earlier spur-of-the-moment impulse he had to kiss her on the lips, but she had looked so cold and lifeless lying there on the ground where he came upon her returning from his neighbour's place, and he reasoned it might have been a revival tactic. But he had to admit in all honesty he had wanted to do that for some time and he just could not resist.

He felt not a little embarrassed when he stooped to gather her up in his arms again. "I am very sorry, young lady, that this had to happen.... Your ankle really must be seen by a doctor. I've got to get you back to Saint Louis." He spoke in a very gentle tone. He hoped his eyes would not reveal the growing love and adoration he had for her.

Cindra then came to the realization of what was actually transpiring. She did not want to believe this was taking place. However, her wish that it was only a dream was totally crushed as the concerned dark-haired man held her in his arms and announced, "The sooner we get started the better."

Chapter 26
Comforting Thoughts

Well, that was that! They were on their way to Saint Louis. They passed the little group of guests who were returning to the Brent cottage. The group members were carrying their snow-shoes, the deep snow having become soggy and wet, melted by the bright afternoon sun. The unhappy occurrence was related to them and all expressed their sympathy to the afflicted one before they continued on towards their destination.

The black limousine resumed its long journey to the city. The patient's vital signs had remained stable during the trip, so the doctor did not think an overnight stay in the hospital was necessary. The X-ray of the ankle proved negative for broken bones and the doctor assured the patient the application of a firm, figure-of-8 bandage was the only treatment needed to the injured site, but he stressed there was to be no weight-bearing, and a pair of crutches was supplied by the Physiotherapy Department. The uncomfortable patient was administered analgesic medication to relieve the dull ache that had settled in the affected part.

She was soon being carried up the steps to the Pindar apartment by the attentive man who felt so much concern for the unfortunate young beauty. The moment of revelation had arrived when her benefactress had to be told. Cindra had been dreading the thought of it, especially so since it involved her boss. She was hoping Phyllis would not have returned from her Thanksgiving dinner, but it was late and Cindra knew she would be there. And one could see the look of displeasure on Miss Pindar's face when she opened the door and saw her beautiful young charge being cradled in the arms of the handsome man. She softened when things were explained: Cindra said she would have to practice at using the crutches before she could walk with them.

Cameron Brent, before leaving with Clarisse and Raoul, said he would have his own doctor come and see his secretary the next morning and check that everything was alright as regards her condition. He also said she was to take as much time off work as necessary, so that her ankle was completely healed before she returned to her job. He assured her that her pay would continue as usual.

After the injured girl thanked him for his generosity and apologized again for having interrupted his Thanksgiving Day festivities so drastically, Cameron left. There was a feeling of sadness in his breast that his dear young secretary was so incapacitated and so disappointed in not being able to enjoy the turkey dinner. He knew there would be some bleak days in store for her and this really bothered him.

As the door closed behind him, Cindra burst into tears, and any bit of scolding Phyllis wished to inflict on her was forgotten. The older woman, undemonstrative as she was in showing affection, put her arms around the golden-haired girl to console her.

After eating the light supper her friend had prepared for her, the injured girl manipulated herself awkwardly on the wooden crutches, attending to her toilette. At last she was in bed, facing the horrible depression that had been creeping up on her. She picked up her father's black book from the night-table. She turned to an entry he had made when he had faced a health challenge. She could vaguely remember his unfortunate accident. There was a terse note therein stating he had sustained a fracture of the left wrist and he had printed, "Use this" beside the following poem he had copied from the writings of John Whittier:

> The healing of His seamless dress
> Is by our beds of pain,
> We touch Him in life's throng and stress
> And we are whole again.

Once more she was amazed at how deeply spiritual her father had been. He was never a one to wear his religiosity on his sleeve, nor to proselytize, but he certainly had a faith, and she wondered if he knew how much that faith was helping her now. Her ankle even felt better and she knew she could sleep. Besides, she had the sweet memory of a handsome, kindly man's lips on hers.

Chapter 27
Affairs of the Heart

Cameron Brent's thoughtfulness and generosity were instrumental in helping the ill-fated lady through this incapacitating period in her life. He had arranged for Raoul to taxi her to her piano lessons; he had his own doctor call in to check on her every day; he sent Shirlianne on a few extra visits, granted at the child's insistence, to see her; and he phoned her daily to see if there was anything she needed. His intuitive nature cautioned him about paying visits personally to this blond girl of his dreams. He knew Phyllis Pindar would disapprove and he had no intention of making things any harder for his beloved secretary.

However, his romantic nature could not be stifled and it was the very next day after the accident that flowers arrived for the house-bound girl. They had been sent at a time when the man knew Miss Pindar would be there to receive them. And what a bouquet it was—the loveliest bright red American beauty roses the recipient had ever seen, two dozen of them, arranged beautifully in an elegant lead-crystal vase, with the most delicate cut-glass tracery! She could not even imagine what it cost, but it certainly caused the older woman's eyebrows to be raised. The envelope accompanying the flowers had "Miss Gold" written thereon, and printed in the lower corner was "Roses from Picardy's-Florists." The card inside was a regular florist's "Thinking of You" card. It was signed simply, "Love, from Shirlianne and her dad." Cindra recognized her boss's hand-writing and tenderly held the card to her heart for a brief moment. She could not deny the loving feelings for him that were stirring within her, nor did she want to.

There were other occurrences coming out of this too. Cameron Brent, true to his word, sent Dr. Robertson to check on the injured one the morning after the accident and Cindra found him just as pleasant and charming as Shirlianne said he was. The little girl had told her dear Miss Gold about him when he had attended her after her running-away escapade. The child had said, "Dr. Rob's my real bestest friend after my daddy, an' you, Miss Gold, an' Auntie, an' Clarisse an'. . . ." The list of names went on. Cindra smiled to herself as she remembered the incident. And Dr. Robertson, before he departed from that first visit, left a Mickey Mouse balloon, saying he was following the instructions of her employer. The balloon, when inflated, caused the patient to laugh; it endeared the perpetrator to her even more.

Dr. Robertson was paying daily visits to the invalid, but in the evenings, saying it was the time he usually made his house calls. However, it was also the time when Phyllis Pindar was there, and the musician noticed, when she was doing her evening piano practise, that the doctor stayed progressively later each visit, chatting and enjoying a cup of tea with the older woman. Cindra was glad he had revealed to her on his first visit that he was a bachelor. She was also glad for her benefactress that she had found a male friend with whom she could relate on a regular basis. *Who knows what might come of that?* she thought.

John Serenity, ("Bless him," she would say), did his little part. His visitations were a joy to the young lady, and he kept her supplied with reading material about the famed city of Saint Louis. "It's for the times when you get bored with all else," he stated. How glad she was the dear man had brought it. She was liking the city even more, now that she had a romantic interest here!

Included in the literature was a copy of *Cherry Diamond* magazine, a publication of the Missouri Athletic Club. The young woman was very interested in this periodical. She had heard so much about this men's athletic club, referred to as "MAC" by the businessmen with whom she was in contact, especially the Brent men. She enjoyed reading the write-ups about the top athletes, teams that had taken part in Olympic competition, the sporting games of squash, water basketball, bowling, billiards, etc., and she was especially impressed by the mention of the ten-mile swim competition in the Mississippi River in 1906.

She read that there was even a Glee Club and in 1909 twenty men presented its first concert. The editor reported it was on the very night the famous Polish concert pianist, Paderewski, (whom she had always admired), and the Saint Louis Symphony Orchestra, were performing at the Coliseum.

Perusing the article further she found that on March 8th, 1914, the club caught fire. Thirty people in the building were lost and seven firemen died when a wall collapsed on them. The building had been completely gutted by the flames. Reading on, she discovered that a new club, more elegant, was erected on the same site at Fourth Street and

Washington Avenue, and opened in 1916. Of great interest to her was the account of the galas and festivities, and the report that golf was introduced as a MAC sport in 1941.

With this type of amusement to break the piano-practice routine the time slipped by, and soon the young woman's ankle was completely healed. She had gradually started doing, four times a day, the foot exercises Dr. Robertson had written out for her, and strength returned to the affected part. She no longer needed crutches. What a blessed freedom that afforded her! She had often thought of how lucky she was that it was not a wrist she had injured as had happened to her dad. She had been able to perform extra piano practise and Miss Grace had been so nice and encouraging towards her.

She even began to regard the accident as a blessing in disguise, so many good things had come out of it. The staff at work sent colourful cards, some humorous, some very beautiful. There was a pretty one from Robert Brent saying he was sorry and that he felt somewhat responsible for what had happened. Of course there were extra letters and cards from home wishing the absent family member a speedy recovery. Jody sent a crude little drawing of a girl on crutches. He had drawn her face with a pronounced frown and drooping mouth which made her laugh. Phyllis strung the bright tokens of remembrance around the room, and they gave much enjoyment to the injured young lady whilst she convalesced.

There was a surprise visit from Leah Frost and Jane Janes. They had come laden with a gift of delicious fruit from the staff at work and with loving get-well wishes.

Best of all, over the weeks she had received two other lovely floral bouquets from her boss, now she had a small collection of exquisite vases. The second floral vessel was a ceramic Madonna with hands clasped in prayer, (no doubt selected by Shirlianne, thought the recipient). The delicate face was very beautiful, and the vase contained an arrangement of pale mauve orchids. To Cindra it was a breath-taking object. The third vase was of alabaster in a fan-like design that had a dramatic greenish tinge; poised daintily in its opening were several gorgeous gardenias, which freely emitted their heavenly fragrance to perfume the whole room. Besides the pampered feelings these extremely beautiful floral arrangements gave her, they also spoke to her heart and the whisperings there, at times, were overwhelming!

It was strange how she wished it all did not have to end so soon. She had derived such enjoyment from the extra visits with the enchanting little Miss Brent; the chats with the kindly doctor who continued to visit, even though it was no longer necessary for any treatment; and the phone calls from her boss, who continued to express his heartfelt concern. But the day finally came when she was to return to work. Well, anyway, it meant she would see her employer. He had sent Raoul with the odd bit of secretarial work for her to do, mainly to keep her in touch with things, he had explained. She had hoped in vain that he himself might come, yet she could see his strategy in not wanting to upset Miss Pindar.

Chapter 28
A Disappointment

Thus a day in late December the completely recovered "Miss Prim" walked to her work place on Olive Street.

Since her living companion had the day off, she found herself alone with her thoughts, and rather glad of it. Her heart beat rapidly when she let her reflections turn to Cameron Brent; it was going to be hard being near him. She hoped she could be blasé and not show her emotions. She was filled with such amorous feelings they just seemed to overpower her. Had someone asked her later what the weather was like outside, she could not have answered, so preoccupied was she with thoughts of him!

She passed through the familiar plate-glass doors of the business building, and after receiving a friendly "welcome back" greeting from Miss Frost and some of the other employees who had arrived for work early, she was soon on her way up to the second-floor office.

Jane Janes made it a point to be there early that particular morning. When their fond reunion was over, she explained to Cindra just what had been taking place business-wise, then handed her some work requiring attention. She was aware Cindra had been taking care of some of the correspondence at home and was therefore not completely out of touch with what had been transpiring.

The prim secretary, on arising that morning, had attempted to make herself look even more prudish, feeling her "disguise" might help to render her more confident when she met her boss. And before long she had to do just that, but her fears were unnecessary. The man got off the elevator with another businessman whom she had met before. He was dressed immaculately in a dark business suit, white shirt, and expensive tie; her heart skipped a beat at the sight of him. However, he greeted her very formally with a handshake, as did his companion. He handed her some papers, which he requested that she file, then the two men disappeared into his office. The prim secretary sat down abruptly at her desk, a pang of disappointment spreading through her. Was this the man who had sent all the flowers? Was this the man who had kissed her? Who had phoned her every single day when she was away, supposedly to keep her informed about business transactions, but really just to hear her voice? Well, she had been mistaken, all his attention and concern was his innate and natural kindness come her way for a while. What a silly girl she had been! She further said to herself, almost scoldingly, *Well, Miss Prim, you are going to grow up and not act like a silly schoolgirl, giving your heart to a man who just wants to be a friend!*

However, when she had gone into her boss's office to take some dictation, he asked that she accompany himself and some other men, business clients, to lunch and take her notebook. During the luncheon session he was very attentive, and she detected a certain look in his eyes that bespoke more than friendship! She was indeed bewildered, but she was determined to be very businesslike and keep her emotions in tow. In a way she wished Phyllis Farrell was still on the scene.

The first day had been the most difficult. Things seemed to settle down and she was looking forward to Christmas. Her mother was to come and spend the holidays with Phyllis and her. She had handcrafted lovely gifts for friends and relatives during her convalescence, some knit, some crocheted, and she was eager to distribute these presents.

She was not unaware that Cameron Brent was staring at her unusually often, and when she would glance at him, he would look away. Well, she would not misinterpret that! *Strictly business, strictly business*, she told herself.

Nevertheless, she knew she was in love with him. She had better luck with keeping her mind on her job at work, compared to her piano practise at home. She felt it was because her work was all business, cut and dried, whereas her music was romantic; it involved the emotions and seemed to fan her passion so that all she could think about was him!

Chapter 29
A Proposal

Christmas went by so quickly. The weather had been mostly sunny and brisk, with very little snow. Her mother had enjoyed a nice visit, taking delight in the attentions of the "Brent Gentlemen," as she called them. They certainly doted on her—Cameron especially. The older woman and the younger man seemed to have a singular understanding of one another.

Cindra's handcrafted presents were much appreciated. Shirlianne especially liked her fancy knit sweater. Cindra recalled the little girl's remarks: "Oh, you beeu-tiful, beeu-tiful Miss Gold, you're so good to me." And her boss, he was quite surprised and really pleased with the cable-stitch sweater he received from her.

It seemed a rather long winter to our heroine. The cold temperature had an adverse effect on her left ankle, and she experienced a dull ache in that region at times.

Yet, on the plus side her musical endeavours were progressing well, and through determination she was able to keep her emotions under control. Her love for the dark-haired man had not lessened, but she had been able to channel these feelings into the fantasy that she was becoming a famous pianist, and nothing was to stand in her way!

These imaginings somehow made it easier to bear.

Also there was her father's little black book with its gems of wisdom. She was so thankful for this legacy from her father. It had been a great comfort to her when she faced the initial pangs of homesickness, and its inspirational thoughts and biblical passages were stirring within her deep soul-feelings that were hard for her to explain.

And there was Shirlianne; her visits were very precious to the two ladies. The younger one missed her companionship at church on the Sundays she was not there. How she adored that little girl! The child was doing very well at her schoolwork, under the guidance of her private tutor, and she was a great joy to those who loved her.

With the onset of spring there was excitement in Cameron Brent's office. He was to go on a business trip to Paris, and one fine spring day he asked his secretary if she could accompany him on this business endeavour. He explained that he needed a person with experience to handle the secretarial affairs, and, judging by her work performance, she was certainly the one in the office who was the most qualified for the important job. He made it clear to her in a very careful and wise way that his thoughts were strictly business oriented.

Well, Phyllis Pindar was of a different opinion. That evening, when the excited girl divulged the news to her during the supper hour, she was absolutely furious, and after the meal the older woman had the superintendent go down to the basement for the young lady's trunk. She told her she was to pack her things and get back home where she would be away from the wiles of such a man. She said she thought he was different, but now she could see he was like all the rest, and she said to the girl in a pitying tone, "To think he would suggest such a thing to you; you can tell where his mind is!"

Cindra was visibly shaken by this verbal attack on the man she loved. She meekly responded, "It's not what you think, Phyllis; his father has recommended a piano teacher in Paris. She'd been a successful concert pianist in her day, and Mr. Brent says that I could study with her, so it's not as though I'd be forgetting my music. Also, his father would be accompanying us."

The older woman did not put her thought of *Silly girl, she doesn't have any idea of what this might lead to!* into spoken words; she just emphasized the fact she must remove herself from this situation, and offered to help her pack.

The young woman could not get to sleep that night; even her father's memo book did not console her. Over and over again in her mind ran the dreadful thought, *How can I go away from the man I love and never see him again? How can I? How can I!* And the more she tried to extinguish the thought, the more insistent it belaboured her troubled mind.

Frantically she turned once again to her revered book and a particular entry caught her attention: "Thoughts held in mind produce after their kind." Her father had scrawled in bold handwriting, "from the writings of Chas. Fillmore." She felt her dad was really being her mentor right then. She took the advice and changed her thought pattern. *Things will change. I do not have to go home, I don't have to leave here.* Several times she repeated it, then, after thanking her Creator for the help she had received, she fell into a deep sleep.

She even slept in, but on awakening the old negative thoughts crept into the young woman's mind. As she pulled up the window shade her eyes feasted on the trees, resplendent in their spring foliage, her ears aroused to the cheerful song of a robin, and she immediately recalled the affirmation she had repeated during the night that things would change for her.

It was difficult for her to hold to such positive thoughts when Phyllis, who had taken the day off work, phoned the Brent business establishment after breakfast, and asked Miss Frost to relay the message to Miss Gold's employer that she was leaving her job with the firm and was returning to Canada.

It was not long before there was an excited knock on the door; the older woman opened it and there stood Cameron Brent! The younger woman had just come into the sitting room dressed in her magenta gown, and her long, blond hair framed her lovely face. The man impulsively rushed past the woman at the door and fell down on his knees in front of the girl he adored. "Miss Gold . . . Cindra, will you marry me and come to Paris with me as my wife?" The man's voice was full of emotion; he looked at her with pleading eyes.

She dropped down on her knees in front of him and he drew her towards him. Her voice rang out as one very sure of the answer: "Yes, I'll marry you."

The older woman, beholding the scene, was flabbergasted. For once she was at a loss for words; but there was so much going through her mind: *What is my precious pianist thinking of! What about her career? What will her mother think? Oh, dear!!*

It was the man who, in his business-like way, sprang to his feet and, after gently helping his loved one up, began to organize things. It was not his nature to ignore the feelings of another person, so he explained to Miss Pindar that Cindra would not be giving up her plans for a musical career. She would be carrying on with her lessons in Paris and he would be taking other office help. Thus his beloved could devote all of her time to her art.

The first thing on the agenda was to call Mrs. Gold in Canada. Much to Phyllis's surprise, the woman was just ecstatic. She told Cameron she would be very happy to have him as a son-in-law and that yes, she would come down for the wedding and probably her daughter Madge with her husband would come too. He was to let them know the date as soon as possible.

"Now we must go and get the rings, my dear, and shop for your trousseau." The dark-haired man spoke decisively whilst looking at his lady love.

The young woman had not yet recovered from the event that had just taken place. All she could think of was the relief she was experiencing at no longer having to hide the deep feelings she had for him. She even unthinkingly put on her office clothes and hastily effected her "Miss Prim" coiffure.

The enraptured couple sped off in his big black sedan, leaving behind the stunned Miss Pindar, who still was unable to fully grasp what had so unexpectedly taken place that morning. She had known her charge admired her employer, but she had no idea that the girl had fallen in love with him.

Chapter 30
A Joyous Occasion

The enamoured couple, after the shopping spree was over, made their way to the Brent business building on Olive Street. It was a rainy day in April but even the raindrops, pelting down on the rooftop of the car, were strumming a love song. The engagement ring, a flawless diamond, had to be shown, and the young secretary's working associates were wishing them well. The women especially were all agog at the huge precious stone in its raised setting.

Mr. Brent, Sr., was very receptive to the thought of Cindra becoming his daughter-in-law. He embraced her and said jokingly that he wished he was forty years younger. The young woman had liked John Brent from the start. His warm caring attitude towards her mother and towards her made her feel accepted in this world of "high society," as Phyllis Pindar called it. Little did she know then how very much she would appreciate his loving support as time went by.

The betrothed couple managed to get past the well-wishers and find seclusion in Cameron's office. It was there, in the privacy of that room, that the handsome man held his bride-to-be in an embrace. Cindra felt her heart was going to burst, so overcome with passion was she. It was then she realized she would no longer be working here. All she could think of was how she would miss being near him during the day. Oh well, she considered, there would be the weekends with him and the nights! She never in the world thought she would be taking the place of Miss Farrell, the glamorous woman who used to visit him in that very office.

It was the man who had to come down to earth and start on the plans. There was so much to do. Jane Janes would take over the betrothed one's job until a new secretary could be found.

Together the couple figured out the wedding date; it would be in two weeks, as the businessman planned to sail to France as soon as possible with his new wife. Cindra suggested to him that she could do the secretarial work; she was so interested in the business dealings, and it would be a challenge. "Besides," she told her fiancé, "I studied

French in high school, Cameron, and I'll be able to help if a language problem arises." The utterance of his name came so naturally to her, so many times had she repeated it to herself, and she loved his name.

They finished the work that had to be done in the office, then took off in the black motor car to the Brent estate in Ladue. The young woman could hardly believe that this would be her home. She thrilled to the thought of it!

Shirlianne had finished her studies for the day and was gathering up a doll in the reception hall when the couple entered through the front door of the mansion. "Oh, Miss Gold, have you come to have dinner with us at the Columns? Oh, Daddy, thanks a lot for bringing her." The little girl spoke excitedly, she was visibly very happy to see her favourite lady and ran towards her with open arms.

The young woman stooped down to give her a hug, and the two of them embraced one another in bunny-hug fashion, neither wanting to let go.

The father spoke gently to his little daughter. "Shirlianne, Daddy is going to marry your Miss Gold."

The child released herself abruptly from the arms of the woman and looked at her father. Her words came fast and fervently: "Oh, Daddy, is Miss Gold going to be my mother?"

"Yes, dear child, she is." The father obviously took delight in revealing this to his child.

"Oh, Miss Gold!" The little girl hollered out the name, and she was in the arms of her beloved lady friend and hugging her even tighter than before. She then switched over to her father and he stooped down to receive the excited little girl in his arms.

"Daddy, you told me not to wish for Miss Gold to be my mother, but I'm sorry, Daddy, I've been prayin' for that." There were tears in the child's eyes as she spoke. She then went back to the lady she had prayed would become her mother and embraced her again, this time in bear-hug fashion, exclaiming zestfully, "My darling Miss Gold, you wonderful lady! Oh, you're gonna be my mother, I love you, I love you."

The man looked at his little daughter. Ordinarily he would correct her when her grammar lapsed into slang, but he let it go this time. He just wanted to enjoy the closeness the three of them felt at that moment, a closeness hard to describe.

Before the little group had dinner, Cindra phoned Phyllis Pindar to let her know she would not be home for supper, with her fiancé instructing her to invite the woman there for the meal; he said Raoul would go for her. However, Phyllis declined the invitation, explaining that she was expecting a guest herself. She did not say who it was, nor did the young woman ask. She detected an odd tone in the older woman's voice, a kind of hurting quality, which aroused a feeling of sadness in Cindra.

Subsequently there was Miss Grace to be called. The pianist just told her she would be unable to take her lesson that night, due to an unexpected occurrence, and she would have to have a talk with her at her next lesson.

It is difficult to imagine the happy meal that the three persons shared together. Shirlianne insisted on saying grace.

"I don't know what you have done to this child, Cindra, but she insists that I close my eyes tightly and thank God for my food. Next thing she'll have me down on my knees!" The father had a twinkle in his eye when he said those words, and they all laughed congenially.

The beautiful young woman thought to herself that at last she had found her true place, and her heart and mind sang with exultant joy that reached to the depths of her very soul. She did not stay late with her new family. The perceptive gentleman could see that she was tired and told her he would take her back to the Pindar apartment. Thus, after she and her new daughter sang a few songs, one of which was "Roses of Picardy," the song that reminded her of the first beautiful bouquet of American Beauty Roses her beloved had sent to her, the three departed in the large black sedan for the metropolis.

Of course, Shirlianne had to go into the apartment and say hello to Auntie, and her appearance acted as a sort of buffer between the older woman and the newly engaged couple. The little girl ran to Auntie and hugged her, Auntie responding in like fashion, such was the love bond between them. Then she saw Dr. Robertson and she shared a hug with her "Doc Rob."

After Dr. Robertson congratulated the couple and fond greetings were over, Shirlianne and her father took their leave, but not before Cameron had taken Cindra's hand in his and brought it to his lips in fond farewell.

The newly engaged woman thereupon went over to Phyllis, tears in her eyes, and when the older woman saw them, she put her arms around the young lady and said in a very sincere tone, "My dear young musician, I'm very happy for you."

"Oh, Phyllis, I hope you're not too disappointed in me, I tried so hard not to, but I couldn't help falling in love with him." The young girl's voice was trembling.

With that, the hurt feelings of the benefactress were assuaged and the two apartment sharers became completely reconciled.

Dr. Robertson asked to talk with Cindra privately. He wanted to advise her in regards to a subject that he, in his sensitivity to the young lady's feelings, knew would be a delicate one. In a kindly manner he told her she would probably have a problem with her husband-to-be; the doctor suspected the man might not be able to consummate the marriage. He said that psychologically the man had suffered great trauma when his beautiful young first wife died in childbirth, and that once, when he counselled him, Cameron had stated he never again would touch a woman and cause her to lose her life! The doctor could see the naive young woman was embarrassed; her fair complexion took on a rosy hue and she was avoiding eye contact with him. He decided not to pursue the subject any further, so he wound up the private conversation by saying, "You know, my dear, when we're going through a difficult experience we think it's the worst thing in the world and we're apt to lose hope, but relationships take a great deal of patience, and even more, understanding, and if these are adhered to, eventually good will manifest itself, if we believe it will."

He then took her hands in his and said, "You've chosen a very kind and caring man to be your husband, and I wish you every happiness. I know you will find it."

Whereupon the good doctor departed, and Cindra, alone in her room, was left to ponder over what he had said. How she wished to be in the arms of her beloved, just to be close to him!

Chapter 31
The Three Phyllises

Phyllis Brent, Cameron's mother, was infuriated by the thought of her son marrying his lowly secretary. The woman, whose marriage plans for him had been thwarted, called the working-girl a gold digger, and wanted to have nothing to do with her. She told her husband, when he asked her what she would be wearing to the wedding, "I'm not going to the wedding. I don't want to be in the same room as that hussy!"

John Brent, though not going along with his wife's ideas, accepted her as she was, and he did not try to change her. To him she was still the beautiful woman he had married, and they had enjoyed raising their children together. The man was quite satisfied with his domestic life. Albeit, there were other ladies with whom he could and did socialize, and he quite enjoyed the indisputable freedom his wife allowed him. Actually, she was a rather superficial woman, and she was quite happy with the life-style with which her husband had provided her. She knew he was still enthralled with her great beauty, and there was a genuine amicability between them that would far outlast any romantic love they might have.

Then there was Phyllis Farrell. She still had hopes that her handsome ex-fiancé was going to make her his wife. She and Mrs. Brent, Sr., had been trying to hoodwink him into changing his mind as regards the engagement breakup. Besides being very fond of her, Mrs. John Brent knew the woman she wanted her oldest son to marry had inherited a fortune. Thus, having her for a daughter-in-law would mean added wealth and prestige for the family. But the two women were unaware of the change in Cameron's affections. Nor could they have understood the bond of love that had grown and was woven like a priceless thread into the lives of the three people who would soon constitute the Cameron Brent family.

And there was Phyllis Pindar: She had kept Cameron Brent in tow as long as she could. Nevertheless, her violent reaction at hearing the news that he wanted to take Cindra to France as his secretary had certainly incited him to action and fostered in him the courage to propose to his lady love.

Those were the three Phyllises in the unfortunate man's life. All seemed to be a drawback to him, somehow: His mother had caused him so much anguish when he made the decision to keep his infant daughter; his ex-fiancée had been instrumental in causing his little daughter to run away, the consequences of which episode threatened the child's health; and Miss Pindar had certainly discouraged him from having any kind of a courtship with the woman he loved.

Chapter 32
Pre-Wedding Arrangements

Plans in plenty were taking place. Mrs. Gold as well as her daughter and son-in-law, Madge and Karl Reidit, were flying to Saint Louis for the upcoming marriage ceremony, and they were bringing with them the couple's son, Jody, who was a year older than Shirlianne. Little Patsy was to remain at home with grandmother and grandfather Reidit.

Madge, when she heard the young child would be going to France with the newlyweds, suggested she fly back to Ontario with them instead. Jody, she reasoned, could ease the pain of separation from her parents for the little girl, with his tales of the farm and its animals and the interesting events taking place there. His mother thought that if anyone could colour it glad, Jody could! Cameron Brent was in full agreement with the plan, but it did take him awhile to convince his bride-to-be that this would be best for Shirlianne.

Mrs. Gold, Marsha, the second oldest Gold daughter, and the Reidit family were to stay at the mansion in Ladue. Barbara May, the second youngest Gold sibling, the registered nurse, was unable to get time off duty for the wedding, so the groom sent her the money for a flight to Saint Louis for a visit after the couple returned from their trip overseas.

The guests arrived as scheduled, Raoul picking them up at the airport in the black limousine, and it was a happy group of people who gathered for breakfast around the large circular table, out on the marble-floored patio, the next day. The splendour of spring permeated the air, the garden was bursting with new life, and the risen sun seemed to be giving its approval by the welcome of its warmth. The birds, not to be outdone, added their songs to the scene, as though heralding gladly the nuptials to come.

All of the domestic staff were buzzing about, making certain the breakfast buffet was just as the master of the house had ordered it. Clarisse was put in charge of ensuring that the guests were comfortable, and that servants were available to see to the visitor's needs when any arose. The master of the house was due back any minute, having gone to pick up his wife-to-be.

Shirlianne and Jody, who had met the night before, became fast friends almost at sight, and that morning the house rang with their squeals of delight. Their abandonment to merrymaking was a joy to behold.

After the arrival of the betrothed couple, the breakfast began. The master of the house had to sit next to Mrs. Gold. She insisted on it, nor did he object. It was obvious the two had become fast friends long before this day. He put his arm around her affectionately and said, "Well, Mom, do you think you can put up with me for a son?"

She looked at him, and, smiling, she responded cheekily, "Well, I picked you, didn't I?" This repartee brought forth laughter from everyone.

Cindra sat beside the children, her precious little girl snuggling close to her. Then Jody, addressing his mother, asked her something, and with that the little girl piped up, "I have a mother too," and she started to hug her adored Miss Gold.

Finally the child's father had to speak to her. "Now, Little Miss, you sit up properly and eat your breakfast, and let your mother eat hers." He glanced at the young woman lovingly, and he thought about how beautiful she looked.

And she did look beautiful. Her lovely blond hair was drawn back softly with a bow at the nape of her neck. He was used to seeing her in her "Miss Prim" hairstyle; his eyes feasted on her enhanced beauty. She was wearing one of the lovely suits he had bought her. It was a buff colour. She had taken off the jacket, revealing the ivory-coloured silk blouse. It had a softly draped scarf-like collar that crossed at the shoulder, one end falling towards the back, the other end to the front, and to secure these in place her betrothed had bought her an exquisite amber pin. As her eyes met his, he made the motion of throwing a kiss with his lips, and they smiled at one another. The happiness she felt at that moment was indescribable.

There was more shopping to be done, so the prospective couple took their leave after breakfast to do just that. Shirlianne insisted on going with her new mother. Finally her father had to reproach her; however, his tone was gentle as he said, "Shirlianne, you're going to have to share your new mother with your father. Remember, darling, she is also going to be my wife. You can go shopping with her tomorrow for your clothes when I'm at the office. Besides, we have to attend to some important business."

The little girl had been content with her father's reasoning, and after a fond farewell was exchanged with her parents, she and Jody disappeared into the garden.

Before the master of the house left with his wife-to-be, he informed his guests that Raoul was standing by with the limousine to take anyone shopping, if they so wished. Then the enamoured couple departed, hand in hand, as if walking on air, as is the way with people in love.

Chapter 33
The Wedding Day

The wedding day arrived, with clouds threatening rain in the morning, but by noon they had disappeared and the sun shone brightly to bless the nuptials of our fair heroine.

The ceremony took place in the small chapel of Christ Church Cathedral on Thirteenth Street. Cindra knew the seating would be adequate, as the guest list was not large. She was glad her husband-to-be had sent her sister Marsha a monetary gift, which enabled her at the last moment to change her mind and come. He had had a hunch the delay in her decision was because of her finances; being in the bridal party would put an impossible strain on her budget.

Seated on the bride's side in the chapel beside her mother and her sister Madge was Phyllis Pindar, the long-time family friend, who was accompanied by Dr. Robertson. Her dear friend, John Serenity, was to have come but was ill at the time. Miss Grace had been invited, but she too was unable to attend.

Of the Brent family, only Mr. Brent, Sr., and Cameron's brother Robert were in attendance. The groom so wished his mother would come; however, he had married, the first time, a woman whom, when it came right down to it, she had chosen. This time he knew he was truly in love, and he vowed that nothing was going to stand in his way! Also added to the Brent list of guests were Clarisse and Raoul. Cindra especially wanted them to be included.

The moment had arrived; the groom waited anxiously at the altar. Jody, in his best suit, was the ring-bearer and carried the rings on a white satin pillow. In his nervousness he tripped on his way down the aisle, and all waited with bated breath, hoping the rings would not go rolling; fortunately they did not.

Shirlianne, looking adorable in her pink organdy dress with its frill upon frill, was the flower girl. She carried a small, white, wicker basket from which cascaded an arrangement of delicate pink sweetheart roses. She followed behind Jody and when she spied Auntie in the scant congregation, she raised a little white gloved hand, waved to her, and the two of them exchanged loving smiles. This caused Auntie to whisper to Dr. Robertson, "At last that dear little thing will have a real mother."

The good doctor nodded his approval.

Marsha, the maid of honour, looking lovely and feminine in her rose chiffon dress, followed next in the small procession.

Then Cindra Gold, on the arm of Karl Reidit, who was to give her away, made her way down the aisle. Gasps came from the onlookers when they caught sight of the beautiful bride. Her gown was a long white satin one, cut on very simple lines. Her bouquet comprised a few white cala lilies, and she carried a white prayer-book in her lace-gloved hands. The radiance emanating from her veiled countenance was breathtaking.

At that moment, with her arm resting on the arm of the young man who was her brother-in-law, Cindra felt the very presence of her deceased father, and the love she felt coming from him brought a tear to her eye. She also knew there was another "presence" surrounding her; it was the Lord of her being, blessing her in that holy sanctuary.

The groom, waiting in his formal striped-pants and black swallow-tailed coat, was almost mesmerized as he caught sight of his beloved, and when he knelt beside her at the altar, he would have described his feelings as sublime.

After the vows were solemnized, the groom was instructed to kiss the bride. He raised the veil from the young woman's face, and his lips sought hers. It was only the second time they had used this caress of endearment, and Cindra's heart was pounding. The sacred pledge had been sealed with a kiss.

The Eucharist having ended, and the signing of the register having been completed, the priest then addressed the congregation, saying, "Ladies and gentlemen," and pointing to the couple, he announced, "I present to you Mr. and Mrs. Cameron Brent."

The happy couple walked slowly up the aisle, her arm on his, to the strains of a familiar wedding march. They were united at last, and there was a little girl following in the recession, who was one of the happiest children in Saint Louis that day. She had her very own mother.

It was a joyous group that congregated outside of the church; confetti was thrown, and hugs, kisses, and congratulations were exchanged.

Cameron had arranged for photographs to be taken in the garden at the Columns, so the wedding cortège headed for the home in Ladue, Raoul driving the black limousine with Clarisse beside him, and the bride, groom, Shirlianne, and Jody therein. Cindra had noticed that the little girl wanted to be near her, so she convinced her husband to have the children come with them.

Robert Brent drove Marsha, Madge, and Karl to the Ladue estate; Mr. Brent, Sr., took Mrs. Gold in his car; and Phyllis and Dr. Robertson chauffered the priest, whom the groom had invited to the wedding feast.

And feast it was! After the photographs were all taken, the little group sat down to a sumptuous meal. There was champagne, laughter, and music; glad sounds resounded in the huge dining-hall with its crystal chandeliers and its windows with the elegant velvet drapes.

The bride had importuned the groom to have Clarisse and Raoul join the guests at the table, and the man finally had agreed. It was not customary for him to have any of his household staff dine at the table with him, but he found himself not being able to say no to the requests of his chosen mate. One could not label Cindra superstitious, but she did take note of the fact that the addition of the revered couple brought the count of those dining from thirteen to fifteen.

Cameron Brent desired to make a toast to the ladies. He started with Mrs. Gold, first saying if it had not been for her, he would not have the beautiful woman who was his bride at his side right now; then the rest of the ladies were mentioned with special little comments befitting each one. When he got to the point of toasting the bride, he became very eloquent and so verbose that his brother finally spoke out good-humoredly, saying, "All right, Cam, you've embarrassed the lady long enough." These words sent a little giggle through the group.

The groom was not happy, of course, about the fact his mother was not there; however, he had quite accepted things as they were and took her absence in a matter-of-fact way, only hoping some day it might be different.

His bride, on the other hand, felt exactly opposite about it. She was aware her mother-in-law was not in favour of the marriage, but she was unaware her feelings of disapproval were so strong that she would miss her son's wedding. The young woman did not reveal to her husband how she was agonizing over this rebuff; in her heart of hearts she wanted so much to meet her as family and to be friends with her. She could only hope that some day things would change and as time went by, during her quiet times, she kept praying fervently for this to happen.

Chapter 34
A Problem Solved

It was a wise decision they had made to have Jody come with his family and have Shirlianne become acquainted with him in her home setting. It eased the parting from her father and her new mother.

When Mrs. Gold assured the child, "Grandma will be going to Canada with you too," the little girl's face brightened.

She spoke with amazement. "Oh, that's right; I have a Grandma too." She looked at the older woman and she could see she was lovingly accepted by her, but she clung until the last minute to her new mother, and at the airport she had her father promise to bring her mother back with him. Then the little group flying back to Canada disappeared after ascending the steps that led into the aeroplane.

The concerned couple had purposely arranged their departure for France to take place after the child was on her way to Canada with her new relatives. And so, it was not until two days after the wedding that they started out on their overseas trip.

The bride was enthralled with the exquisite wardrobe that she now possessed. The lovely clothes gave her such pleasure, and she felt very relieved at having shed her "Miss Prim" image. She gloried in her beauty and femininity.

All on board the ship could see Cameron Brent adored his wife. But it was not long before Cindra realized he had put her high on a pedestal. He almost worshipped the ground she walked on, but the young woman was not satisfied with that. She was not a goddess, she was a live human being and he was the handsome man she had married. Her passion for him was great. He stirred in her feelings she found difficult to control.

Had time been not so pressing, she would not have chosen for the wedding day the date on which it occurred, as for her it was an inconvenient time of the month, conjugality-wise; however, they were several days out to sea and their marriage had still not been consummated. He was loving enough as far as it went, with holding hands, lip-kisses, and other fond gestures, but she wanted him too as a lover, and eventually she wanted to bear his children.

She was becoming very frustrated. She wondered if there was anything wrong with him physically. She even began to wonder if he preferred men, but that thought she soon scrapped as there was no indication of it.

She went through a whole gamut of feelings from anger to hostility to peevishness. She tried to calm herself by reading her father's memo book, but she ended up throwing it across the state-room! And Phyllis had made accusations about the man, saying he wanted to take her on this trip as his secretary, for erotic reasons! "What a joke!" Cindra exclaimed out loud.

She would try womanly wiles on him! She started flirting with other men and she realized what a dangerous tactic that was! She was practically having to fight them off, and her knight in shining armour (and she thought how true, in armour!) was allowing her to have a fling, watching with sad eyes and always there when things were seeming to get too hot for her to handle!

Oh, how she loved her husband! He was everything she wanted in a man; perhaps she would have to settle for a life of celibacy and try to control her passion. She knew the mystics did it. She would pray about it, she believed that God answered prayer, and she pleaded, "Oh God, will you please help me?"

A few minutes later she thought of Dr. Robertson and what he had tried to tell her when he had the private talk with her. A voice within her was telling her to talk to the ship's doctor. She had met him, Dr. Coniker. She was glad he was an older man and presented himself more as a fatherly figure. She was embarrassed, but she just had to talk to someone.

She arranged an appointment with Dr. Coniker. Though the young woman was shy and ill at ease in discussing such delicate matters, she found that he was very understanding and lent a sympathetic ear.

The good doctor had a talk with the man in question, and they discussed his great fear of losing another wife in childbirth. Dr. Coniker pointed out to him that this irrational dread was disturbing his psyche and causing impotency. Ways of preventing conception were enumerated and the doctor cautioned the man, saying that his wife had her needs and if he did not fulfill his matrimonial responsibility, he might find himself the father of another man's child!

The man was visibly shaken by what the doctor had told him as regards his wife; he realized how self-centered he had been, and he felt remorse at not having identified the problem. But it had been so long....

It was then that the trip miraculously changed for the young wife. She was loved with a passion beyond her fondest dreams, and the conjugal bonds were cemented, strong and firm and beautiful!

Chapter 35
Paris in the Spring

The sea voyage agreed with them both. Cindra, not being much of a sportswoman, was content to watch her husband at the various activities. She did join him for a little swimming, and of course the dancing at night was a pleasure they both enjoyed.

However, when it became known that Mrs. Cameron Brent was a talented musician, she was in demand to give some renditions on the piano at the cocktail hour, and the proud husband was overjoyed to see his wife happy and jubilant again, and feeling fulfilled.

The young bride was hoping they would set up a little housekeeping apartment, but her spouse dissuaded her. He wanted her to be free to pursue her piano studies. A secretary was arranged for him, a piano was brought to their hotel suite, and Cindra was able to spend as much time as she desired on her music when her husband was working.

The teacher, whom Mr. Brent, Sr., had recommended and contacted, was expecting the newlywed couple. Thus, one evening they visited her at her villa, which was not far from Paris. What a delightful evening it was! The country estate, heady with the fragrance of its spring flowers in bloom, was beautiful; Mrs. Veronique Beauchamp was charming, and the two ladies took to one another on the first meeting. It was obvious that the retired concert pianist, now teacher of music, held John Brent in high regard. Cameron Brent was beginning to understand his father's frequent visits to France (in connection with business, of course)!

There was a trip to Austria and in Vienna they waltzed in a magnificent ballroom where the lilting strains of the music of Johann Strauss matched their mood and their love. They worshipped in Notre Dame Cathedral, and Cindra's thoughts returned to the little chapel in Saint Louis where they were married. She experienced the thrill all over again by remembering how she felt when the priest presented them to the congregation as Mr. and Mrs. Cameron Brent.

They attended the opera, watched a ballet, toured the Luxembourg Gardens, laughing with the French children who were sailing their toy boats in the pool of those gardens. They walked under Napoleon's Arc de Triomphe, and ascended, via an elevator, the Eiffel Tower, where they indulged in a scrumptious meal in one of the grand restaurants. They wandered along the lovely tree-lined avenue, the Champs Élysées, and strolled arm in arm by the River Seine, two people filled with the magic and the charisma of Paris, and the indulgence of their intense love.

Chapter 36
A Choice

Cameron Brent's business trip was successful and all went well. Mr. Brent, Sr., knew that with his oldest son at the helm, it would be so.

The young wife had made great strides in her piano technique; Mrs. Beauchamp suggested she stay in France to study further. When Cameron told Cindra what the good lady had said, the young woman gasped, "Oh, Cam, to be away from you, I couldn't bear it. I don't care about a musical career, I just want to be with you, and there's Shirlianne."

They were in the bedroom of their hotel suite. The young woman sat at the dressing table, brushing her golden hair. The pink hue of her negligee matched the rosy glow on her face; she was radiant. Cameron came towards her and took her in his arms. His voice was soulful as he spoke: "Oh, darling, you are my Cinder of Gold, it would break my heart to leave you here and have to part from you." His kisses were hot on her lips, and they were wrapped in each other's arms, away in their land of ecstasy.

Chapter 37
The Voyage Back

The parting of the piano pupil and Veronique Beauchamp was an emotional one; they had grown very fond of one another. They had laughed when Cindra told the woman of her first piano lesson with Miss Grace in Saint Louis and how frightened she had been. She expressed thanks for the invitation the kind woman had given her to stay with her at Beauchamp Villa and further her musical studies, but she said she wanted to be with her husband.

The divorced woman said she understood completely how Cindra felt about separating from the man she loved and sending him back to the States alone. She confided to the younger one that she wished John Brent could come to Paris more often, and from the expression on Mrs. Beauchamp's face, the piano pupil surmised that they were lovers.

Cindra knew she would miss the dear woman and that she would leave a bit of her heart in Paris. She would never forget her visit! She now had such wonderful memories of her sojourn in France, the land of one of her favourite writers, Alexandre Dumas, who had written of the French Revolution in his novels *The Count of Monte Cristo* and *The Three Musketeers*. She loved the latter book, especially as her husband's second name was Aramis. This name was chosen by his mother, who was a romantic and had named her firstborn after one of the famous musketeers.

She had almost the same predilection for Alexandre Dumas the Younger, who, like his father, was a novelist. One of his novels, *Camille,* had provided the plot for Verdi's opera *La Traviata,* which she had so enjoyed whenever she heard it on the Saturday afternoon radio broadcasts back home in Canada. How long ago it seemed! Ah, the memorabilia, and she was still adding to it with this remarkable honeymoon! How truly pleasurable it would be to look back upon, she mused. But alas, these musings had to cease, and she had to pack for their return voyage. The thought of going home to the Columns and to her new role as mother of the child her husband and she loved so much spurred her on.

The sea voyage back to America was just wonderful, unlike the journey to Europe, which had been marred by the adjustment the husband had to make to married life. They could revel in their love, and that is just what they did.

They stood side by side at the rail on the promenade deck, talking and making plans for the future; they enjoyed deeper discussions on the meaning of life, and though their views were not all alike, they were compatible. Sometimes they watched the starlit sky; they felt in tune with the universe and their spirits were uplifted! Cindra, on pondering these things, came to the realization that she had not only found a kindly man for a husband, she had also found a soul-mate!

Chapter 38
A Happy Reunion

Back home there were some adjustments to be made. The master bedroom had to be altered to accommodate a woman as well as the master. The first Mrs. Cameron Brent had separate sleeping quarters, but that did not satisfy the second one. So the master of the house changed the adjoining bedroom into a sitting-room for his beloved.

There was also another bedroom, which the man of the house modified. It was a large room and he had it stripped of furniture. He had a bedding firm construct a very large, thin, circular mattress, and he announced to his wife that that was where their exercises before dinner would take place. Cameron had to laugh at the astonished look his wife gave him. He drew her close and spoke enthusiastically: "My darling, once you get doing them you will enjoy them, and I'll wager you'll not want to miss them."

All Cindra could do was to laugh skeptically and marvel at the way her husband could talk her into such a thing, and she knew he had!

The day after the couple arrived back from France, Shirlianne returned from Canada with her grandmother Gold. What a reunion that was! The little girl did not know whom to greet first, so she grabbed them both around their legs, and the father had to sweep the child up in his arms to prevent them both from losing their footing! Hugs and kisses were exchanged, and after this Shirlianne went into such an accolade about the farm and Jody and baby Patsy that her father had to silence her, saying that her grandmother must be given a chance to speak too. Mrs. Gold laughed at the exuberance of the child. She remarked, "My land, I don't know where that child gets all her energy!"

When they arrived home at the Columns from the airport, the entire staff of servants lined up to welcome home Shirlianne. It had been the first time the child had been away for that long a duration, and they had missed the happy little girl's presence.

Again at dinner the same night, the child was full of chatter. She told her new mother and her father about the farm animals and about Jody's dog, "Spooky." Then she said something that caused her father to cringe: "And Daddy, Jody's mother had baby Patsy, and she didn't die, and I'd like a sister just like baby Patsy."

Cindra noticed her husband's reaction to the child's remark, and she knew she would have some convincing to do if Shirlianne ever got her wish.

Later in the evening, when the new wife's mother was having a private chat with her, the mother told her that, on seeing Cindra's step-daughter, the people back home surmised that she had married a black man.

Chapter 39
"The Wishes"

Before Cameron Brent's mother-in-law left, he and Cindra took her to his bank and arranged for a draft to be drawn up in her name for the purchase of the home in Belleville on which the good woman had had her eye and had told the man about when he had visited in the Ontario city. She never dreamed he would eventually purchase it for her. However, it stuck in his mind, and with his wife's approval, he implemented the plan that was to give the lady the fine new residence that had been her dream house.

"Sonny, I never in the world thought I'd fly up in an aeroplane like the rich. You've seen to that, and now the dream house!" The woman's voice was ecstatic as she continued, "You're spoiling me, and I love it."

Cameron genuinely liked his mother-in-law, and he liked her directness; he gave her a big hug and told her that she deserved it, for giving him such a beautiful wife.

Living became, indeed, a wonderful experience for the little family who lived in the house called the Columns. Every day was a day to celebrate life!

Shirlianne was progressing favourably with her schoolwork; actually, the tutor said she was brilliant. She had loved her stay at the Reidit farm and she was missing Jody very much; however, her dad promised her another trip to Canada, which at times he wished he had not, as she kept asking when.

Cindra had resumed her piano lessons with Miss Grace; the latter was amazed at the progress her pupil had made whilst studying abroad. And, of course, with the lifestyle she now had, she could spend as much time as she wanted at her music. She thanked God every day for that privilege. But there was something gnawing at the very heart of her: it was the feeling of separation she was experiencing in regard to her mother-in-law. She wanted so much to be friends with her. She could only think of her with love, because she was Cameron's mother, and she had raised such a fine son.

One night, after their nightly sing-song, Shirlianne and her new mother put their heads together to figure out a name for the lovely old mansion where grandmother Brent lived. The two Brent properties were adjoining; thus they could see the huge brick estate off in the distance. The child's mother said that in her father's little black book she had read that if you kept saying and believing in forgiveness in a situation, it would take place.

The little girl was very pensive. "It's like wishin' and prayin', isn't it, Momma?"

"Yes, Shirlianne it is. So what shall we name Grandma Brent's house?"

"Let's call it 'The Wishes,' Momma."

"Oh, that is a nice name." The mother put her arm

around the child as she uttered these words of approval.

"And we'll wish every time we look at it, eh Momma?" She was very serious when she said this, but then she clapped her hands and exclaimed, "It'll be fun!" And the two of them hugged one another.

Cameron Brent had settled into his work at the office. He had a new secretary, but he missed "Miss Prim" in that position. She had been so efficient and had read much material, which rendered her very knowledgeable in his business affairs. But the recompense started when he went home at night. His family would be ready and waiting, and after he changed into his sportswear, they would do their exercises. At first, their attempts at performing these exercises seriously were turning into fond embraces by the amorous couple, and they were ending up in each other's arms. It was the husband who had to take control of the situation, and he made sure the half-hour session was completed before the amorous feelings were allowed to come into play.

Shirlianne was glad to see her parents so loving. It was something for which she had wished and prayed, not just for a mother, but for somebody who would love her father and make him happy; she was quite content having him share his love for her with her new mother.

Chapter 40
The Attention Seeker

Mrs. John Brent was a real socialite who loved the Country Club scene, and her husband would take her to the various social affairs, quite happy to be with her at these functions when he was not away in France. Both of them revelled in the party atmosphere. They were well liked, and they had been members so long that they felt as though they were the founders of the club. John made sure the children took advantage of the activities associated with such a fraternity, so they were all skillful at golf, tennis, horseback riding, etc. His wife, being a genteel lady, was not interested in athletic endeavours, but she enjoyed seeing the family participate in the different sports and would cheer them on during any of their tournaments.

The same lady had her ways of getting attention from her son. At times she would phone his home and complain to him that her high blood pressure was bothering her, and she would ask him to come to her house to check it. She knew he had the sphygmomanometer and stethoscope from his medical training days. Cameron was aware that it was just a ploy. Nevertheless, he humoured her and would go. Actually, he was glad of an excuse to go over and see her. He considered it had been her right to be unaccepting of his infant; so many people felt the same way, but it was doubly hard for him when she took the same attitude towards his wife. He always managed to keep the visits pleasant, because he loved his mother dearly, though he wished so much that things were different, and he would have given anything to have the two women he loved so deeply visit back and forth and be a comfort to one another.

At the Columns the lady of the house was quite accepting of her husband's trysts with his mother. Indeed, she was glad they got together; however, it did annoy her when the lady would request him to go over there when they were in the midst of dinner, or at some other unsuitable time. But she resolved not to make a fuss about it because the woman was her elder and she was brought up to respect her elders, especially in the case of parentage.

Chapter 41
Cameron Introduces His Wife to High Society

Great plans were taking place at the Columns: Cameron Brent was throwing one of his fancy balls. This one was for the purpose of introducing his wife to his neighbours (most of them the Country Club crowd), and friends, including some of his business associates. There were invited a few mutual acquaintances, but the majority would be complete strangers to the young woman.

Previous to this, the proud man had his wife pose for a portrait to hang in the entrance hall. It replaced that of his first wife's, which was given a less prominent position in the hallway on another floor. He would not cease to admire it, as the woman had been extraordinarily beauteous, though delicate and with a lack of ardour, but she was the mother of his child and he respected that.

On the other hand, the current oil painting, when it was completed and hung in place, was, as her husband described it, "breathtakingly beautiful" and captured the warmth and magnanimity of the lovely lady it depicted.

The guests had all gathered in the huge reception hall with its black-and-white checkered marble floor. They were waiting for Mrs. Cameron Brent to appear. And that lady was having the last-minute touches done to her hair, which was arranged in a soft puff, framing her face, and swept back into the French roll with a diamond-studded comb nestled therein. The beauty's husband had appointed Clarisse as her official hairdresser and "lady-in-waiting" (he did pamper his wife).

Shirlianne was in her mother's room helping her to dress. When she saw the beautiful gown on the lady she could not help but exclaim, "Oh, Momma, you look so bee-utiful, just gor-jus!"

The master of the house, very handsome in his tuxedo, was waiting at the foot of the wide stairway that descended through the centre of the spacious reception hall, and down those steps walked a beautiful creature in an elegant rose taffeta dress. She was wearing shoes to match. As she met her husband, he took hold of her gloved hand and kissed it, then, placing her arm on his, they wandered through the bevy of guests, and the host proudly introduced to them the lady who had brought such meaning into his life.

Cameron knew that Cindra would be a little nervous as she made her entrance down the flight of steps, and that was why he purposely stood waiting for her. When she saw him, she smiled and relaxed; his presence gave her the confidence she needed to face all the people gathered there anxiously waiting to meet her. Thus was born a little tradition, one which over the years, just as that night, would see the radiant princess joining her Romeo prince. When their eyes met, it was, and would continue to be, like a flame lit for eternity!

The princess was glad to see some of her friends amongst the many strangers. When she saw Phyllis Pindar, she emitted a little squeal of delight, put her arms around her, and hugged her. Of course Dr. Robertson was at Phyllis's side and after he gave Cindra a little hug, he pointed to his companion's third finger, left hand. The young woman saw the sparkling diamond ring that her ex–living companion was wearing; she gave a gasp of joy and hugged her dear friend again.

"Oh, Phyllis, I'm so happy for you. That's wonderful." Her words were spoken excitedly, and she went on, "Have you set the date yet?"

It was the doctor who spoke up. "Well, I can't get her pinned down to a date yet"—he looked lovingly at his fiancée—"but I'm working on it." The two women laughed and the doctor squeezed Phyllis's hand.

Then Cindra spied John Serenity. He was standing a little behind the doctor. She had not noticed him, but when she did, she just flew into his arms. "Oh, my dear Mr. Serenity, I missed you so much at the wedding, I was sorry you were sick."

The old man held her tightly in his arms. His voice was choked with emotion: "My Little Miss, and now you're all married, I so often think of you, how hard you worked at your music. Oh my, oh my!"

Little Miss looked at him with love in her eyes. She never would forget how kind he had been to her when she was a newcomer to Saint Louis and everything had been so strange. She took hold of his hands and looked straight into his eyes: "Dear, dear John, don't you worry about my music, I'm still taking lessons from Miss Grace, and I'm able to practise all day if I want to." After saying that, Cindra gave him a little smile, then added, "And I'm so happy."

This brought a smile to Mr. Serenity's face, and he shook his head in approval as she passed on.

The couple continued along the line of guests, the handsome lord of the manor introducing his charming wife. They came to Dr. Eric Bonn, who was a good looking, blond aristocrat, Austrian by birth, and who belonged to the country club crowd. He had been watching the lovely lady since the time she made her graceful entrance down the carpeted stairway. He could not take his eyes off her. To him she was divine, and he thought to himself, *How did Cameron Brent find such a woman?*

As the object of his attention held out her gloved hand, Dr. Bonn took it in his and looked deep into her eyes, the most beautiful blue eyes he had ever seen, and he had met many beautiful women. After he kissed her gloved hand, she smiled demurely at him, then she and Cameron proceeded to meet the next guests—Eric's lady friend Julia, his mother, Greta, a widow, and his sister Claudia, who was unaccompanied by any swain.

Claudia was a dark-haired beauty. She had always been interested in Cameron Brent. They would meet often at the country club or on the golf course, and actually she had been invited to one of his fancy balls as his date, but he had seemed so distant, and there was the matter of his little daughter! Only now, she regretted having lost him.

When introductions were completed, the dancing began. The mansion had a ball-room that could be extended by including the huge dining room, and for large occasions like this, the dancers often spilled over into the reception hall.

Of course, the lord of the manor and his lady, according to custom, were the first couple on the floor. Cindra felt that she was floating on air, with Cameron's strong arm around her. It was as though she was in heaven. An orchestra had been engaged, as usual for these affairs, and the music added to the deception that it was indeed heaven! It was a Strauss waltz, and after the first few opening strains the host motioned for the guests to join in.

What a picture it was—the ladies in their long gowns

in a variety of pastel colours, the men in their black tuxedos. The hostess of the manor felt like Cinderella. It was as if her fairy godmother had waved a magic wand and voilà, she was there. But unlike the unfortunate Cinderella, who had to disappear at midnight, she could stay with her prince forever!

Chapter 42
Their Social Life

Life was very full for the little family at the Columns. Shirlianne was working enthusiastically at her school work, and her momma was applying herself diligently to her musical studies. The two of them would look over to the Wishes and say a prayer that things might change, but so far nothing had happened. Both of them would remind each other that they had to be patient.

Attendance at church on Sundays continued to be a priority in the young wife's life, and likewise in Shirlianne's. There was an Episcopal church in their vicinity, and though they did not like to leave the cathedral in the metropolis, they were glad of the extra time gained for the household to be together by not having to travel so far. As for the husband, he was just happy to be with the two people who meant so much to him, no matter where the place.

Thursday of each week was almost an anathema to the lady of the manor. It was the day when the lord of the manor was involved in his auxiliary duty in the navy. However, when she saw him in his naval officer's uniform, the lady felt very proud, and there was their reunion the next day and that made the parting worth while.

John Brent was pleased with the way his business was flourishing. He gave most of the credit to his oldest son, who had always been a clever student, and he knew it was through Cameron's expertise that the company was back on its feet. But a price was being paid. The son began drinking fairly heavily with the clients. He discovered that it was good for business, as many large deals were finalized by way of the social scene. His lady was not averse to his pipe-smoking. Her father had smoked cigarettes, and she, unlike her mother, accepted her father's habit graciously; she just adored the smell of her husband's pipe tobacco. But in the case of his drinking of spirits, she felt differently; she had a fear that it might get out of hand, even though it was mostly associated with business.

The master of the Columns continued to enjoy his workouts at the athletic club and the occasional golf game at the country club. Nevertheless, since his wife was not interested in belonging to the country club set, the good man centred most of his social life around their home. There were sumptuous dinner parties, with Cameron always toasting the women individually. On one of these occasions Mrs. Gold and her daughter Barbara were there for a visit, and Barbara loved it when he said that Canadian nurses were always in demand in the States.

At these same dinners, after coffee was served, and before the dancing began, the master of the house would escort his lady into the drawing-room, announcing to the guests words from *The Merchant of Venice*, by one of his favourite authors, Shakespeare: "here we will sit, and let the sounds of music creep in our ears...." And the accomplished lady would give a mini-concert on the beautiful grand piano, which she could hardly believe was hers. Often included in the short repertoire would be several magnificent bars of Rachmaninoff's "Rhapsody on a Theme of Paganini" as requested by her lover.

Dr. Eric Bonn and his sister and mother would often be invited to these affairs, and since the lord of the manor was usually talking and drinking with business clients who had been invited, the doctor would dance with Cindra as much as he could without making it obvious that he was monopolizing the beauty. But the lord of the manor would watch his lady, drinking in her beauty and throwing her kisses from across the room when her eyes met his. And when he claimed her for a dance, his lady would blush, and she would get the feeling as though she was still at high school. Her heart would beat fast when she was in his arms; she was filled with adoration.

Then there were nights at the opera. Those evenings held a special mystique for the budding pianist. When her escort appeared in his tuxedo, evening cape, top hat, white scarf, and gloves, she felt she was in fairyland. The limousines would drive up to the main entrance of the stately place of the arts, bejewelled ladies and their gentlemen escorts would alight, and the excitement of the thoughts of the pending performance sparked the evening air! And later, as the operatic story unfolded she was truly lost in the land of make-believe!

Very often John Brent and his exotic-looking lady would be in attendance at these musical galas. Cindra had the greatest desire to go over to their box-seat and beg the proud lady to be friends with her, but the voice from her inner self advised against this course of action, and, even though she considered she could tolerate a rebuff, she would end up letting her divine guidance overrule. But how she longed to socialize with her husband's elegant mother! Nevertheless, there was consolation in the fact that her own mother visited frequently and Cameron Brent, by his attentions and caring, gave the visitor from Canada the feeling she did indeed have a son!

Chapter 43
A Babe Is Born

As time went by, the governor of the Columns was finding it extremely difficult to ignore his wife's wishes that she have a child. He argued that it was too soon in their marriage, and that she should be a little older. These objections were met with a negative response, so the governor gave in to his lady's wishes, and one day it was announced there was going to be a prince or princess joining the little family at the Columns.

Once the expectant mother was past the initial unsettling feelings of the gestation period, the family was back to the usual routine, which meant that the before-dinner exercises were resumed, but the protective father-to-be made sure his lady performed the exertions passively and without strain.

Shirlianne was exultant at the prospects of a baby, and she was fascinated by the expanding measurements of her mother's abdomen. One night at dinner she startled her father with the remark, "Oh, Daddy, wouldn't it be nice if Momma had quintuplets?"

Cameron looked at his wife in a panicky way, but when she laughed uncontrollably, her mirth served to dissolve the imagery the startling remark had conjured in his mind and he laughed along with his wife, much to Shirlianne's delight. Needless to say, Cindra avoided playing the "Quintuplet's Lullaby" during the remainder of her pregnancy. She did not want her imagination stimulating her fertility.

The time seemed to fly by for the family at the mansion with the columns. They had such fun planning together for the new little arrival. Much to the expectant mother's objection the father-to-be arranged for a nanny for the infant and for nurses round the clock until such time as the new mother would have her strength back. The lord of the manor said he wanted his pianist back at her music as soon as possible.

Likewise, special plans were being made for Shirlianne; she was to go to Canada and visit Jody and baby Patsy. When the child heard that, she squealed with delight, then responded, "But Momma, I shouldn't leave you."

And Momma's remark was, "Now, darling, I have your daddy. I'll be fine, and when you come back you'll have a new little sister or brother, and we'll be all together again, and so happy!"

The thought of going back to the farm and seeing her friends, as well as all the animals, was great enticement to the little girl. She was eager to get packed and was soon bound for Canada with Grandmother Gold, who had come to accompany her back to Ontario and the Reidit farm.

Then one Thursday night, when Cameron was away on naval reserve duty, strict orders having been left for his wife to call him if she should, perchance, go into labour, she herself received a strange phone call. It was her mother-in-law, asking to speak to Cameron. When she heard that her son was out, she told the young woman in a hostile tone that it was her prerogative to see her grandchild when it was born, and she intended to take that right.

It was a coincidental phenomenon that she should call then, as Cindra's uterine contractions were starting. They caused her to lose complete control of reality and she had visions of the unfriendly woman trying to kidnap her child. She was terrified at the thought of her baby being wrested from her; it threw the young woman into such a frenzy that she packed a bag for herself, including a receiving layette for the baby. She stealthily ordered a taxi and was gone before any of the household staff was aware.

The expectant mother's contractions were becoming stronger and closer together, and the cab driver, frightened by the situation, took her to the closest maternity hospital of which he knew. It was a small Catholic maternity hospital run by the Sisters of Charity. Before long she was confronting a nun dressed in the habit of her order. The scared young woman, between her labour pains, told her story— that she was running away from a malicious someone who was threatening to steal her baby.

The religious sister could see how distraught the poor woman was, so she did not belabour her with questions, but tried to calm her, assuring her she would be safe here and that God was taking care of her. Cindra found her words and her calm, gentle manner very reassuring. The nun then assigned Sister Mary Margaret to be with her, and she was wheeled into a little cubicle and placed on a narrow bed, over the head of which hung a bronze crucifix. What a comfort it was! It reminded her of the suffering of her Lord, and she vowed that if He could endure the pain of the cross, she could endure bravely the birthing of a new soul into the world!

The young woman, in her birth pangs, thought an angel had been provided for her in the form of Sister Mary Margaret, who eased her through the last stages of labour with such understanding that when her time arrived for the child to be delivered, she experienced no fear. She felt the very presence of God in the "prayed-up" atmosphere of her surroundings. The first cry of her baby was the most joyous sound she thought she had ever heard!

But then the realization came to her with full force: Cameron did not know! Oh, what had she done! How she wished she could have shared it with her husband! How she wanted to call him, but her unbridled fear took over and she could not bring herself to reveal her whereabouts. She was so thankful Shirlianne was with her family in Canada and away from the heart-breaking ordeal.

However, when a sister laid the little boy beside her, her whole being was filled with wonderment! The tiny fingers, so perfectly formed, the chunky little thighs and little legs: This wee soul had come out of her body! All she could think of was, *What a miracle! miracle! miracle!* And back in her room, when again the swaddling infant was laid on her breast, Sister Mary Margaret came in with some of the other sisters, wanting to take a peak at the wee one. Cindra's mind wandered back to that scene long ago, and she could appreciate how Mary must have felt when the shepherds came to adore the Christ Child!

The harrowing experience Cindra had gone through, with her beloved not being there, played havoc in her mind. Her paramount thought was that she just had to keep her baby safe! Consequently, two days after her delivery she decided to flee with the child to her dear friend Phyllis Pindar. She knew she could trust her. The sisters aided her in making arrangements. Since others had come wearing wedding bands, which very often meant nothing, they did not know but that she was an unwed mother going out to battle the world the best way she could. Most certainly, the fleeing young woman was grateful to them for not asking questions.

The concerned nuns gathered together the necessities the new mother would require to properly care for the infant, so she left in a taxi with the tiny one nestled in a crude wooden cradle, surrounded by piles of diapers and other baby things, and with the many blessings of the Sisters of Charity resounding in her mind.

Chapter 44
To Seek and Find

When the master of the Columns returned on Friday morning and discovered his wife was missing, he was furious with the household staff. They had never seen him in such an angry state before. "Where in hell is my wife?" he remonstrated.

And no one knew. Clarisse had been away on a day off, so she was as much in the dark as her employer, and likewise very much worried.

The man, crazed with grief, hunted through every room of the mansion. He feared he might find his wife in one of the rooms, dead, after giving birth to their child. He was relieved when it was not the case, but he got busy and began to phone any friends who might know of the whereabouts of his wife. He also phoned the many hospitals listed in the phonebook. One of these institutions was unwilling to divulge any information about a certain mysterious woman who had come there stating there was a danger her child might be kidnapped. The young mother's confession was honoured, and consequently Cameron Brent's attempt to locate his wife was foiled!

In his panic he had quite forgotten to contact Phyllis Pindar. "That's it," he was thinking out loud, "she went to her old friend's place. Besides, Doc Robertson would be there." It was Friday night and the bewildered man sped off in his big, black sedan to the Pindar apartment. He had been listening to the radio back at the mansion, in case any news concerning a missing blond woman might come over the air waves, and ironically the piece of music being played was, "Through the Dark of Night, I've Got to Go Where You Are"! That song came back to him as he made his way to the Park Plaza Apartments. When Phyllis, responding to a knock on her door, opened it, she was startled to see Cameron Brent. He was unshaven and he presented a dishevelled appearance.

"My God, Cam, what is it? Where's Cindra?" The woman expressed her astonishment.

"That's what I'm trying to find out, Phyllis. She disappeared when I was on auxilliary duty Thursday night. I was hoping she'd come here!" The man tried hard not to show how upset he was that his wife was not there, but he moaned, "Oh, God, where is she?"

The unhappy man told Phyllis he had private detectives working on the case. He also asked the concerned woman to let him know if and when she heard anything, and with that he was gone.

Consequently, on Sunday, when Phyllis got the phone call from Cindra, she was not surprised, and urged her to come there as soon as possible. It was not long before the taxi arrived with the pale young blond woman, who looked even more beautiful in her frail state, and the crude wooden cradle with its tiny, sleeping occupant. The good friend was waiting at the door with anticipation, and she rushed down to the taxi as soon as it drove up.

"Oh, my precious Cindra, what in the world has happened? Cameron is just about crazy with worry over you. How could you do this to him?" She uttered the condemnatory pronouncement rather unthinkingly, because when she helped the young woman out of the car, she could see how unsteady and weak she was, and when she observed her sad countenance, she only said, sympathetically, "Oh, my dear!" and put her arm around Cindra affectionately.

Cindra, at this show of tenderness, began to cry, much to her regret, as she had promised herself she would not do that. However, it proved a good catharsis and she felt better for it.

Dr. Robertson had followed his fiancée down to the taxi, so he was the one who had the honour of carrying the cradle, with the sleeping babe, into the apartment. The cabman followed, conveying the large pile of baby things. That done, the doctor settled with the cabman, who then left.

The older woman immediately told her dear friend that her husband had been there, and that he was almost beside himself with grief, wondering what his wife's actions were all about.

When the layette was put away in the new mother's unoccupied room, the three adults sat down in the sitting-room. Cindra was now having severe pangs of remorse; she was dreading the thought of facing her husband. She confided to her old friends the telephone conversation her mother-in-law had had with her, just before she left on that fateful Thursday night.

It was Phyllis who spoke first. "But, Cindra, surely you would have known Cameron wouldn't let his mother do such a thing as kidnap the baby!"

"Oh, Phyllis, the contractions were starting to come, and I began to panic." She took a breath. "I was alone and scared; I just had to make sure my baby wouldn't be taken from me."

"Well, my dear, I must call Cameron. I promised him," the older woman spoke decisively.

There was a look of panic come over the young mother's countenance again, and the blood drained from her face.

It was then that the doctor took over. He first checked Cindra's blood pressure with the appropriate equipment from his little black bag. When he found it was dangerously low, he asked his fiancée to make her a cup of strong tea, then he spoke gently to the young woman. He told her she was in such a state because of her fear, and he was able to make her understand that there was no way her baby could be taken away from her.

With the drink of tea and the counselling of the doctor, the young mother's spirits seemed to be lifted and she began to look at the circumstances realistically. She agreed that her husband should be called and only hoped he would understand why she had suddenly disappeared.

Cameron Brent must have exceeded the speed limit, as it seemed no time at all from when he received the phone call till when he appeared at the Pindar apartment. He looked older and haggard, owing to the deep anguish he had been through. At sight of his beloved wife he said nothing, but straightaway went over to her and took her in his arms, gently stroking her fair head. He just wanted to hold her and never let her go.

"Oh, my darling, please don't ever leave me again. I didn't know if you were alive or dead!" He spoke compassionately.

All fear left her when the young wife was in her husband's arms. The strength and support she experienced there flowed into her, and her equilibrium was restored.

The whole situation was explained to the man, and with his great understanding he held his precious one closer. He told her how much he loved her, how much he needed and depended on her, and how his life had no meaning now without her.

The baby began to stir. It was Phyllis who went to pick him up. "Oh, you beautiful little darling. You want to be in on it all too, don't you!" She held him closely.

However, baby had his own needs and before long his faint mutterings developed into a lusty cry. It was his feeding time, but only his mother could satisfy that need, so she retired into her former room to suckle the infant. Soon after being fed and changed, he was asleep again in the nun's wooden cradle.

The little family was soon on its way to the Columns. No conversation took place between the new parents; they were enjoying the bond of love they felt in the silence, just happy to be in the same space together.

The household staff was lined up in the huge entrance hall, eager to welcome back the mistress of the manor and to see the newborn prince of the estate, who remained asleep in his wooden bed. And the mistress noted there were several new additions to the staff, one of whom was a registered nurse in a white uniform. She was to attend to the baby when the mother was tired or chose to effect her piano practise. The lady of the manor looked at her handsome husband. She almost said something about the added expense, but thought better of it and just smiled.

The fond greeting of the staff gave Cindra the encouragement she needed to make her feel reinstated as mistress of the house, since she felt she, besides being unfair to her husband, had also let *them* down by taking off the way she did.

Clarisse and Raoul had not been with the rest of the staff. They now made their appearance, and there were more fond salutations. Then Clarisse went to the wooden cradle. Kneeling by it, she picked up the sleeping babe at the suggestion of his mother. She held him close to her heart and rocked back and forth. There were tears in her eyes, but they were tears of relief in the nightmare of her mistress's disappearance being over, and tears of joy that there was a baby to hug!

After this, the master of the house decided it was time he asserted his fatherhood, so he gently took the waking infant from Clarisse's arms. Holding him tenderly, Cameron walked up the stairs with him, saying he was going to acquaint his little son with his newly decorated nursery. However, the babe began to cry lustily, and it was as if it were an omen for the years to come, a prediction of woe, which none of them, at that time, could even vaguely imagine!

Chapter 45
A Name for Baby

The morning after his wife's return, the man of the manor announced to her he was going to sell the Columns, and they would move away from the threat of his mother's caustic influence on their lives. Because he was averse to causing his wife any embarrassment, he did not tell her that his mother had denied having threatened to kidnap the baby. She had said, "There you are, Cameron, I was opposed to you marrying that girl. Surely this proves to you how unbalanced she is!" The son could not tolerate any verbal attack on his precious wife. He decided he would move his family from the vicinity, to avoid any further trouble.

Nevertheless, on hearing his plan, Cindra became very upset, reasoning that it was Shirlianne's home. She put up such resistance that all the poor man could do was rescind his proposal, but he muttered whilst shaking his head, "I hope nothing like what we've been through will happen again!"

It was decided a name for the baby should not be chosen until Shirlianne returned home. And what a greeting it was at the airport, when the new parents took their baby son to meet his step-sister. The little girl only had eyes for the small bundle that her mother was carrying.

"Oh, Momma, he's white. I didn't know if he'd be brown or white!" The child, in her naïveté, had been genuinely perplexed about the issue, and before she did anything else she had to find out for herself the skin pigment of the new family member. Her curiosity having been satisfied, she then went into a great hugging spree, spurred, of course, by the sight of her beloved parents.

Mrs. Gold, who had accompanied the youngster on the flight, went over to her daughter and took the sleeping infant from her arms, cooing over her new young grandson. "Cameron, he's just the spitting image of you, the lucky little fellow." Mrs. Gold had a way of saying just the right thing to please her son-in-law.

The man laughingly responded, "Mother Gold, you must have kissed the blarney stone this morning and it's just showing up now!"

Towards the car walked the jolly group. Shirlianne hanging on tightly to her mother's hand; her remark about her mother's tummy being flat brought forth a little giggle from all.

Mrs. Gold stayed at the Columns for a couple of

weeks, supposedly to help look after her new grandson. "Land sakes, Cameron, you didn't need to get those nurses for every shift. I could have taken over for the day shift, anyway, if you did think nurses were necessary." The woman was sincere in what she said.

"Now, love, you brought up your family. I don't expect you to come here on one of your rare visits and work all the time. The same goes for Cindra—I want her to have time to keep up with her music. She's busy enough nursing our son." The man, pointing in his mother-in-law's direction, continued, "And see all the work you've done on those lovely baby things you're making."

Mrs. Gold proudly held up a pram cover she was crocheting for her grandson. She thought to herself that it was so like her son-in-law to notice her efforts.

At the first meal the family had partaken together, the subject of a name for the baby was discussed, and the name "Peter" was favored.

"Oh, goody, Momma, Peter was the name of Jesus' disciple." The little girl had not forgotten what she had learned at Sunday school when she was in Canada with Jody.

That remark settled it, and baby was given the name Peter Cord, the latter being one of his grandfather Brent's names.

Chapter 46

Another Baby

Cindra had received many lovely vases with flowers from her husband, some from their courting days, if one could so call them, and some very recent ones. Consequently, when her birthday rolled around, her husband, asked her what she desired in her heart of hearts. Her response was a wish for a little cabinet where she could display these exquisite containers. Accordingly, on that particular anniversary of her birth, her Prince Charming presented her with a huge, curved glass cabinet. It was of rich mahogany wood, matching the furniture in the drawing-room, with mirrors inside to reflect the precious ornate jars, and interior lights that caused the objets d' art to shimmer in all their glory.

The young woman was thrilled with the gift and the devotion of the man who had given it; she could not help thinking what an especially thoughtful person he was. She hoped that what she had done on the fateful Thursday night would not come between them; they had such a special kind of love. It almost seemed that he idolized her more because of it!

The little family returned pretty much to their regular routine. Peter was nursed before the exercises that preceded dinner, so he was included in the activity of the group, even if only to lie on his own little mattress near the big one, and move his arms and legs in infant fashion. It was his fussy time, but if he fussed too much, the nurse would come to his rescue, (and needless to say, that of his family) and check on his particular need.

Time continued to roll by, as is its nature, and Peter Cord grew by leaps and bounds. He had been sleeping through the night for some time, so the shift nurses were replaced by a nanny. He was a precocious little fellow and would soon be drinking cow's milk from a cup. The old fallacy of a nursing mother had been put to the test and was disproved; soon there was to be another addition to the little family. It could not have pleased Shirlianne more, and when Carol Lynne joined the family tree, the girl was overjoyed at having a baby sister.

Along with the infant came another exquisite vase to the glass cabinet, gift of Cameron Aramis Brent, who this time paced anxiously in the maternity hospital waiting room and prayed that nothing untoward would happen to his wife. The expectant mother had requested to go to the Catholic maternity hospital of the Sisters of Charity, where Peter Cord had been born, and the nuns were all very happy to see there was a concerned father. It also gave Cameron a chance to thank the sisters for taking such good care of his wife the first time. He finally gave a sizable donation to their order, which had always been his intention.

Peter's step-sister, though she loved him, was distraught at some of his antics, especially since he had begun to walk. She was delighted to have a baby sister, whom she could hold whilst sitting in a big arm chair, one who, like her dolls, would stay put and not move about mischievously.

One night, at Shirlianne's special time with her mother and father, when Cindra and she would sit at the piano and have their musical hour, the child remarked to her mother, "Momma, God has given me you to be my mother, and Peter and Carol to be my brother and sister. He's answered every prayer I've ever made, except He doesn't answer my one for the Wishes." The young girl had a wistful look on her face and she had pursed her lips.

"I'm sure He'll answer that prayer some day too, Darling."

But this response belied what Momma was thinking, as she had a kind of hopeless feeling about a reconciliation ever occurring between herself and her mother-in-law. Cameron had been drinking more heavily, and his mother was blaming his wife, even though the episodes were client-oriented and had to do with his business deals.

There were nights when he would come home inebriated and Raoul, who was now his personal butler, would put him to bed. Then Cindra would lie down beside him and hold him and pray. He would look so white, she was afraid he was dying!

The young woman felt she was somewhat responsible for her husband's behaviour, thinking that possibly it was the estrangement from his mother. She blamed herself for this, especially since there had been no contact between mother and son after the fateful night of the mysterious phone call, when she was in labour with her first child.

When the young mother would voice this to her husband, he would just laugh. One of these times he responded, "My darling, it's just that I never could drink much—it doesn't agree with me, but my drinking with the clients is surely getting us the business. Now don't you worry your pretty little head about my mother and me. Until she accepts you and Shirlianne she can go to hell!"

"Cam, please don't say that. She is your mother, and I think you should visit her a little, like you used to." The young woman spoke sincerely; strange as it may seem, she felt no animosity towards her mother-in-law. She just felt that she must be a very lonely woman, whose husband she knew had a very good female friend in Paris. She was aware her father-in-law had recently returned from another visit to France, and she could not help but feel sorry for the older woman.

The handsome husband began to tease a bit. "Now you take my mother-in-law, if she'd been around as much as you were before we got married, you would have had a great deal of competition."

With this remark, Cindra began to laugh, and her husband drew her to him. Their love was still as passionate as it was in Paris on their honeymoon, despite the vicissitudes their lives were facing.

Yet, as time passed, there was something else that troubled the young mother, besides the mother-in-law problem: Dr. Eric Bonn was a frequent visitor. He had the children calling him Uncle Eric. He lavished them with gifts, and she felt he was spoiling them. He had hardly even acknowledged Shirlianne, which really bothered her. She could not tolerate seeing her precious one rejected in any way. She had discussed these things with her husband, but he took a very casual attitude towards the whole matter, presenting Eric as a lonely man who could not seem to find the right mate. He expounded the merits of his friend by informing her that the good doctor had taken into his home his mother, along with his sister, Claudia, when his father had died. Despite this praise of the man, Cindra still had her misgivings as far as he was concerned.

One night the master of the house had one of his grand balls planned. He was unavoidably detained that night at work. The musicians had arrived, as well as the guests, so the mistress of the house had to make her appearance down the elegant stairway without, as their tradition was, her Prince Charming to greet her at the foot of the stairs. She was radiant in a lovely gold lamé gown, and who was at the bottom of the stairs to receive her but Dr. Eric Bonn. She was furious; however, she had to hide her feelings for the sake of the other guests.

Then, on top of this, Cameron had imprinted on the invitations the notification "Dance cards for the women," which meant the men were to mark on the cards, claiming the different partners for the numbered dances. His explanation was that it added variety and an aura of excitement to the evening. The golden-haired beauty's dance card was filled up before her husband joined the party, and, of course, honour was the order of the day. She was devastated! Her husband was not very happy about it either; he had to watch his wife in the arms of Eric Bonn for many of the dances. It would be some time before he had that kind of a dance again!

Chapter 47
Brumby "Goes"

There was a period when the young mother and her son Peter became very close. He was quite musical, and showed promise as a student of the violin. Carol Lynne, on the other hand, found her piano studies toilsome; she certainly had not inherited much of her mother's musical talent.

Cameron's imbibing of spirits continued. Many nights occurred when the beautiful wife was all dressed up for some special occasion and her husband would not show up. The son would come and sit with his mother and look at her. The boy adored her, and it bothered him to see her hurt. On more than one occasion he saw her cry. He was beginning to dislike his father.

There would be no fuss between the parents when the man did show up in an inebriated state. Peter, though he had gone to bed, would hear his father stumble up the stairs, and his mother, who had taken off her finery, would get into bed with the master of the house, whom Raoul had assisted to undress, and the forgiving woman would hold her husband. She would stay in bed with him the next day, until the effects of the alcohol wore off. It was a strange thing, but those were the times when she felt very close to him and she agonized over him, so strong was her love for him.

Occasionally, on Saturdays, a group of friends would meet at the Columns for breakfast, then proceed to the country club stables where the lord of the Columns kept his horses. The lady of the house would go along, her husband making certain she had a gentle horse, since she was an inexperienced rider.

On one of these riding occasions, Cameron was helping Elaina, an attractive brunette, an old acquaintance of his from the country club. She asked for his assistance in mounting her horse, as she had confided, to him alone, that she was going blind, and she did not want anyone else to know. His compassion for the young woman was great. He was proceeding to help her, when suddenly there flew past them his wife on the steed he had banned anyone from riding. He was on his mount as quick as a wink, yelling back to Robert to look after Elaina whilst he pursued the runaway, "Brumby," so named because he was as wild as the Australian horses from whence came the appellation. He rode fiercely, ordering the beast to stop; Brumby would rear on his hind legs, and the man was terrified that his wife would be thrown to the ground. However, the worried husband had the opportunity to catch up to the beast, and, grabbing the reins, slow him down and rescue his terribly frightened wife, whose chest was heaving in short shallow breaths. He stopped the two horses near a fence and, dismounting, tethered them there. Then, cradling his wife in his arms, he lifted her down off Brumby and sat under a tree with her. Cindra was still breathing irregularly. She was an ashen colour; Cameron was afraid she might have a heart attack. He could not bear the thought of losing her. He loosened the clothing at her neck to help free her airway and spoke to her gently, instructing her to take deeper breaths. Gradually her respirations slowed down and the colour returned to her face. He was reminded of the time he first kissed her, when she had sprained her ankle. He desired to kiss her now but thought better of it, so he lifted her onto his horse and the two rode back to the Columns with Brumby following behind.

The riding group was expected back at the Columns for lunch. A message was left with the staff for brother Robert to take over as host. The lord of the manor chose to remain with his wife. She was very upset about the whole thing, saying that she had been jealous and had acted stupidly. She told him she was very sorry and that he should go down and be with his guests. She felt weak and began to sob.

He looked at her lovingly and thought to himself of the number of times she had stayed with him when he was drunk. He told her, "Don't cry, my darling. I can't stand to see you cry. It's alright, Cindra, it's kind of nice to think you were jealous." He thought this approach might help, and yet both of them knew there was no need for jealousy. Their great love had endured and over the years had increased, so that nothing could stand in the way of it or make a difference one way or the other to it. It remained steadfast and flourishing!

The regretful young woman vowed then and there that she would not behave so childishly again!

The lord of the manor also had a vow and stuck with it, though his was immediate. The very next morning he sold Brumby; that act, however, had sorrowful repercussions!

Peter would sometimes go to the stables with his father, and the young lad had a particular fondness for Brumby. The horse seemed to sense this and would tolerate the boy touching him. This was unlike his behaviour with other children, or with most adults, for that matter, whom, by balking and stomping, he would warn to keep their distance! But Peter would give him some lumps of sugar, which he would take calmly. The young boy's voice must have had the right quality to soothe the beast, for Brumby became docile when he was around. When Peter heard that the horse, his horse, had been sold, he went into a rage, saying he hated his father.

"Peter, you are not being very fair. Just because you had a good relationship with him doesn't justify keeping him." The father was finding the conversation very painful; he tried to convey to the boy that he did not want to hurt him. He continued, "You know your mother had a very terrifying experience with that animal. Fortunately I was able to intervene and save her. It might happen again to someone else, and it could end tragically, my son. I just cannot take that chance."

Pleading with the young boy was futile; he could not be consoled. It would be a long time before the son would forgive his father!

It so happened that Peter, at this time, had a friend who was going away to boarding school, so this gave him a notion—he begged to go away to the same private school as his friend. His mother was reluctant, but his father thought it was a good idea. He knew the boy was still angry over the sale of Brumby, so he thought it would be good for him to get away. "Perhaps, my dear, it will help him to forget!" he reasoned with his wife.

It made Shirlianne shudder at the thought of it. Of course, she had been younger when the same suggestion came forth in her life; however, she felt sorry for her brother and promised to write to him often. "And, Peter, I'll feed your fish for you, and when I write to you, you write back and let me know how you're getting along." The sister paused. "Oh, Peter, why do you have to go away? I may never see you again!" The young girl had tears in her eyes. It made one wonder if she perhaps had some kind of premonition. She held on to him tightly when she said good-bye.

Peter bid farewell to his step-sister in her bedroom. She had not been feeling well, fainting spells being one of her symptoms, and the doctor gave orders for her to stay in bed and get plenty of rest.

Peter was somewhat embarrassed. He said, "Oh gosh, silly, you rest and get better, there's summer holidays." He parted from her abruptly and ran to the car, where his father, mother, and sister were waiting to take him to the train station.

Chapter 48
A Sad Farewell

Shirlianne's condition, even with extra rest, did not improve. She was losing weight, and Dr. Robertson said she must go into hospital for tests. Cindra was very concerned; she thought if anything happened to this girl she loved so much, who was now in her adolescent years, and her confidante, she did not know what she would do.

It was a sad mother who packed the patient's suitcase for her stay in the hospital.

Shirlianne helped her mother, on whose face she saw such a look of concern. "Don't you worry, Momma. You know God will take care of me and Jesus will be with me." She spoke with assurance as she put into her bag the picture of Jesus that she had been given at Christ Church Cathedral in those bygone days when the woman with her now was just a dear friend.

The mother was glad her daughter had such faith. She had to admit the girl's attitude was helping her. *Oh,* she thought, *what a precious one she is!*

The blood tests of the young girl proved positive for leukemia; the prognosis was not good. Cindra spent most of her time at the hospital. One day the patient said, "Oh, Momma, you're going to get so far behind in your piano practice. I feel bad about that, and what will Daddy say?"

And Momma responded, "Your father is just as concerned as I am, Shirlianne. He likes me to be with you."

Auntie Phyllis, too, was a frequent visitor, and one day she brought John Serenity. How happy the girl was to see her dear friends! Though her mother could see the extra excitement was tiring for her, she loved to see the expression of delight on her daughter's face when such friends did appear.

The day came when the doctors said there was nothing more they could do for Shirlianne and she was discharged. She was very weak, so her father carried her up to her room and laid her on her bed. She was frail and listless, the observation of which tore at her father's heart. She had been such a healthy-looking child and had grown into a fine-looking teenager, strikingly beautiful. Oh, how could this happen, he thought, but it did, and like it or not, it had to be accepted.

The girl suddenly looked startled. "Daddy, I forgot all about Peter's fish. They must be starving!" Even in her weak state she thought of her promise to her brother. She continued, "And I told Peter I'd write to him often. I'll have to write him a letter, Daddy."

"Now, Raoul has been looking after the fish, and you can write to your brother when you're feeling better. Your mother writes to him, you know, and she phoned him last Sunday." The father reassured his daughter and she seemed pacified after hearing that her brother had not been forgotten. It was obvious she was very fond of her step-brother. Once he grew out of the toddler stage, they had become close friends.

The young girl never did get up from her bed. Her father arranged for nurses round the clock to attend to her needs, and he read to her in the evenings as he used to do, with her step-sister, Carol, in attendance as well. He also had a piano moved into her room, not just an ordinary piano, but the little white piano that had been in Cindra's room at Auntie Phyllis's apartment. His aim succeeded, as it brought back to the girl such loving memories when she and Miss Gold would sing together after that lady had finished her piano practice. "Oh, Daddy, you brought me the Dove, the dear little Dove. Oh, thank you!" The girl's eyes lit up with joy as they feasted on the musical instrument.

And the mother spent many beautiful hours with her precious Shirlianne, playing for her the music she loved so well. The young woman thought to herself that it was no Steinway, but the remembrances it conjured up for her were soul-stirring: memories of a dear little motherless child and of a dark-haired man with whom she had tried so desperately hard not to fall in love, but who crept into her mind as she practiced, until she could hardly stand it.

The mother and step-daughter, with Carol Lynne joining in, sang Shirlianne's favourite melodies: "Roses of Picardy," "Just a Song at Twilight," "Nocturne for Shirlianne" (they had put words to that), and, of course, "The Quintuplet's Lullaby." The young girl still had the basket, with her favourite five dolls, in her room!

One evening, after Carol had gone to bed, Shirlianne requested that her mother stay with her and play "In a

Monastery Garden" on the piano for her. When the song was finished, she began speaking to her mother, in a weak voice, "Momma, ... Momma, ... I could see Jesus ... standing in that garden.... His arms were stretched out to me ... and I could see right into His heart of love...." The girl's breathing had become shallow, and her voice increasingly weaker. Cindra sent the nurse to summon her husband to come immediately. The young girl raised her hand with great effort and motioned for her mother to lean down to hear her and she whispered, faintly, words that Cindra would never forget: "Thank you, dear Miss Gold, for being my mother." At that moment the girl fell asleep, a sleep from which she did not waken to this earthly plane.

Cameron arrived at his daughter's bedside and held her in his arms until her heart beat its last throb, but Dr. Robertson, whom the nurse had called, did not get there until after she had passed away. He was the one who made out the death certificates.

Cindra gave the deceased loved one a kiss on the forehead, then went out of the room and wept uncontrollably. Auntie Phyllis had come with Dr. Robertson. The bereaved mother was most grateful to her old friend for coming to be with her, and they shared their grief together. So many memories they had of a precious little girl who had come into their lives and brought them so much love.

The funeral took place in Bofinger Chapel in Christ Church Cathedral, the same little chapel where Cindra was married. And the young woman's thoughts went back to it. What a happy day it had been for Shirlianne when her dear Miss Gold became her mother!

Peter Cord, on bereavement leave from boarding school, and Carol Lynne sat with their beloved Grandmother Gold, who had come from Canada, along with Madge and Karl Reidit. Jody remained at home. He was very upset when he heard the news, holding back the tears as best he could. He had blurted out, "Why did she have to die? We were going to get married when we got older!"

Cameron Brent could not give in to any emotion at all, as his wife was literally overcome with grief, and he had to practically hold her up. Seeing the old friends to whom the child had endeared herself—Auntie Phyllis, Dr. Robertson, John Serenity, Clarisse, and Raoul—just started her weeping again. She made a great effort to control herself when John Brent and his son Robert appeared; she was so glad they had come.

At the cemetery, when the undersized white coffin was lowered into the ground, Cameron had to support the grief-stricken lady to keep her from falling into a faint. He was glad when someone in the small group came forth with smelling-salts; these were effective in reviving the swooning one.

In bed the same night Cindra was weeping again. Her husband told her gently that she could not go on that way.

"But she was our love child, Cam, even more than if she had been born to us! Oh, why, why, why?" After this querying exclamation, the broken-hearted lady drew away from her husband. She continued to weep silently, and she did not want him to know.

Chapter 49

Tearless Morn

The young woman continued to grieve much longer than she should have. She belaboured her mind with thoughts of the child. She recalled how they had bathed baby Peter together and the little girl had wondered why, unlike her, he had a "little tail," as she had called it. They had sat, each in a rocking chair, the mother with baby Peter, the child with her quintuplet doll, Cindra, and rocked them together until Shirlianne would say, "Momma, they're both asleep." How those beautiful memories tore at her heart! Even Peter's visit home from boarding school had not helped. And her music was forgotten. She explained to Miss Grace that she was just not feeling up to the piano practice.

Cameron thought if she had another child it might help his wife, but after she had become pregnant she became more depressed, and he wished he had not caused that to happen. He plied her with gifts and brought her breakfast in bed. One evening he came home with a lovely mauve-and-blue-flowered chiffon frock, with parasol to match, and he said he wanted to see her wear it. The sorrowing lady looked at it, managed a wan smile, thanked him for it, then again lay back listlessly on the lounge in her bedroom.

During this period it was a bleak world in which the man had to live. Carol Lynne gave him much comfort. He had allowed her to take over the spot in his heart left void by Shirlianne's death, and his life was enriched. The child was a darling little girl, every bit as intelligent as his first daughter.

Carol Lynne herself missed her step-sister. Shirlianne had nurtured her since her babyhood, as older sisters often do. Added to this she had to deal with Peter being away at boarding school—the two babies had been born so close together they were almost like twins. His absence made the demise doubly difficult for her.

Thus the father and his second daughter became close

friends, much closer than the girl would ever be to her mother!

Though Cameron Brent had no deep religious convictions, he was not agnostic, and one night, as he lay in bed with his wife beside him, closed off in another world, you might say, he contemplated how much he missed their closeness. He said to her softly, "Cindra, where is your God?"

That very night the young woman had a dream. She saw her husband with another woman, a beautiful fair-haired woman. They were laughing together. In the morning, she woke with a start. She chastened herself verbally: What was she doing? How could she jeopardize their love? With her grief she had set up a barrier to their relationship. Shirlianne would not want that! How could she have been so selfish! Her husband had the same grief to bear, and so did Carol.

Then Cameron's remark came back to her. Yes, where was her God? She ran for her father's black memo book, and, opening it, she came upon an entry that seemed so fitting for the situation. Her father had copied therein the verse of a hymn she remembered singing at church, "Oh Love That Wilt Not Let Me Go." He had written down the author's name, "George Matheson," and had noted that he was a blind preacher. She sang the inspiring words of a joy that can come through pain if one opens one's heart to God, and by tracing the rainbow through the rain, the promise that the morn shall be tearless will not be in vain.

She repeated it several times, and its true meaning came bursting into her mind. Ah, yes, it was time to dry her tears! She had closed her life to joy! She was letting her troubles, like the rain, engulf her! Well, she was going to trace the rainbow through the rain. What a lovely thought!

And for her that morn had magic; she seemed a new

person, ready to tackle the day. She would go down to her husband's office and surprise him. She put on the new flowered dress he had bought for her. She could just get into it, as her tummy had started to expand; however, it was flouncy and, when she looked at herself in the mirror, she liked what she saw. With the addition of a white hat and dainty white gloves, she was ready to go. She no sooner got out of the room than she remembered the matching, frill-edged sun-umbrella, and ran back for the pretty thing.

It was the new chauffeur Faulkner's day off; therefore, Raoul drove her down to the Brent Company Building in the black limousine. His greeting was, "Oh my, Milady, you do look beautiful!"

And it was Robert Brent who met her as she alighted from the limousine. "Well, hello Cindra, nice to see you out." His greeting was sincere. He went on, "Cam and some of the others have gone to the track—it's race-horse day. Come on along with me, have a bit of fun. You've been moping about too long."

The young woman could not have agreed with him more. What the heck, what a lark, she did feel like some fun. So they sped away in his yellow sports car, chatting and laughing, their cares left behind.

Meanwhile, at the track, Cameron was ensconced in a box-seat. Beside him sat Phyllis Farrell. There was no danger, he thought, that he might get romantically involved with his ex-fiancée; she had been so cold. But he noticed a change in her. He found her warm and caring: She expressed to him how she regretted the way she had acted with Shirlianne, and how sorry she was when she heard the girl had died.

The handsome man was about to respond, when his eyes spied the vision of loveliness coming on to the grounds, a vision in a familiar mauve-and-turquoise flowered dress, with a parasol to match. She was laughing with Robert, who was accompanying her. She was vivacious, and she was beautiful. He was down to her side like a shot, but not before she had seen him with Phyllis Farrell. So that was the blond woman in her dream!

She looked at him coquettishly and said cheerily, "Hi, Cam. I thought I'd take in some of the fun too."

He did not need much encouragement; he was a slave to her love and he was glad to be back in that position again. "Come on, we're getting out of here." He spoke decisively whilst putting his arm around her. He gave his brother his racing forms and spoke again. "Robert, take care of Phyllis, will you? Tell her my wife is sick and I have to look after her."

With that, Cindra gave him a tap with her umbrella, saying, "You prevaricator, I feel great."

He laughed as he led her to his car, and the young woman's heart was beating fiercely within her. It was as though they were dashing away on a first date. He drove off the road at the top of a hill, on to a pull-off area, then he drew her towards him and told her, "You've been away so long, Cindra, it's wonderful to have you back. I don't know what I would do without you."

"Oh, you'd find a beautiful blonde soon enough, I think," she teased him, and they both laughed at that remark.

After embracing her, he drove on to a little lodge of which he knew, and that day they renewed their love bonds. They laughed, joked, danced, and ate a sumptuous dinner in the elegant dining-room beside a decorative fountain, into which Cameron kept flipping coins. "All for good luck, my darling," the happy man said.

They had phoned home, on their arrival at the lodge, to tell Carol Lynne of their whereabouts, and again, before retiring, they phoned her to tell her they would be staying at the lodge overnight, and would see her the next day.

The night they spent there at the lodge would be one the beautiful woman would remember. It was a night of which dreams are made!

Chapter 50
Good for Uncle Clive!

Cindra did have moments when the old feelings of depression infiltrated her mind. It was at these times she would persistently affirm the words of wisdom from the Book of Job, which she had found in her father's blessed black book: " . . . thou shalt forget thy misery; and remember it as waters that pass away." She surmised her father had opened his book and read the verse often, as it was underlined, and the particular page on which it was penned was dog-eared.

Decidedly, Dad Jack had had his share of troubles: His wife had a sister, and because Bonnie May had married Dad Jack, of whom their wealthy father disapproved, the latter left his fortune to the sister, Beatrice. She eventually married a man, a projectionist in a theatre (and, unbeknownst to her, a gambler), who squandered the fortune, leaving poor Beatrice a sick woman, destitute on the doorstep of her sister, Bonnie May. Dad Jack took her in, and the couple nursed her through successive heart attacks until she died. Cindra remembered her Aunt Beatrice sitting and crying because of her misfortune and the fact that she could have helped her sister's struggling family had she not been so unwise. That unusual occurrence took place when she was very young, but it was, indeed, a lesson in forgiveness and compassion that was engraved on Cindra's mind indelibly.

And now, the mansion known as the Columns was again filled with music. The young musician was back at her usual practice. It was true that she avoided playing some songs, but there were many others. Carol Lynne enjoyed singing to her mother's accompaniment, just as much as her step-sister had, and she could carry a tune just as well. Sometimes she was able to convince her father to join in, but the man, sitting by his wife on the piano bench, would start feeling amorous, and Carol would scold, "Now Dad, stop kissing Mother and sing with us."

During this time Cameron's drinking bouts with his clients were almost nil; he was too concerned about his wife's health, especially as the time for the delivery of their third child was drawing near.

The bundle of joy arrived early one clear morning at four o'clock. The little girl replacement for Shirlianne turned out to be a boy. But the bonnie wee babe, Andrew John, won his mother's heart! And Carol too took delight in her new brother. Of course, father was as proud as could be and handed out cigars down at the office.

The new family member brought much happiness into the home. The father insisted on extra help for his wife. There was a nanny to look after the wee fellow, which allowed the mother more time to spend at her music. He was very proud of his wife's musical talent; Cameron had never forgotten what Veronica Beauchamp in France had said, that Cindra could have had a brilliant career as a concert pianist, had she stayed in Paris and studied.

Andrew was a few months old when Peter Cord came

home for the summer holidays. Peter felt very sophisticated, being a "boarding-school boy," stiff upper lip and all that, but when he saw his baby brother he was just as pleased as the rest. At the times when he found himself alone with the little one, he played with him, retrieving the rattle the youngster had dropped. Peter giggled at the way the child would accelerate the movement of his arms and legs in excitement when he would hand back the plaything. The baby, too, would smile, as he made baby gurgling sounds.

One fine summer day it was announced that Uncle Clive had arrived from India. He was Phyllis Brent's only brother, an "eccentric bachelor," she called him. He was a very wealthy man, but none knew exactly how he made his money, or rather more money, as the Porter-Gale progeny had inherited an ancestral fortune.

He was staying at the Wishes, and when he heard that his sister had never met her oldest son's wife, in that capacity, he could hardly believe it. His remark was, "What sort of an odd-ball is she, Phyllis, that you've never met her, and you live so close?"

The man's sister went into a tirade of faults she found in her daughter-in-law: "Why, she sent her young son away to boarding school, I hear she's very chummy with her domestic staff, and she's having one baby after another." She went on enumerating other defects, then, wanting to change the subject, she queried her brother about his work.

But he was not about to leave the matter of his favourite nephew Cameron's wife, and let her get away with all the invective she had heaped upon her. "How do you know so much about her if you've never met her, Phyllis?" He went on, "Don't forget, you had five children, and very close together, as I recall. One easily forgets, doesn't one?" He paused for a moment, then continued, "Well, I'm going over there to see for myself."

Phyllis knew that once her brother had made up his mind, there was no changing it, so she said nothing. But as he left for his nephew's house, to make sure he heard, she vociferated, "Don't forget, Clive, I'm having a little gathering of your old friends this afternoon, in the garden!"

Clive waved his hand, both in acknowledgement that he had heard and to signify that he was leaving.

It did not take him long to walk over to the neighbouring estate. At the back of the mansion, as he approached the marble tiles of the patio, he heard the sounds of a piano being played, ethereal sounds, he thought. Then he spied the vision of the most beautiful woman he opined he had ever seen. She wore a pale blue silk gown, and her blond curls were gathered back, at the nape of her neck, by a blue silk bow. Beside the piano was a wicker bassinet from which were visible two chubby baby arms and legs moving rapidly.

The young woman looked up from the piano and was rather startled to see a gentleman with bushy gray sideburns approaching. Then it dawned on her: "You must be Uncle Clive!" Exclaiming thus, she got up and walked towards him.

"Yes, my dear, and you must be Cameron's wife. I'm so glad to meet you. And who's this young fellow?" He glanced towards the baby.

The proud mother went to the bassinet and picked up her little son. Turning to the man, she said, "This is Andrew John, and he's the best baby!" The little fellow smiled and cooed, as if to verify what his mother had just boasted to his grand uncle.

"Well, isn't he the happy one." Uncle Clive then changed his expression to one of seriousness. "Now what's this between you and my sister? You know, Phyllis has always let her pride interfere with her true feelings. From what I can gather, she's carelessly set up a wall between you, and her haughtiness won't allow her to give an inch!"

Dear, dear man, thought Cindra. *How understanding he is!*

Before she could interject anything, the uncle continued, "Well, she's having a garden party this afternoon, and she's invited some of my old friends, but I'm not going unless she invites you!"

The young woman looked at him in amazement. "Oh, Uncle Clive, you mustn't do that!"

Clive gave her a little pat on the shoulder. "Don't you worry, I'm going right over there now and tell her so, and believe me, she'll be phoning you."

With that, he was gone, and it was not long before the lady of the house was summoned to the phone by her parlour maid. It was Mrs. Brent, Sr., asking Cindra if she would please come to her garden party this afternoon. The young woman, eager to heal the rift that existed between them, accepted graciously. Consequently, that afternoon the young mother, having added a large white hat and gloves to her apparel of the morning, hand in hand with her two children, the baby having settled for a nap, walked over to The Wishes. It was a moment for which she and Shirlianne had earnestly prayed!

Coming to meet her over the stretch of velvety green lawn was a most elegantly dressed woman, very stately and superbly self-confident. Cindra thought she looked even more beautiful than when she had met her in Cameron's office, such a long time ago, it seemed. Uncle Clive was escorting her, and it was he who spoke first.

"Phyllis, this is your daughter-in-law, Cindra, and your two grandchildren." He purposely made a formal introduction to stress the absurdity of the estrangement. *Imagine,* he thought, *close members of a family having to do that after all those years!*

Cindra stretched out her hand to her mother-in-law, but it was Peter who spoke first, and his words were caustic. He looked straight at his grandmother and said, "Why have you treated my mother so badly, as though she weren't even alive? I think you're mean!"

The young mother was embarrassed. "Hush, Peter!" She had tried not to show her nervousness as regards this meeting, but now she had trouble controlling it.

The older lady had been thinking what sweet children they were, though she didn't know now if she would call the boy that. Well, the judgement was passed, and the woman could not deny what he had said. "The boy is right, Cindra." Then her voice became very soft. "He is your champion, and that is good. I remember how Cameron used to stick up for me. Now do come and have some lemonade and meet our other guests." Mrs. John Brent used her charm as best she could under the circumstances and led her family over to where the other guests had gathered for the introductions.

Clive could see what an impact Peter's bitter words had on his sister. He knew how expert she was at hiding her feelings and said to himself, *Well, that's good, there's to be no more of this silly nonsense!*

Clive Porter-Gale felt very proud of his strategy, and he used the same tactics for the gala dinner party Phyllis was holding in his honour the same evening. He told his sister that if she did not invite Cameron and his wife to the affair, he would have dinner at the Cameron Brent house. He told the woman he was doing this for her own good.

The master of the Columns was a surprised man when he came home from work and his wife told him about their invitation to dinner at his mother's. "Darling, are you all right? What on earth has happened?" The man wanted an explanation.

"It's all the doing of your Uncle Clive, Cam. What a wonderful man he is!" Cindra then told her husband about the whole day's proceedings, and the man was overjoyed at the incredible news.

It was a happy little group that did the usual exercises that afternoon. Then, after baby was fed, and Carol and Peter had eaten, their parents having joined them to chat with them, the couple got ready for the unexpected dinner at the Wishes.

The evening seemed magical, the air was heady with the fragrance of summer flowers—petunias, roses, a sweet-smelling potpourri—and the evening star was prematurely making its celestial appearance. The lord of the Columns and his lady walked over to the Wishes, both a little nervous at the prospect of socializing with the former's mother, from whom they had been estranged so long—Cindra especially, as she had never been in her husband's family home. Cameron sensed his wife's apprehension, and before they entered the mansion he took her in his arms and kissed her in an effort to reassure her that all was well.

If the young woman thought the Columns was luxurious, she had only to look around at the sumptuousness of the entrance hall she had just entered to see greater opulence; she mused to herself how truly magnificent it was. And fitting into those surroundings perfectly was the stately figure of her mother-in-law. How majestically she came towards her son and his wife. He dutifully gave her a kiss on the cheek, then, putting his arm around Cindra, he said, "I think you have met my wife, Mother."

The two women looked into each other's eyes. It was the older woman who walked towards the younger one and put her arms around her, then cried out "Oh, Cindra, I am sorry. Can you forgive a foolish woman?"

By this time Cindra had tears in her eyes and responded lovingly, "I never could hold anything against you, dear mother of Cam. You have given me such a wonderful husband."

The husband looked at his wife. He was never prouder of her than he was at that moment.

His mother gently pushed the young woman an arm's length away. "Let me look at you, Cindra, you dear beautiful lady." Turning to her son she said, "Oh, Cameron, she is so lovely!"

The son nodded and smiled; he had purposely come early, as he had not known what to expect, and he was so glad they had those moments alone. Now the other guests were being announced by the butler, Gaynor, as they arrived. Brother Robert escorted Phyllis Farrell; Apparently they had been dating since the day at the race track, and though she was older than Robert, they seemed to be very interested in one another.

Dr. Eric Bonn was there with Elaina, the girl whom Cameron was assisting to mount her horse when his wife flew by on Brumby. Later she told Cameron she had been receiving treatment for her eyes and her sight was improving.

Eric's sister, Claudia, arrived on the arm of a male friend from the country club. He was also a mutual friend of the Brent family. And accompanying them was Eric's mother, Greta, who had been invited as a partner for Uncle Clive. The confirmed bachelor had scolded his sister for setting him up with a date, but when he saw her, a voluptuous redhead, he was more than pleased. His sister knew her brother and figured as much!

Three other couples, old friends of Clive's, were included in the guest list, bringing the total to eighteen. There was a grand march into the dining-hall, and Cindra, on the arm of her father-in-law, felt like royalty as they led the way into the huge oak-panelled room. Cameron followed, escorting his mother. The rest continued in the procession, and soon all were seated and indulging in a gourmet meal such as the daughter-in-law had never tasted before. It was both nourishing and delicious, causing her to think what a fine hostess Cameron's mother was. The conversation at the table was both animated and interesting. Uncle Clive, especially, was enjoying his dinner companion.

After the meal, coffee was served in the drawing-room, along with liqueur, if so desired, and socialization resumed in an amicable manner. Uncle Clive kept it lively with his tales of India.

Before the soirée ended the gifted musician was asked to render some musical numbers on the piano. Looking very regal in her long sapphire blue chiffon dinner gown, she sat down in front of the grand Steinway in the magnificent drawing-room. This was her forte; she had spent so many hours practising her music that any nervousness she had she could keep well under control. She played as she had never played before, mostly familiar works of Chopin, which displayed her virtuosity and brilliance of technique to perfection. Phyllis Porter-Gale Brent, sitting beside Cameron, turned to him and remarked, "Oh isn't she wonderful!" With that she burst into tears.

Her son put his arm around her and offered her the fresh linen handkerchief he had in the pocket of his tuxedo. "Mother, don't cry, we're together now, that's what counts."

The woman shook her head sorrowfully. "I've been so wrong, Cameron, so very wrong!"

She was still sobbing, and her husband, noticing his wife's emotional trial, came over to her, leaned down towards her, and gently patted her on the shoulder. "Now, now, Phyllis, there's no use looking back, my dear," he spoke softly. "You have plenty of time to rectify things; don't be so hard on yourself."

My husband is right, she thought. *Crying over spilt milk never did help anyone.* Well, things were going to be different, she vowed!

Cameron and his wife were the last to leave. His mother requested this, as she wanted to talk to the couple alone. The older woman put her arms around her daughter-in-law; she did not want to cry again, though she could not hold back the tears. "Cindra, Cindra, I missed your wedding. Dad said you were the most beautiful bride. I've missed so much, and I've made it hard for you, but things are going to change, I promise you!" She spoke sincerely, looking straight into her daughter-in-law's eyes.

Cindra too could not hold back the tears, but hers were tears of joy. "Mother Brent, I have always admired you from afar and wanted to be friends with you. Now it's happened, and I'm so glad. Please, don't chastise yourself with such self-reproach. I just want us to be happy."

The older woman felt almost juvenile as the younger woman expressed her thoughts. Ordinarily she would be indignant at the younger person advising her how to think, but this was no ordinary occasion, and she could see that her brother Clive was right. She had been letting her pride rule her. Well, she must stop it, so she said to her daughter-in-law, "I'm afraid, my dear, I have a lot to learn. This has made me come to my senses.... Thank goodness, no matter what our age, we can change!"

There was the feeling in the little group that they did not want to part company; however, the young mother had to get back and nurse her little son, so fond good-byes were said, and the master and mistress of the Columns returned home.

Later, as they lay in bed, the master of the house held

his wife in his arms close to his heart. "My darling, I don't think you can even guess how much I love you!" His words were like music to her ears.

The moment was too lofty for anything but silence. Their souls seemed to be soaring high above the world, in the ethereal place called heaven, and Cindra felt sure that Shirlianne, in her eternal home, knew her unanswered prayer had finally been answered!

Chapter 51
Cameron's Resolution

Mrs. John Brent was a most happy woman in the days that followed. She enjoyed her grandchildren immensely and was thankful that her oldest son's estate was neighbouring hers. There were other grandchildren: Her daughter, Nancy, who was married to Jeremy Beck, had three children, Carrie, Krystin, and young Polly. They lived in another part of the city, and she did not see them very often, a state of affairs she had previously blamed Jeremy for. She was opposed to his heavy drinking, but she could see that she, alas, had played a part in causing the alienation, and since she had taken the vow to change, her attitude towards him had softened.

Phyllis Brent spent many summer days in the beauteous gardens of the Columns. She and Carol Lynne would read out of the little girl's books, most of them inherited from the child's step-sister. Carol told her that her latest book had been given to her by her grandmother in Canada, whom she had recently visited. This disclosure caused her father's mother to lament as she thought of the many hours that had been lost because of her foolish pride. Yet it made these hours all the more precious, and she enjoyed them to the full.

She did not become too well acquainted with Peter at first, as their relationship was a little awkward. However, when the time came for the boy to leave for summer camp with a group of boys from the church, they were on fairly good terms. Still, the woman mused to herself, almost out loud, *Oh, he's just like me, that barrier of pride. It's going to get him into difficulty in his life too!* The grandmother did not realize how right her prediction was!

Meanwhile, Cindra continued with her music practice and that pleased her mother-in-law, who enjoyed listening to the lilting refrains that floated out through the French doors of the drawingroom. But the older woman's main delight was when little Andrew's nanny would wheel his carriage out to where the stately older woman sat and place the child in her welcoming arms, so happy was the grandmother to hold and hug her little grandson.

There were reciprocal meals shared between the folks from the Wishes and those from the Columns, and living became a beautiful shared experience between the two families. Phyllis Brent was especially appreciative of this when her husband was away on business in Paris.

In late summer there took place two weddings. Robert Brent married Phyllis Farrell, much to the satisfaction of Mrs. John Brent, as it meant the Farrells' fortune would be joining that of the Brents', since Phyllis Farrell was sole heiress to the former. The other wedding, which was at last taking place, was that between Dr. Robertson and Phyllis Pindar.

Thus, excitement reigned high for all, but especially for Carol Lynne, who was flower girl twice, first at the Robertson wedding and then with her cousin Polly Beck, who was also a flower-girl, at her Uncle Robert's wedding. Polly's two sisters, both teen-agers, were bridesmaids at the latter affair.

Mr. and Mrs. Cameron Brent could not have been happier than when they saw the two couples being married. Cameron was glad Phyllis Farrell had softened and had at last found a mate. He could not say that he had ever really been in love with her, not after he had tried very hard not to, but had fallen so desperately in love with his secretary. He wished for his brother that his love for Phyllis would continue to grow, as his had for Cindra.

And Cindra was glad to see her dear friend of the Park Plaza apartment days so happy, coming out of the church on the arm of her husband, as Mrs. Jack Robertson.

The colourful weddings soon became memories. Time passed by quickly, as it is wont to do, and Cameron started to have the odd drinking bouts with his clients again. One night his wife got a dreadful fright. He came home with his head thickly bandaged, and Dr. Robertson was with him. Raoul was helping the inebriated man up the stairs when Cindra came out of the bedroom; on seeing her husband, she cried out his name. He kept repeating, "Cindra, darling, I'm sorry, I'm sorry."

She demanded, almost hysterically, to know what had happened. The good doctor said he had come along home with Cameron for two reasons. First, he had to explain to the young woman what had occurred, that her husband had fallen when leaving the club, had struck his head on the pavement, and was then taken to hospital. The doctor stated he had been summoned to go to the emergency department, thus he was able to assure her that skull Xrays proved negative for fracture. The other reason was to remain with him, as Cameron had refused to be admitted. He told her that her husband had sustained a deep gash to his head, which had been sutured, and that his level of consciousness would have to be checked periodically, so he had come home with him and would carry out head-injury routine throughout the night.

The concerned wife thanked "Dr. Rob," thinking to herself what a dear, precious friend he was. She asked if she could carry out the routine of which he spoke and relieve him, but he told her to get her rest and not to worry. Then he phoned his wife to inform her of his whereabouts.

It was to no avail that Dr. Robertson told the anxious wife not to worry. She had a very fitful sleep and in the morning she was pale and nervous as she awaited his report on the condition of her husband. Dr. Robertson said, "He's going to be okay, my dear. He slept well and his level of consciousness remained stable." These were words she was glad to hear.

Cindra stayed in bed with her husband the entire day. He was full of remorse. He told her his drinking days were over, that he never could tolerate alcohol and could see it was going to ruin him. "You know, Cindra, I've always wondered if you regretted not marrying the medical student boyfriend you had in Canada. What would you say if I went back into medicine?" He looked at her directly as he spoke.

"It's whatever you want, Cam. It'll be you who has to do the studying." She really had to think about it, it was such startling news.

"Well, dear, Dad's business is going well. Robert is taking right ahold now; his marriage has made a difference." Since his wife did not say anything, he continued, "I would really like to be a diagnostician. I think if Shirlianne had been diagnosed sooner she might not have died—research also appeals to me."

This made her fully realize just how deeply the death of his daughter had affected him.

"Where would you have to go, Cam?" That was what she wanted to know!

"That's the only thing, it's most sensible to go to Indiana University, where I began. I could probably get in right away. It's almost the same distance as Kansas City from here, only in a northeasterly direction." He mentioned Kansas City, as his wife had been there and it would give her some idea of the distance. He paused then. "I'd come home whenever I could." He was well aware it would be difficult for both of them.

They continued to talk about it. Cindra thought maybe his head injury had made her husband irrational, and yet, when she saw how serious he was, and how feasible was the plan as he divulged it, she became very grave. She thought to herself that perhaps it was what he needed, a challenge, a goal that could possibly end his drinking days. She was all for that!

The formalities did not take long. The man was right: Since he had been an excellent student, he was accepted immediately into the Indiana University Medical School. Thus Cameron Brent left the Brent Paper and Printing business, with his father's blessing, and that of his mother as well, since for him to become a doctor had always been her wish. For Phyllis Porter-Gale Brent, it was a dream coming true.

Chapter 52
Life Goes On

The master of the Columns was glad that the separation between his mother and himself and his family had finally been healed and he felt better about leaving his wife and children; actually, it was a factor in his making the final decision.

Mrs. John Brent was now very supportive of her daughter-in-law the musician, and she would let no one say anything against the young woman. The bonds of love grew very strong between them, and this indeed helped Cindra to face the bleak thought of her husband being away from home for such a long time.

During her husband's absence the young mother involved herself in her children's activities. Peter had returned from boarding school. The father thought his oldest son should be the man of the house now, whilst he was away. Though sports were high on the lad's list of interests, and his mother encouraged him in these, it was during this period that he became quite a virtuoso on the violin, and his mother was very proud of him.

Carol Lynne, conversely, was not keen on her piano lessons; she took them mainly to please her mother. She became very involved in swimming and went on to acquire life-saving awards. Her mother, determined to have her take advantage of her talent for swimming, but also at the girl's request, enrolled her in synchronized swimming classes, and ballet classes as well, the purpose of which was to help her in the performance of the "Synchro Swim" figures.

Andrew was growing out of babyhood; he was a delightful little boy and the apple of Grandmother Brent's eye. After all, he was named after her husband—the second name, that is! Some would say he was a "slow" learner, but his grandmother would not hear of that term being used to describe him. "You just wait," she would say. "He'll be just as bright or brighter than the other two as he develops. Just mark my words." And she helped him with his childhood studies, assisting him to read, even before he started his schooling. She also had his grandfather play chess with him; the man would give him helps and assists here and there in the game, but there eventually would come a day when this was not needed, and grandfather had to concentrate well to stand up to the young fellow's cunning strategy in the game.

Cindra was content during this stage of her life to see that her children were well educated. She, influenced by her upbringing, made sure her progeny's spiritual life was nourished, so they were in church every Sunday and belonged to the appropriate church groups, according to their age. Off and on, this met with complaints from the children, but these soon passed and their mother had her way.

The musician, of course, continued with her piano practice and her music lessons. She had been saddened by the death of her music teacher, Miss Grace. They had become endeared to one another, and Cindra missed her very much. But in the course of time she found another teacher, a Mr. Connor, a slight little man, but an excellent tutor. He was also a professor of music at one of the universities. His instruction seemed to be exactly what the beautiful virtuoso needed to perfect her technique, and she felt she was progressing further in the art for which she had such innate talent. Although the rigours of her practice were tedious, she was loving it!

Eric Bonn would occasionally make an appearance on

the scene, saying that he had promised Cameron he would keep an eye on things whilst he was away. Nevertheless, Cindra did not encourage his visits. He indeed 'kept an eye' on her, as was his wont, and she did not like it!

There were nights on rare week-ends when she would awake and see a naval officer's hat on the dressing table, indicating her husband was home on auxilliary duty. He would be in the den studying, not wanting to waken her. Though she would waken, and later she would say to him, "I just felt it in the 'vibes' in the air that you were here." She would hasten to where he was, in her filmy negligee, with long blond hair flowing, and there would be such a wonderful reunion, one that ended, for that night, the studying of a man who hungered for his wife's caresses.

Chapter 53
A Bitter Quarrel

There were not many things on which Cameron Brent and his wife disagreed. They had had several minor flareups over household finances; Cindra, not having been brought up by wealthy parents, always had the feeling they should cut down on expenses. But recently there was dissension, this time of major import, over another matter, and the lady of the house was insistent about it. Carol Lynne had complained bitterly to her father, "Daddy, mother expects me to wash my own underwear, and vacuum my room, and also help the maids with the cooking on the weekends. Gosh, I have enough to do with my studies at school, and my Synchro lessons, and ballet, and piano; to please her I'm learning knitting and crocheting at school, so I can make gifts for special occasions, Mother says." She did not wait for him to respond but continued, "I told Gran Brent about it but she just says, 'Oh, your mother knows what's best for you. Do as she says.'" The girl imitated her grandmother's voice.

The father looked at his daughter, the apple of his eye. He felt sorry for her and expressed it. "Well, that indeed is a heck of a lot for a young girl. I'll speak to your mother about it; you just leave it to me."

Thus Cameron brought up the matter of their daughter's heavy schedule to his wife, and the latter's irritation showed in her voice, though she tried not to get angry.

"Cam, just because you were brought up with a silver spoon in your mouth and have been able to keep a similar life-style as an adult doesn't mean that Carol will; she may fall in love and marry a man who is not rich and who needs a wife that can run a household on very little."

"Come on now, Cindra, have a heart. The poor dear came to me in tears. Now, she's my child too." The father felt he had to defend the girl who was counting on him.

"You go away, Cam, and leave me to raise the children and then all you can do is criticize!" She had now become angry and it showed both in her voice and in her facial expression. She added something that afterwards she wished she had not: "Look at your sister, Nancy. She's really unable to cope with caring for her family properly because she didn't learn to be a housewife. Now that has caused troubles, and Jeremy goes out drinking to get away from it!"

Cameron in his turn became angry too; in response to the criticism he said, "Well you certainly haven't had to use any of the housewifely skills you learned!"

The altercation took place just before it was time for

the man to leave for the university, and he walked out of the house without the usual fond farewell that the couple would share, pledging their undying love until his next visit home.

The unhappy wife was in tears after her husband left. They had never had such heated words before, and it was tearing her apart. She had said some other abusive remarks that were troubling her. She recalled reading in her father's black memo book some words of Holy Scripture she wished she had put into practise: "Not rendering evil for evil, or railing for railing, but contrariwise blessing... seek peace and ensue it." She knew her father had used them in his life, as her parents had enjoyed a most compatible relationship. She promised herself she would argue no more with her husband about the matter but she would try to convince him in a gentle way that her ideas had much merit. She wished she had given him a blessing on his departure instead of those caustic words. "Oh, what if something happens to him before he arrives there?" she whispered to herself, and she prayed for his safety en route.

However, before the despondent woman retired to bed that night, she received a phone call from her husband. He said whilst he was driving he had been thinking over all that had taken place and that her way of bringing up the children was praiseworthy. He complimented her on being a good mother, then said he was sorry they had not patched up their quarrel before he left and that he was aching to take her in his arms now and alleviate the hurt.

Cindra was just glad he had phoned. She told him she was trying to do her best for the children, stating she did want them to grow up to be responsible people, but also, as an appeasement, that she was willing to help their daughter with her domestic chores.

Cameron next talked to Carol Lynne, explaining to her

that her mother was trying to make sure she became a capable person, and there would come a day when she would thank her mother. He told her her mother said she would help her with the work she had to do at home. Lastly, he asked her to do as her mother requested, without complaint, assuring her this would make it all easier.

Before the phone connection was cut off the husband spoke to his wife again, words of endearment, encouragement, regret and love!

Chapter 54
Events at the Columns

There was an expense the lady of the Columns did agree upon—the abolishment of the outdoor swimming-pool and the construction of an indoor pool. Since Carol was taking her synchronized swimming lessons very seriously, her father decided she should have a pool at home in which to practice. He even arranged for Raoul, who was an excellent swimmer, to act as life-guard for the young girl when she would be using the facility. Raoul and his wife continued to be very valuable domestic staff members of the Cameron Brent household and more so since the master of the house was away most of the time. Actually, they had become like members of the family, and now the ex-chauffeur would be assuming a further role in its concerns.

Cameron's remark, "A pool will encourage us all to take more exercise," caused his wife to smile in amusement. The man, though he continued an exercise program at the university, knew his wife had lapsed from the routine of physical activity before dinner, the regime being done only on the weekends when he was home. Her explanation to him was that there was not enough time in the children's day.

Consequently, a huge swimming pool, all glass enclosed, was constructed on the west side of the mansion, and the area where the outdoor pool had been, in the lower gardens, was levelled, becoming a tennis court in the summer and a skating rink in the winter. The children learned to skate on this home rink and so did the lady of the house. Though ice-skating was popular in her country, there was never enough money in her family to afford a non-necessity like ice-skates. But once the lady, assisted by her husband at first, had learned to skate, she was just as avid an enthusiast of the sport as were her children. She enjoyed it, especially when the master of the house had music transmitted to the area and she could glide to the lovely tunes, feeling uplifted and free.

On Christmas day, if the temperature allowed for ice, there would be a large group of family and friends out on the rink sometime in the afternoon, and the laughter and fun was exhilarating to the body as well as to the soul. Grandmother Brent along with Grandmother Gold, if she was there visiting, would sit out on a bench, with a car-rug draped over their legs, and join the hilarity, humming the tunes and singing, if they knew the words. Truly, a festive mood was the order of the day!

And, as the children grew, Christmases at the Columns, besides being occasions of splendour, were as well ones of accomplishment. The children would be encouraged by their mother to make their gifts. For Carol Lynne it posed no problem, as she had her knitting and sewing skills. Likewise, Peter could craft things of wood in the workshop of the mansion. But Andrew, in his younger years, needed help with his gift-making. This help came first from his mother, then later from the chauffeur Faulkner, who, you might say, was an artificer in woodwork. Finally the lad managed very well on his own.

For Cindra, the main event of the celebration of the nativity of the Christ Child was the midnight Mass; it had always held a certain sacred mystique for her, which she hoped to be able to inspire in her kin. As each child grew older that child would be included in the attendance of the family at the church in Ladue, to commemorate the birth of the Lord, in the holy Eucharist.

During these years, at this annual festive season, the master of the manor was home for the holiday; joy and good humour reigned supreme. Of course he was very happy when Grandmother Gold was able to join them. She would sometimes be accompanied by Cindra's sister Barbara when she got the holiday off from her nursing job, and because these times were rare, Auntie Barbara was fussed over royally by the children.

Always the lord and lady of the Wishes were invited to these merry celebrations besides other relatives and friends. The table in the dining-hall was extended to accommodate the celebrating souls and troubles all being forgotten, the Cameron Brent residence was vibrant with mirth, joy, and gladness—and of course music! Cameron's toast to the ladies, one at a time, was met with pleasure by them, but the boys would snicker, and as it went on, they would end up placing their hands over their ears, looking laughingly at one another.

Yet Cindra, over these years, was faced with another family member's absence. Peter, at his own insistence, after three years of his father's absence, had gone away to a private military school in Indiana. Though she wanted what was best for him, his mother missed him more than she was willing to say.

Chapter 55
Claudia's Conspiracy

The years passed by quickly, so the children would have said. For their mother it was different. She virtually ticked off the days, one by one, of her husband's four years at medical school—the two years of pre-clinical, then the two years of clinical experience, until they were completed and he was at last ready to graduate and receive his doctor of medicine degree. She was very proud of her husband; he was to be valedictorian at his graduation exercises.

The graduate had been working on a certain experiment for a thesis. It had to do with leukemia research, and he had become so engrossed, one weekend in the project, that time became immaterial. It was not so for his wife. They were to attend a ball that night. Cindra was ready and waiting. At last the telephone rang; the anxious young woman ran to it. It had to be him, she thought. She was quite surprised when she heard Eric Bonn's voice on the other end of the line. It had been arranged beforehand for the two couples to attend the affair together. Eric seemed rather upset; he said he was calling from Elaina's house. She was his date for the event. His information was that she had just twisted her ankle, having tripped on her way downstairs; he explained that he had given her first-aid, but that it would be impossible for her to go with him. In turn he was surprised when Cindra, in a disappointed tone, informed him that Cameron had not arrived home from Indianapolis yet. Eric said he would be right over.

When a car pulled up in the driveway of the Columns, the young Mrs. Brent thought it was her husband. Instead it was Dr. Eric Bonn. He rushed in, not waiting for Dalton, the butler, to announce him. His coat flew open, revealing his well-cut tuxedo. He did present a handsome dashing appearance, and the beautiful woman, looking especially radiant in her lime green evening gown, with her golden hair drawn back and cascading softly in curls, wished so very much that her husband was there.

Eric spoke in his decisive, "doctorial" way: "We'll go to my place and pick up Claudia. She can be my partner for tonight; I phoned her to get ready. We'll wait for Cam over there."

Whilst the golden-haired lady looked at him in an "I would rather not" manner, the high-spirited man placed her wrap on her shoulders, and, after giving instructions to the butler to send his employer to the Bonn residence when he arrived, he ushered her out the door and into his car.

Cindra had been in the Bonn mansion before, but the sumptuous European-style furnishings still impressed her. Mrs. Bonn was out at the country club for a game night. "She'll be sorry she missed you," was Eric's remark.

Claudia came down the winding stairs looking very glamorous in a pale blue evening gown. "Hello, Cindra, so Cameron hasn't arrived yet!" The young woman spoke with a German accent.

Cindra was quick to make excuses for her husband. "He's been doing some research at the university for a thesis and he tends to lose track of time."

"Well, we'll have a little drink. I'm sure you could use one." With that pronouncement Claudia went directly to the liquor cabinet and mixed drinks for the three of them.

Cameron's wife had informed her that she preferred a little sherry; however, the lady mixing the drinks told her they were out of sherry, but she would fix her a nice drink.

The young Mrs. Brent began to relax as she sipped her drink with Eric. Claudia had disappeared and they were alone. Soft music was playing in the background, setting a dreamy, romantic mood. Having emptied their glasses, the couple seemed almost mesmerized.

Eric drew closer to the young woman beside him on the divan. His thoughts were heady; she looked so beautiful in the candle-light's glow. He had to admit he had always been in love with her. For him, just to touch her was thrilling!

The object of his dreams, on her part, was not resistant to his advances; for that matter, she felt powerless to resist. She was in his arms and passion, in all its aspects, prevailed!

Cindra awoke to the reality of time and the situation. She knew she had let happen what she had not wanted to happen, but there had been a driving force within her and she had had no power to resist it.

Even Eric ended up having remorse as he could see how devastated she was when she faced the reality of it all. Whilst he drove her home there was complete silence. He stole a glance at her now and again; he kept thinking of how he adored her!

As they drove up to the front door of the Columns, Cameron, in evening attire, was just leaving the house. On seeing his wife, he rushed over to the car to assist her in alighting from the vehicle.

"Sorry, Darling, I should have started back sooner. I got tied up this morning with the experiment I've been working on. It was a crucial time . . . ." His voice trailed off. Cindra spoke not a word. She just got out of the car: she could not look at him. She went through the front door, which he held open for her. She did not even say good night to Eric; Cameron expressed that formality.

In their bedroom Cameron, suspecting she was distraught over his late arrival, began to apologize again for his thoughtlessness.

"It isn't that. I wish it were!" She spoke with a fierceness.

"Then what's happened, Cindra? What is it?"

To answer, his wife started talking in riddles, so he thought. "Do you want a divorce, Cameron? I'm not the saintly wife you thought you had. Eric and I . . ." She could not finish; she hated to say it, and what she had said was uttered with a mixture of displeasure and disgust.

He approached her and spoke to her gently. "It's me who should be asking if you want a divorce. Are you in love with him, Cindra?"

She knew his love for her was great, so great that he would sacrifice his own happiness for hers. She ran to the bed and buried her head in a pillow, in tears. Sobbingly she said, "You're the only man I've loved or will ever love. I don't know what came over me."

He went over to the bed and sat down beside her. "Then I don't know what the big fuss is about." With those words he seemed to shrug it off as a mere perchance incident.

But she could not; her sense of impropriety was gnawing at her. He took her in his arms and said it was all his fault. She winced. *Ah, my gallant gentleman,* she thought. *Why had he not come?*

"Darling, don't torture yourself over this. It's done, we can't go back, so forget it. If you don't love him and don't want a divorce then let's chalk it up to my mistake. I'd been away so long this time, it was unfair to you.... Now, I hope you're all packed. It's my graduation next week, and we leave to-morrow for Indianapolis." He purposely changed the subject to get her mind off the event that was playing havoc there.

She lay still, saying nothing. He took her in his arms and told her that nothing in this world could interfere with his love for her, that he practically worshipped the ground on which she walked, so lofty were his feelings for her. And with tenderness and love he consummated their union, as though to impress on her that their marriage was still intact. He had another reason too, besides his desire; he had to defend her honour, just in case.... She was a young woman and still of child-bearing age!

However, the young Mrs. Brent could not settle to sleep; she kept waking her husband. Her concupiscence seemed insatiable. He asked her what she was given to drink at Eric's place. She told him the whole story of what had happened. He was not surprised when he found out who had mixed the drinks.

He spoke as though talking to himself. "So it was Claudia! She spiked those drinks with some sort of aphrodisiac!" The man knew Claudia had always had designs on him and she probably thought this was a good chance to break up his marriage, so he figured it.

Wanting his wife to have a good night's sleep, he went to his black bag, took out a vial, needle, and syringe, and injected the lady with a tranquilizer. Before long she settled down in his arms, and he stroked her fair head as she fell asleep. *I must help her not to suffer over this,* were his introspections before slumber claimed him for the rest of the night.

Chapter 56
Graduation at Last

The spring morning dawned beautiful and bright. Cameron had been called to the Wishes at daybreak. His mother was having an attack of pain in the abdomen similar to that which she had had some years before, and the son remembered it had been diagnosed as cholecystitis. On examining her he felt it was a similar attack. Against her wishes he arranged for her to be admitted to the hospital.

She argued, "But I want to go to your graduation, Cameron. It's always been my dream." Nevertheless, she realized it was to no avail and acquiesced, instructing her maid to pack a bag for her. Severe pain had struck again, causing her to gasp and hold her breath; she knew then and there her son was right! She tried to convince her husband to go to the event without her, but he said his place was here with her, so that was settled.

The disappointed man went back to a wife still in bed. She was awake but very groggy. She said she could not possibly go with him, explaining that she was too sleepy and too upset. And when she was informed of her mother-in-law's plight, she also said she was worried about her.

"Dad is staying with Mother." He put her mind at rest about that matter. "Now, my darling, you have to go. All my confrères are wanting to meet you. I've told them about you, how beautiful you are, and how accomplished...." He was about to say more but she cut him off.

"Yes, and now you'll have to tell them how improper I am!" The thought of the occurrence of the evening before was cutting into her like a sword, and she chastened herself bitterly.

The man could have laughed at her naïveté. Little did she know about some of the women she was going to meet, wives of the men with whom he studied, and the tales they would tell about them, and of the illicit amours that went on at the country club, but he did not tell her.

"Cindra, you have never been judgemental towards others who have had lengthy extramarital affairs, so why are you so hard on yourself, just for one slip?" With this pronouncement he was trying to get her to take a rational view of the situation. "And it's not as though you did it deliberately."

A soft knock on the door interrupted their conversation. It was Dalton with their breakfast tray. With persuasion the troubled young woman ate her share.

The master of the house had to take command of the situation. He explained to Carol and Andrew where their parents were going and arranged for them to be taken to church by friendly neighbours. The domestic staff, who were very proud of their employer's accomplishment, wished him Godspeed and promised to look after the much-adored children with care and affection.

Clarisse was summoned; she helped her mistress complete her toilette and style her hair. She related to the young Mrs. Brent that she and Raoul were also going to her husband's graduation. She said that Cameron had said, " 'You are like family and I want you there.' So, Ma'am, I'll be your coiffeur, besides help you dress, for all the things taking place." The maid sounded very pleased to be included in the important event. She went on, "And of course it gives me and Raoul a chance to get away together. We'll attend the graduation, of course, but we'll be on our own. Raoul has some things planned for us two." By this time the trusty servant could see that her mistress was under some sort of stress, so she added in a sympathetic tone,

"Now, don't you worry, I'll be there to do your hair when you need me."

Accordingly, the two couples left in separate cars, headed for the event that would fulfill Cameron Brent's destiny. Cindra sat quiet and motionless in the Brent limousine. Her husband feared she might go into a depression as she did after Shirlianne's death. He considered it must be her religious convictions that were causing her such anguish. Realizing this, he knew he must get her to talk about it. He started the conversation.

"Cindra, at church the priest talks about the 'grace of God' and 'unconditional love.' Where is that unconditional love of God, which you claim is so great, that makes the mistakes of life forgiveable? You were able to forgive my mother for her years of slight against you, which I so admired in you, yet you can't forgive yourself. Cindra, if God, as you claim, is such a great God of love, then let that love of God come through to you."

Cam is right, she thought. *He is not much of a churchman, but obviously he absorbs what he hears.* She looked at him, contemplating how handsome he was with his dark hair greying slightly at the temples. How distinguished he appeared! He glanced at her briefly and their eyes met, then he spoke words she felt had a great deal of truth in them.

"You know, my darling, I think it's your pride getting in the way. You can accept the imperfections of others, but you expect yourself to be perfect."

Finally she responded, "I guess you're right, Cam, but it's just that I feel I betrayed a trust . . . and you."

"Well, I don't feel that way at all. If there was any betrayal it rests on my shoulders. It was so thoughtless and selfish of me, I should have gotten home and taken you to the dance. It would have served me right if you decided to leave me for Eric. I wouldn't have blamed you." He said this with the intention of impressing on her the fact that had he been there, she would not have been placed in such a vulnerable position.

They continued to talk; Cameron could see the pained look on his wife's face gradually disappear, so that, at the end of the long journey, when they arrived at their hotel, she expressed interest in the oncoming course of events, much to the relief of the graduating doctor.

The convocation hall at the university was filled with dignitaries and bigwigs the night of graduation, as well as relatives and friends of the graduating students. When his turn came, Cameron Brent stood at the lectern poised and confident as he gave his valedictory address. He mentioned in his speech how those of them who were married with families and with their homes a great distance away owed so much to their wives, who had kept the homefires burning and raised their children practically alone. He then added something that had come to him en route in the car. He said that when they are administering to the needs of their patients and caught up in the business of their profession, they should not forget their life partners at home, who have needs too, and include these persons in their caring. Then he asked his life partner to stand up and he proudly introduced his wife, saying she had been very instrumental in his success at arriving at this important day in his life.

Cindra, in her softly tailored peach-coloured suit, seated near the front, arose. She managed to hide the nervousness that a previous unfortunate incident had caused her, turned slowly round, and with a friendly little gesture of her gloved hand acknowledged the applause given her.

The valedictorian looked down on her with eyes of love; never did he cherish her more than at that moment.

Her beauty and charm made quite an impression, and as she sat down, she shed a little tear, not the involuntary tearing of her left eye, as droplets fell from both eyes. Her husband's public recognition of the part she played in the attainment of his degree touched her deeply and endeared him to her more than words could express.

There were celebrations taking place through the week for the graduated doctors, but Dr. Cameron Brent prescribed a restful regime for his wife. There was room service to their suite for some of their meals. He put his wife's mind at rest as to the children by phoning them every day. Both mother and father spoke at length to each one, listening to their happenings at home and filling them in on what was taking place in Indianapolis. Carol kept them informed of her Grandmother Brent's condition, letting them know she was not going to need surgery.

Pampering his wife, Cameron had given Clarisse a written schedule of the times she would be needed as coiffeur for his beloved. The faithful maid adhered to the schedule, and the young woman made her appearance at the different functions in most elegant style.

One afternoon the gifted musician, whose husband had heralded her talent, was to render a few selections on the grand piano in the palatial lounge adjoining the hotel lobby. It was a request of the new doctor's class-mates. Cameron Brent was forever seeking ways to make it possible for his wife to practice, so he had scored again in this regard. He escorted the beautiful pianist to the musical instrument with dignity and aplomb, holding her hand high, as though she were a princess, and truly she did look very regal in her pink gown of silk moiré. He kissed her hand affectionately before she sat down and received from his lady love a coy but flirtatious smile in return. He, almost mesmerized, watched her every movement, and he could see she was in her world, poised and confident, perfectly at home in the art to which she had dedicated so much time. Those who were there all agreed they had never heard the selected Chopin pieces nor the Strauss waltzes played so brilliantly. The encores persisted, but the man of medicine, with his trained eye, deduced something of which the pianist was not aware—that she was becoming tired, and, by placing his hand gently on her shoulder, he indicated to her the concert must end. He escorted her away from the piano. There were so many people wanting to meet her; her husband made the introductions and showed her off in a way that bespoke her being a priceless treasure in his life.

According to custom, midday tea was served to the gathering, but after as much socializing as etiquette required, Dr. and Mrs. Cameron Brent returned to their suite. When the doors closed behind them they stood there, looking at one another. He was a doctor at last! The realization suddenly came to the young woman that this was what he had wanted since he was a young boy. And in the doctor's mind there were thoughts of how lovely she was, and how gloriously gifted, and in this blissful moment they drew close to one another. He kissed her passionately. Suddenly she backed away, saying she was afraid the episode, which had happened in bed last Saturday night, would occur again. Cameron laughed and remarked, "Don't worry, darling, I have plenty of needles with me."

The comment caused them both to laugh and Cindra felt complete sanity return to her. The old cliché her father oft repeated was once more confirmed: "Laughter is the best medicine."

Finally the love tryst had to end; it would soon be time for Clarisse to come and assist her mistress with her grooming for the evening's event. Then Cindra suddenly remembered her oldest son, who was in military school in Culver, not far from them. "Oh, Cam, I completely forgot about Peter. He should have been here for your graduation!" The fair woman was abashed; caught up in her own frayed emotions, she had forgotten about the boy she adored.

"Don't worry, my dear, I sent him an invitation, but he's involved in some military exercise and could not get away." Actually, the truth was that he chose not to attend. Anyway, the concerned mother felt much better when her husband put a phone call through to Culver, and she had a lengthy conversation with the military student.

Clarisse came promptly and helped her mistress prepare for the night's fête taking place in the magnificent ballroom of the hotel. The gala was sponsored by the university and it was Cindra's privilege to meet there many of the professors and doctors who had been her husband's instructors. But those learned men would have said it was their privilege to meet her and enjoy her charisma and charm. She indeed sparkled with wit and vivacity that night.

Sunday evening's affair concluded the week's festivities. There was a sumptuous dinner with speeches, which took place in the banquet-hall on the campus of the university. Dr. Brent, on observing his beautiful wife, could not help but marvel at her poise and confidence. His mind wandered back to when she had been his young secretary, accompanying him for business lunches with his clients. And he considered how those had been such valuable learning experiences in the development of her conversational skills. He could not help but feel great pride and joy as he watched her commune with his tutors and colleagues, and just be the brilliant jewel she was meant to be. And if she had been asked, she would have said her composure and self-assuredness were the result of her husband's gentle care and guidance, and that, just recently, it was his common sense and logic, as well as his faith, that were responsible for her being able to forgive herself.

Chapter 57
A Mother's Compunction

On the couple's return home, the master of the house immediately contacted the Wishes. He was glad to hear that his mother's gall bladder attack had subsided and that she was back at home. It was not long before the graduated doctor and his wife walked across the gardens to the neighbouring estate, and there took place a happy little reunion, with the mother embracing both her son and his wife. Cameron, after cautioning his mother to stick to her diet, was handed an envelope. It contained a congratulatory card with a cheque from both of his parents for an enormous amount of money. The immediate response that came to his mind was to tell her it was too much, but his mother stood there, obviously bursting with pride over her son's achievement, so he thought better of it and, expressing his sincere thanks, accepted it graciously.

His mother then became pensive; suddenly tears welled up in her eyes.

"What is it, Mother?" He was very curious, he could see that whatever she wanted to say was difficult for her to express.

She seemed to gather up courage and almost blurted out, "Cindra has told me what love you gave to Shirlianne, and just what a beautiful little person she was." Obviously the woman was now regretting those years she made him and the child suffer, and she was thinking how she could have done so much to help.

Cameron could not deny the fact that a great hurt was there, and that this was a very delicate situation. But he considered the ordeal his mother had just been through. She looked so pale, and he was sure a cholecystectomy had not been performed because of her elevated blood pressure. Perhaps she thought she might die and wanted to get this off her chest.

The sorrowful woman spoke again. "I'll not blame you, Cameron, if you can't forgive; it was very cruel."

The retrospective man looked at his wife and thought about how this dear one, having been slighted for years, forgave his mother instantaneously. And he had thought many times of how his decision to keep his dear coloured child really put a burden on his mother; society had to be blamed for that. Well, it was all in the past, and this was the present. He promptly stepped forward and embraced his mother tenderly, all the while thinking about that unconditional love of God, about which he had preached to his wife, and how it applied to him as well and must be operative in his life.

Phyllis Brent, after a little crying session in her son's arms, pulled herself together and reminded herself that she was the hostess, so refreshments were ordered and shortly thereafter the three family members enjoyed tea and cookies in the drawing-room. The older woman, appearing as though a heavy weight had been lifted from her shoulders, beamed with pride as she visited with her son, now a medical doctor, and she praised her daughter-in-law for her self-sacrificing role in her son's achievement.

When the doctor and his wife took their leave, the farewells were fond and loving, with promises of getting together again very soon.

It must be stated that it was not only Grandmother and Grandfather Brent who gave congratulatory tributes to the new doctor. Carol Lynne and Andrew John were very excited and filled with admiration, which they freely made known to their father. Carol presented him with a meaningful card along with a sweater knit in his university colours (she told him it had taken her since Christmas to make it). Andrew gave him a wooden letter-opener, which was rather crudely crafted. One could see the carving of the medical insignia had given him some trouble, but the effort had to be appreciated, and so it was by the grateful father. Accompanying it was a card, fashioned out of art paper and displaying a bulky, lab-coated figure, from whose ears hung a stethoscope. The message inscribed thereon was "Well done, Dad."

The unpretentious man was lauded as well by numerous other relatives, by his household staff, and by his many friends, but there was not a word from Peter. Cindra, who had great love for both her husband and her son, felt the boy's indifference was inexcusable and she planned to reveal these feelings in her next letter to him. Nevertheless, after discussing it with her wise life partner, who reminded her of the perilous times the youngster was put through during his business-drinking days and the episode of the horse Brumby, she decided not to interfere, but to leave it to her prayers alone to heal the relationship.

Chapter 58
Hurray for the Children

Cameron Brent, M.D., was glad his clinical years in medicine were behind him. Wanting to locate in a hospital in Saint Louis so that on the nights he was not on call he could be home with his family, he applied and was accepted for internship at the Saint Louis University Hospital. It offered rotating internships, and thus would enable him to spend some time in each of the hospital's medical departments. He was sure his field was pathology, and he had hopes of becoming a diagnostician. His professors confirmed the belief he had in himself as being very astute at diagnosing cases according to the presenting symptoms, and even though it would mean another year or two as a resident doctor, there seemed to be a driving force within him urging him to attain that goal.

This meant the man's stipend would be very meagre; hence, Cindra was concerned about finances. She was worried that they had gone through a fortune already, since her husband had changed careers, and suggested that they cut down on the household staff, but he would not hear of it. He just laughed and told her not to worry her pretty little head. To put her mind at ease he enumerated their assets: his naval pension, the interest from his numerous investments, the congratulatory cheque from his parents, and Uncle Clive's noble-minded contribution.

In fact the enterprising Clive had generously shared a portion of his huge fortune with the couple. He had stated, "You know, Cameron, you've always been my favourite nephew, and your wife, well, I became her worshipper the first time I met her."

Nevertheless, the lady of the Columns, with her frugal upbringing, was eager to economize wherever she could. She had always encouraged Carol Lynne to handcraft things, so the girl became skilled at knitting and dressmaking, not to mention culinary accomplishments. She had been enrolled in a private day school for a number of years. Mother said it was not necessary; father disagreed, but it was Carol herself who complied with her mother's wishes, explaining to her dad that she had many friends, and friends more to her liking, who went to the proposed public school. These were the ones she preferred to be with. The girl, like her mother, was no socialite and had no desire, as did her private-school chums, of having a debut. The father was very touched by his daughter's selfless decision and by her admiration of him, especially when she told him she wanted to go into the health care field, like him, and become a nurse.

Peter Cord had won an academic scholarship, which helped with the fees of the private military school where he was enrolled. He had worked hard at his studies, as he knew of his mother's financial concerns, and she was very pleased with his efforts.

Then there was Andrew John, or Drew (a nickname some of his schoolmates had given him). His hair was just as black as Peter's was blond. Everyone said he was the image of his dad; he also had the same mild temperament as his father, and he was liked by all. True to Grandmother Brent's prediction he was doing very well at his studies and was always at the top of his class. His grandfather and he would play chess for hours on end, and when he won against an adult in a chess tournament and brought home a trophy, there was almost no end to the congratulations he received. The boy said it was all his grandfather's doing; he had been his painstaking coach and must be given the credit where it was due!

Chapter 59
A Dream Come True

There was to be a series of fund-raising concerts at the Kiel Auditorium and Cindra's music teacher, Prof. Connor, had submitted the musician's name for her to be a guest artist at one of the concerts. The young woman felt honoured, though she had many qualms about it, especially when she saw the proposed list of names of the other performers. He chuckled when she said to her tutor,"But, Professor Connor, I'm an unknown. The other artists have made names for themselves. How could I possibly draw even a small crowd to a concert?"

"You leave it to me, young lady. The way you play Rachmaninoff's Concerto is out of this world. It's unfair for the public not to hear it; now I have some promoting to do." And promote he did. The pianist had to have her photograph taken for the programme for her evening's performance. And the professor researched and wrote up a spiel about her that caused her to laugh. In large letters was printed: "The talented Cindra Gold-Brent, child prodigy & gifted pianist, studied in Europe under the celebrated Veronique Beauchamp..." and on it went.

The man had posters plastered all around his university, as well as on buildings in the city and other public places. It made her feel like a real celebrity, though she had not even played in that capacity before.

The excited woman perused through some old newspaper articles that John Serenity had given to her on the history of the Kiel Opera House and Auditorium. It was certainly not unfamiliar to her. Many were the nights she and her husband, who had annual season tickets, sat in their reserved box enjoying a feast of music, whether opera, symphony concert, or whatever was scheduled at the time. Mr. and Mrs. John Brent were also subscribers. She reminisced back to the days when there would be glances exchanged between the occupants of those two reserved boxes in the theatre; at that point in time Cindra had so wished that the momentary looks from her mother-in-law, lorgnette poised in her hand, were not hostile. During intermissions the élite crowd would gather in the luxurious lounge and sip drinks of their choice—the women in their fine evening apparel, the men in their tuxedoes—socializing and discussing the presentation for that night. Mrs. John Brent would stubbornly remain in her place and chat there with any of her close friends who dropped by to pay the elegant lady their respects.

The introspective woman, rousing from her reverie, read from one of the newspaper clippings, dated November 1934: "The Dream of a Decade Realized—a $6,000,000 Structure." It stated, "The opera house is separated from the arena by a completely equipped stage, with a proscenium serving both the opera house and arena, equipped with sound-proof curtains so the stage may be used in connection with either unit." The clipping further explained that the ground floor of the building was devoted to exhibition space and conventions, and that there were rooms available for the press, concert rehearsals, dressing rooms, etc.

In another newspaper article she read about some of

the singers who had performed at the Kiel the first year after its opening, in April 1934. The list was impressive: Lucrezia Bori, a famous soprano who sang "Mimi" in *La Bohème*, one of Cindra's favourite operas. And the name Rosa Ponselle brought back memories. She, a dramatic soprano, was prima donna of the Metropolitan Opera Company in New York at the time. Her mother had some recordings of Miss Ponselle. These records she often played on their gramaphone, and her mother would say, "That woman is known as the 'Caruso' of sopranos."

Whilst gathering the odds and ends of clippings for filing, the aspiring concert pianist discovered an interesting news bulletin dated November 8, 1934. It was a rave review of the performance the night before of a certain Russian composer and pianist, Sergei Vassilievich Rachmaninoff. Why, that was the composer of one of her choices for her evening concert's repertoire! Her tutor had suggested it, her husband had requested it, and, of course, the latter's wish was her command. She avidly read the details; "Rachmaninoff has composed his 'Rhapsody on a Theme of Paganini' twenty-five years after his third piano concerto. It was completed between July 3rd and August 18th of this year and had its premiere last night in Baltimore, the composer appearing as soloist with the Philadelphia Orchestra, conducted by Leopold Stokowski. The Rhapsody includes some of Rachmaninoff's most fascinating music, and his twenty-four variations on it combine poetry with a dazzling brilliance. As in all of his works for piano, the technical demands upon the soloist are extraordinarily exacting, and the resources of the instrument are exploited to the utmost. A spectacular performance it was, by a spectacular artist. The applause, indeed, was thundering."

Cindra could not help but wonder if the great composer ever performed at the Kiel Opera House. Goodness gracious, she thought, now she was to play there as a guest artist. Oh, why did she let Prof. Connor talk her into it? That man, to encourage her, said she had been ready years ago.

The rehearsal with the Saint Louis Symphony Orchestra, the day before the concert, could have gone better. The pianist had been fighting a headache most of the day. She figured it was her nerves and hoped for the best on the following day.

Peter Cord, a handsome boy in military uniform, was granted special leave so he could attend his mother's concert. Mr. and Mrs. John Brent, instead of using their reserved box, which had seats for only six people, obtained tickets for choice seats in the exclusive Mezzanine Dress Circle, enough to accommodate the whole family and their friends. There were the two donors, the Cameron Brent family of four, Clarisse and Raoul (with surprisingly no remark from the senior Mrs. Brent), Phyllis and Robert Brent, Leah Frost, Dr. and Mrs. Robertson, John Serenity, Cameron's sister Nancy and her family, Dr. Eric Bonn, Bonn's mother and his sister Claudia, and a few other close friends, making a grand total of twenty-eight! The concerned pianist made the remark to Mr. Connor, "Well, at least twenty-eight tickets are sold!"

The day of the concert the pianist, as was suggested by Prof. Connor, took it easy. She concentrated on some of her favourite passages in her father's black memo book. Her prayers seemed to steady her and strengthen her. She found solace and experienced a great calm in the act of thanking her Creator for the fulfillment of her dream.

Soon she was there! The members of the orchestra had assembled and tuned up their instruments, then the master of ceremonies escorted Cindra Gold-Brent to the stage and presented her to the audience. She looked radiant in her long black velvet gown. Her golden hair was arranged softly and elegantly in a French roll in which was tucked a long diamond-studded comb, a gift from her husband. She looked out at the many faces, not twenty-eight, but scores of them. If one could have read her mind, the exclamation "oh, my goodness!" would have been spelled out clearly. But then her eyes caught sight of her family as she rose from her introductory bow, and she had the feeling she was in the drawing room of the Columns. She sat down at the huge concert grand piano and played as she had never played before, or so her family thought. She had a captive audience. They were spellbound. Some would have said it was her charisma; Prof. Connor said it was her technique and talent; Cameron Brent said it was because she was a goddess; she herself said it was a dream, but a dream that had come true!

As the concert progressed, two visions seemed very close to the musician: One was of her father, who, she thought, would have been very proud of her, and who, she felt sure, was aware of this moment, wherever he was on his eternal journey; the other was of Shirlianne, the precious one who, after she first heard her play, had been such an ardent fan of hers through the short span of her life on earth.

At the end of the performance, after the almost endless applause and the customary laurels, which she received with gratitude and modesty, came the best of all—the man who was waiting for her in her dressing-room. She thought of the piece of music, "Dance, Ballerina, Dance," and how sad it was, because in the lyrics the dancer had given up her lover for her career. As for Cindra, her Prince Charming stood there, so handsome in his formal evening attire, with a bouquet of exquisite red roses from Picardy's and a heart bursting with love for his real goddess. And she felt fulfilled. She had proven that she could have been, and actually for a night was, a true concert pianist. Still, she was content with her career as mistress of The Columns and the mothering of her little family, which gave her such joy and pleasure.

Chapter 60
A Joy Repeated

There were rave reviews in the newspapers the following day as regards Cindra Gold-Brent's concert. One critic said she had appeared from nowhere and became famous overnight; most of them referred to her as a "mystery star." One of the reporters had left off the name Brent, and, referring to her as Cindra Gold, stated, " . . . and truly her performance was pure gold." She was not pleased with the omission; she had debated the name with Prof. Connor and had told him emphatically that the programmes were to include her married name. However, her husband was able to soothe her ruffled feelings by telling her he rather agreed with the man.

There were requests come for her to make guest appearances at different concerts throughout the year. Cameron would have favoured her accepting at least some of these engagements, if not all. The pianist declined every one, saying she did not want the world's acclaim. All she wanted was to raise her family with poise and dignity, teach them the true values in this world of unrest, and be there for her husband with her support and encouragement, helping him to advance in his chosen field of medicine. But that was not to say she was giving up her music; she continued to practice just as avidly as before. But her main purpose in life, since she had married Cameron Brent, remained the same: to create a happy home atmosphere, where growing and caring were the main ingredients.

Shortly after the concert the telltale signs that there was going to be another blessed event at the Columns were developing within the body of the mistress of the mansion. The new doctor was elated and modestly protective of his wife.

Peter Cord, when he received the news in a letter from his mother, in the reply that he sent back, expressed annoyance with his father. And to this correspondence that criticized his father, Cindra responded promptly, explaining that he did not know the circumstances, and that his father was a wonderful man of whom he should be proud.

Carol Lynne, at first, was not overjoyed when she was told she was going to have a new brother or sister, but when she started knitting outfits for the baby-to-be she became very enthused and earnestly looked forward to the occurrence.

Andrew John, involved in his baseball and in the improving of his skill at chess, was too busy to give much thought to a new member joining the Brent clan. Nevertheless, as the months went by he became aware of the expanding dimensions of his mother's abdomen, and by the time the event occurred, he was quite ready to accept the expected one.

If asked, the master of the Columns would have said that this was the first time he had not experienced dread of his wife going through pregnancy or fear at the time of delivery. He stayed with her through her labour and assisted at the actual births. Unexplainably two heart-beats had been detected only at the onset of labour, so the multiple births were quite a surprise. Dr. and Mrs. Cameron Brent were the proud parents of beautiful, dark-haired twin girls, one destined for fame.

Thus, Ruth Gail and Rebecca May, with the second names to honour both grandmothers, joined the Brent household, providing the lusty crying and the breaking of routine, but also the joy, the thrill, and the love of newborns.

Carol Lynne, could she have had her way, would have taken over complete care of the new babies. Her mother had to step in and monitor the time she spent with them. She had to agree with her mother, realizing she knew best, but the time she did spend with her new sisters, she confessed, was all the more precious.

Indeed, the whole family, including the household staff, doted on the twins. Their paternal grandmother was delighted. She would sit with them whilst their mother worked at her music, and one at a time she would hold each one close and tell her how beautiful she was.

And as the years passed, they were to become little stars in the doctor's life. Once in a while he would take them to the hospital with him on a Sunday and proudly show them off to the staff; there was always someone free to visit with them whilst he gave his opinion on a case into which he had been called.

Both little girls retained black hair like Cameron's, so he was convinced he was their father. There was another man who would like to have thought otherwise, but he held his peace and became "Uncle Eric" to them, along with the rest of the children.

Christmases at the Columns were both magical and hallowed. The birthday of the Christ Child remained, as always, the main theme, but as the little twins' perception increased, Santa Claus again made visits to the grand old home. And the young people continued to create the customary handcrafted gifts. One year Peter Cord, on holiday leave from the academy, had fashioned little wooden pull-carts for his baby sisters, an act that pleasantly surprised his mother.

Cameron Brent's toasting of the women who sat at the Christmas dinner table came to the fore as usual, and the happy home was filled with song and dance and the mystical beauty of the Yuletide season.

Summer holidays, spent at the cottage at Lake of the Ozarks, had great appeal for the whole family. The doctor had the dwelling renovated and added rooms to it, thus promoting the comfortable accommodation of his expanding family and household staff. There were sailing, water-skiing, and all the fun things that take place at a lakeland resort. Cindra had such poignant memories of the place— of a little girl singing a song about five babies, of a twisted ankle, of a missed turkey dinner, but mostly of the first kiss of the man who she never dreamed would become her husband.

Chapter 61
The Offspring Mature

The passing of the years saw Cameron Brent, M.D., finish his two years of internship, and his two years of residency at Saint Louis University Hospital, and finally become established as a diagnostician, and, as the years went by, one of prominence. He gave most of the credit to his wonderful wife, who had been so supportive over the years, nurturing their children and encouraging him during the residency period, when he knew she wished him to be home. But it was worth it all, they both agreed, as it made the moments he was at home even more precious.

Peter Cord, graduating from the private military academy, chose to remain in the army and to enter the field of medicine. Certainly he did this not with the intent of following in his father's footsteps, but because he felt a natural inclination towards that study. But, since he still remained at odds with his father, if asked he would have had to admit that competitiveness was involved.

Despite his troubled relationship with his father, Peter always enjoyed the different holiday breaks from school, first from his boarding-school days, and then from the military academy. He and Carol cherished a very close bond between them, and Carol was truly proud of her older brother, who looked so handsome in his military uniform. Andrew almost worshipped his brother and, in his turn, felt very proud when he accompanied the uniformed fellow to any of the social functions they attended. Last but not least, the little twins, once they had made their appearance, crept into Peter's heart, as babies have a way of doing. He lavished attention on them as much as did the rest of the family.

Despite Cindra's pleadings that his father had not touched a drop of liquor since he left the Brent Company business, her oldest son continued his judgemental attitude towards his paternal parent. His dysfunctional association with him worried his mother, especially when in later years, Peter, attending university in Indianapolis, had rented an apartment in Saint Louis (with the financial help of Uncle Clive), and the family seldom saw him during those times he was in the city on holidays. The young man was proud of his army affiliation and of the fact that he did not have to rely on his father for his medical training, or for anything.

But as time passed, the concerned mother's continuing prayers were answered by a strange course of events: Peter, in his high school days, had met, at a party in their home, a friend of Carol Lynne's. The girl, unbeknownst to Carol's brother, had become enamoured of him, so much so that she could not forget him. Peter after years away, had a chance meeting with this girl, and, though a budding romance had the proverbial "rocky road" evolution, the young lady was instrumental in convincing Peter to become reconciled with his father. Thence came about a wedding, but that story must be told elsewhere.

Carol Lynne, unlike Peter, adored her father and the feeling was mutual. The little girl had been such a consolation to him at the time of his first daughter's death and they became true friends; it was a friendship that grew over the years. The young girl, a couple of times, had the wonderful opportunity of accompanying her father on business trips to Europe. His specialized medical practise was such that he could devote time for the benefit of his father and do business abroad as representative of the Brent Lumber and Printing Company. On the two aforementioned occasions the twins had been suffering with childhood ailments, and Cindra chose to remain at home to help nurse them back to health.

The lovely young Carol progressed favourably in synchronized swimming. She enrolled in different swim competitions, in which she displayed her prodigious skill and brought home prized trophies. As the twins grew she taught them the graceful aquatic sport. Raoul found himself guarding at the Brent mansion's pool, for hours on end, almost every day.

Cindra's first biological daughter grew to respect her mother exceedingly. She valued the simple trustworthy qualities that her maternal parent nurtured in her brothers and sisters and her. She noted well that this dear talented musician had really fulfilled her aim to be a concert pianist, but she gave up the plaudits and acclaim of the world for the rearing of her flourishing family and for sharing her talent freely by playing the piano at different functions at their church in Ladue.

She also marvelled at her mother's civic pride and the interest she took in the affairs of the city. The studious lady knew the history of most of the beautiful old buildings that graced the downtown area. Sitting around the fireside occasionally, after music time was over, the family would listen to stories of the different landmarks in the city. Everyone was especially enthused about the relatively new Gateway Arch, which, in the good woman's estimation, she designated "the finest monument in North America." "Why, it's three hundred and twenty-eight feet higher than the Statue of Liberty." Then, excitedly, she would add, "And the distance across the base is the same as the height!" Cindra related how Eero Saarinen, an architect, had won a competition, launched by the Jefferson National Expansion Memorial Association, for the design of a structure, which was to symbolize the "Gateway to the West," a tribute to those who spent their lives committed to taming and settling the West (and to memorialize the Indian tribes who lost their lands to those new settlers). "That was a couple of years after I arrived in Saint Louis, but the work on the Arch didn't commence until 1961, the year in which the clever man died." And she described how sad she felt that he never did see the marvellous monument he had designed.

Built at the Mississippi riverfront, the stainless steel

structure had been a civic dream of Saint Louisians for twenty years. Finally, in the fall of 1965 the last section of the Arch was placed into position. And there was an annual excursion of the Brent family to the fine commemorative edifice. The children delighted in the souvenir shops inside the Gateway Arch and regarded it a special thrill when their parents would get tickets to sit in one of the eight capsules, which would take them to an observation platform in the top; there they could look out of the aeroplane-like windows, viewing the city of Saint Louis to the west, and to the east the Mississippi River and East Saint Louis.

It was a disappointed mother who finally had to agree to let her oldest daughter leave for Canada to go into nurses' training. The girl had had it in her mind for some time to train at Toronto General Hospital. Her Aunt Barbara had graduated as a nurse from there and, no doubt, influenced her in her choice. Her mother wanted her to stay in the States and apply to a hospital in her home city, but her father, seeing how determined she was, agreed to her plan. To convince his wife he supported his remonstrance by saying, "You know, dear, Canadian nurses are held in very high regard, and Canadian secretaries are the best in the world." Giving her an impish smile, he continued, "She'll have her grandmother and the others close in Belleville and that aunt of yours in Toronto whom you're so very fond of."

The concerned mother was not so sure. She felt that Belleville was so far away; however, she knew the so-called aunt, who was not really a relative, but a close friend of her mother, would welcome into her home anytime the young student nurse.

Carol did come back from Ontario a graduated nurse, though with a bleeding heart after a broken romance. This episode grieved her mother. Next, there were some odd happenings in the nurse's career (she did work in that capacity in a hospital in Saint Louis), but, as in anyone's life, matters were straightened out, and she eventually married the doctor who had been eluding her. Alas, it is a love story in need of a separate tome in order to do it justice.

Andrew John, on thoughtful deliberation, figured there were too many doctors in the family. Thus he decided to follow his leanings towards the judicial system and, in the course of time, became a lawyer. His life story, as regards the affairs of the heart, was rather strange. Nevertheless, after several misadventures, it would end like a fairy-tale romance.

Likewise, Andrew's narrative, and that of the twins, are legends in themselves, requiring documentation in another volume. Suffice it to say that Rebecca inherited her mother's musical talent and did, in fact become a concert pianist.

When the grandchildren came along they were loved and cherished by the doctor and his wife. As it happened, because of tragic circumstances, the first one, granddaughter Carla, the fortunate couple had the privilege of raising through babyhood. And again the fine home was blessed with that special joy that only a baby can bring.

Chapter 62
A Tradition Ends

The master of the Columns visited Canada many times over the years. He particularly enjoyed the brief excursions he and his wife and mother-in-law would make sometimes in the autumn to a place called Combermere. Having flown from Saint Louis, they would take off from Belleville in the car they had rented at Toronto International Airport and, visiting the Reidit farm on the way, they would travel north through the hilly countryside, a countryside on fire with the changing colours of the leaves on the maple trees. The man and his companions found the variegated panorama more breathtaking each time they went. And, every time, Cameron would implore his wife to recite her poem "The Waning of the Year," one that she had composed in high school and that, she proudly boasted, her English teacher said was greatly inspired. It was an ode to the pumpkins and the corn shocks clustered in the fields, to the bees retiring and the birds flying south. The last verse Cameron would have her narrate several times, and she, in a rather melancholy tone, would recite

> Yet there is a loveliness
> charming, although sad.
> Something stamped upon the soul
> that makes one rather glad.

The man agreed with the English teacher that the sonnet was inspirational. He said it stirred within him nostalgic feelings as regards summer's ebb, and the sentiment that autumn's beauty could not be denied.

The three travellers would always find amusement in the strange belief of some of the townspeople that Cameron was Cindra's second husband. They, having seen the little coloured girl who visited at the Reidit farm, years ago, were still under the impression the woman was first married to a black man.

Those were most memorable sojourns for the three

people. After the demise of his mother-in-law the doctor said it would be some time before he would take the trip to Combermere again, and it so happened he never did.

Cindra had not been aware her mother had suffered a heart attack at the time of her concert at the Kiel Auditorium. The woman, not wanting to alarm her daughter, said nothing about it. And the pianist had thought her mother was not interested! She always felt badly about it, though her mother did live on for a few years afterwards.

The last festive gathering of kith and kin of the Cameron Brent family, in which the master of the mansion was included, took place in mid-winter in the mid-1980s. The dining-table was extended into the drawing-room to accommodate all family members and guests who attended. The women were resplendent in their elegant dining-gowns, and the men, not to be outdone by the fair sex, were dressed formally.

The master of the Columns, as usual, toasted all the ladies who were present, singling them out one by one. He proclaimed them "the most beautiful women in the world." He left until the end the tribute to his wife, and, looking at her with eyes filled with love, he confessed to them all that she was his "real goddess." He proceeded to thank her for the wonderful family she had given him and for the great love they shared. He next said something that turned out to be an omen: "My dear, no matter what befalls us, I want you to be happy." Before he sat down, he walked over to her, raised her hand to his lips, and kissed it. Then, passing by his mother on the way back to his chair, he fondly gave her shoulder a little love tap.

The host at one point left the dinner table, which caused his wife to be concerned, as she detected lines of strain on his countenance. However, he nonchalantly said he would be right back, which he was. But after dinner, when coffee was being served in the drawing-room, he again left the gathering and retired to his bedroom. Cindra, alarmed at his unusual actions, followed him, asking Peter, who had long since been reconciled to his father, to come with her. Her handsome prince was lying on the bed; seeing his wife, he held out his arms to her, and the last words he uttered were "my darling."

Cindra stared in disbelief at her husband, whose breathing seemed to have stopped; she demanded, in a voice filled with anguish, that Peter do something. Thoughts raced through her mind and she made them audible: "Why, dear Cam, not long ago you toasted all of us women." She was holding her hands tightly, confident her doctor son could save his father.

Paul Craig, M.D., who was Carol's husband, and Andrew had followed the anxious woman and her oldest son to the bedroom. The two doctors carried out resuscitation procedures, mainly to satisfy Peter's mother. Their exchanged glances confirmed in each other what they both felt, that the dark colour of the father's face indicated there would be no return from the vale called death.

Andrew, meanwhile, had phoned for an ambulance, which soon arrived, and the hopeful wife, escorted by her two sons and her son-in-law, followed the stretcher on which her husband lay. A hasty trip was made to the hospital, with the paramedics applying their life support skills, albeit to no avail. The lord of the manor called the Columns would not be returning there.

Carol Lynne, who was trying to keep all the grandchildren in tow, on seeing her father being carried out on the stretcher, knew with her trained eye that by his appearance, his traditional toasting of the ladies that day had been his last. She recalled how his salute to her mother had been like a farewell. With deep inward sorrow she bade a silent good-bye to the dear man whom she loved so much, the man who had not only been her father but a trusted friend.

A hush came over the gathering of dinner guests as they became aware of what was taking place. All were hoping the good doctor would recover. They were indeed saddened at the news of his passing when the sorrowful family members returned from the hospital and told them. The feeling of a great loss pervaded each one.

Cameron Brent was buried beside the grave of the precious child who had drawn him and his beloved Cindra together. And when the grieving wife placed a red American beauty rose from Picardy's on her husband's casket as it was lowered into the ground, she afterwards put one of the fragrant flowers on the gravestone of the young girl. The mourning widow was consoled by the thought that just as the two souls were united in life, they were now together on their eternal journey. She was able to transcend her silent tears and thank God for His solace, which seemed to clothe her like a mantle, even though her thoughts wavered paradoxically between sorrow and comfort.

Chapter 63
The Greatest Is Love

In the days following his father's death, Peter Cord was worried about his mother; she continued with her piano practice, often playing "In a Monastery Garden" and "Roses of Picardy," nostalgic pieces that she had not played since Shirlianne's passing. He was concerned that she might go into deep depression as she had when his stepsister died; now there would be no loving husband to see her through. As well, she had shed no tears, unlike his aged grandmother Brent, who for some time afterwards kept a fresh supply of handkerchiefs nearby.

Carol Lynne too noted her mother's behaviour with vigilance. Often, when calling on her, would she find her sitting at the little white "Dove," and the woman, bereft of her mate, would explain in her calm way that it drew her closer to the Lord of her being and thus close to Cameron.

At first, her children, supporting the grieving process, encouraged their mother to tell them about her first meeting with their father. She told them how she became Cameron's secretary when she started to work at the Brent Printing & Supplies Company, how she sprained her ankle whilst snow-shoeing at his cottage, and how he had sent her American beauty red roses from Picardy's. She had interpreted the gift as the second sign of any romantic feelings he might have for her, and she thought of how the beautiful blossoms had indeed told the truth.

The curious offspring wanted to know what was the first sign of romantic feelings he had for her, and she was forced to tell them about the kiss he had given her as she lay almost semi-conscious in the snow, and how he had explained it as a means of "reviving" her; at this the intent listeners laughed.

Cindra, in her private reveries, would recall how Cameron had always been the romantic; she had loved his romanticism. The way his eyes followed her at galas when they were a room apart; the way he would send her flowers on a noncelebration day, with a little note saying, "...just because"; and the way he would genteelly kiss her hand in the presence of others—so many things! She would sit by the curio cabinet (another of his gifts to her) and admire the numerous exquisite vases that had been sent to her by her lover. She would recall and relive the moments when she had received each one; the exotic flowers, contained in each, were vividly stamped in her memory.

During this time of grieving, her personal lady's maid, Clarisse, that long-standing close friend and confidente, gave her mistress special care and attention; it was actually she who finally talked the gifted musician into resuming her music lessons.

By now, Dad Jack's black memo book was showing the signs of much use. The gems of wisdom therein were her mainstay, and as her soul was nurtured within she became energized to do something in the without. The pained expression on the faces of those children in impoverished countries, which she saw on television, struck a chord in her that would not stop vibrating. She decided she must offer her talent to God, a sacramental offering, and so, having gone back to the serious study of the art at which she was gifted, and spurred on by her offspring, she began to play professionally. The interest she had stirred up in the music world years ago at her concert at the Kiel Auditorium had not been forgotten; also, Prof. Connor, her eager promoter, helped launch her into the courageous endeavour. Glad was Cindra to be putting her musicianship to good use. She played not for acclaim, but for the benefit of humankind, donating the money she made to the Children's Relief Fund. Yet the plaudits were there: "Inspired," "brilliant," "superb technique" were terms the critics used to describe her performances.

A year later, as winter gave way to spring, and the earth sprang to life with growing things, the family, especially Peter and Carol Lynne, started to encourage their mother to accept the attentions of Dr. Eric Bonn, who they knew had for some time been trying to call on her. The young woman reminded her mother that in her father's last salute to her he said he wanted her to be happy.

The two perceptive offspring stated that everyone knew "Uncle Eric" had always been fond of her, and that it was time she began to have some companionship, especially when he was interested too. No one but those involved had known of the love tryst the two had had one evening in the distant past and the regrets the lady experienced over the erotic episode; no one, that is, except Carol, and her mother had told her about it because of a certain happening in the young nurse's life.

Cindra did not know that Eric Bonn had broken off his betrothal to Elaina after Cameron died. Nor did she know of the love-stricken man's attendance at every one of her concerts; he hoped in vain for a night, after one of the performances, when there would be no one to escort her home and the honour would fall to him. But, alas, there were always some members of the family waiting for her in her dressing room: of the married couples, usually Carol and Paul, sometimes Ellen and Peter, when they were in town; occasionally Jenny and Andrew; and, consistently, Ruth, the young teacher, who lived with her mother. But rarely was the professional pianist, Rebecca, in attendance, she being away on tour much of the time.

Persuaded by her family's insistence, Cindra began seeing Eric Bonn. There were dinner dates at exclusive restaurants and evenings spent together at the opera, for which they had a mutual predilection. Nevertheless, though she enjoyed his company, she was quite aware she was not in love with him; there was a certain mild-tempered man, the remembrance of whom still filled her mind. Eric could hardly control his passion, but she managed to discourage his amorous advances, albeit regretfully, as the thought of frustrating him dismayed her. Not only the dejected man, but her offspring too, were disappointed;

Carol encouragingly said to her one day, "Why, mother, if you marry Eric Bonn, you won't even have to change your initials!"

On an unseasonably cold evening, very late in the spring, Dr. Bonn escorted his beloved to the opera; he knew it to be one of the lady's favourites, Puccini's *La Bohème*. Alas, it turned out to be frighteningly prophetic—just as the prima donna in the libretto, Mimi, dies of consumption, our heroine in this story "took a chill" that night. Unremittingly a virus invaded her body, and by mid summer, when the song of the cicada was again heard in the land, her terrestrial life ebbed away.

Eric Bonn, whose hopes had been rekindled lately, thinking the pianist's more hauntingly beautiful musical renditions were inspired by him, was devastated and blamed himself for his cherished one's illness. But the "nieces" and "nephews" blamed him not; they felt their mother had been pining inwardly and had had a strong desire to join her loved ones in the paradise of eternity.

Cindra was buried beside the man who had always remained the one of her dreams. The brokenhearted Eric was a bit of a romanticist himself; when the group of mourners left the graveside, he was seen to place, on the grave of the woman he so admired, nay, adored, an American beauty red rose from Picardy's.

Thus ends the saga of a beautiful girl who had a dream, and a dream that came to pass. But the unfolding of her life far exceeded that dream, as she found fulfillment living life with the man she loved. Though they had had their differences, they had worked them out, and the storms in their life they had weathered together. Their marriage had been a sublime union, allowing for growth and joy and beauty, and reverencing the most important component of all, that name for God, which is love.

Epilogue

Carol Lynne Craig became the grateful inheritor of Grandfather Gold's black memo book. In one of her mother's last wishes she had bequeathed the priceless treasure to her child. Cindra always regretted that her oldest daughter had gone so far away for her nurse's training; her feeling was that, had she been in Saint Louis, a certain ill-fated occurrence, in the young nurse's life would not have happened. She hoped the book would be a trustworthy mainstay for Carol Lynne as it had been for her.

Ruth, a teacher in the elementary school system, stayed on at the fine old mansion in Ladue. She had suffered through the loss of those closest to her: first her father; soon afterwards her teacher fiancé, who was killed in a car accident; then her mother. The young lady was a great comfort to her grandparents at the Wishes, who were advancing in age. She spent much time with them; they filled the void her deceased parents had left. Eventually she married another suitor, and they raised their children in the grand old family residence.

And so, there remained a home in Saint Louis, a familiar setting, where twin sister Rebecca, after a gruelling concert tour, could return. The gifted young musician assumed the stage name of "Rebecca Gold," which would have pleased her Grandfather Gold. When she was in Europe on tour, she would make special visits to Paris, to "Beauchamp Villa," a place of which her mother so often spoke. Rebecca became endeared to the aging, illustrious Mrs. Veronique Beauchamp, who welcomed the granddaughter of Mr. John Brent with open arms. "She is just like her dear mother," Veronique would say.

Uncle Eric proved a great blessing to the bereaved

family. He felt part of the brood; especially dear to him were the twins. In the course of time Elaina became his wife, and the Bonn domicile became like another home to the growing Brent household.

Clarisse and Raoul continued on as loyal servants at the Columns, though the Brent clan, like their parents before them, regarded them as kinsfolk. They were included in all of the family gatherings, when the beautiful mansion resounded heartily, as of old, with joy and cheer and song. The piano music many could provide, with Peter, for variety, bringing forth his violin, but when Rebecca was home there flowed from the magnificent Steinway grand piano such glorious music that all were reminded of another time and of another person, whose tremendous talent still lived on.